SUPERNOVA

SUPERNOVA

KASS MORGAN

LITTLE, BROWN AND COMPANY

New York Boston

Little, Brown and Company
Hachette Book Group
1290 Avenue of the Americas, New York, NY 10104
Visit us at LBYR.com

Little, Brown and Company is a division of Hachette Book Group, Inc.
The Little, Brown name and logo are trademarks of Hachette Book Group, Inc.

The publisher is not responsible for websites (or their content) that are not owned by the publisher.

First Edition: October 2019

alloyentertainment

Produced by Alloy Entertainment
1325 Avenue of the Americas
New York, NY 10019

Library of Congress Cataloging-in-Publication Data
Names: Morgan, Kass, author.
Title: Supernova / Kass Morgan.
Description: New York ; Boston : Little, Brown and Company, 2019. | Sequel to: Light years. | Summary: As the war draws closer and secrets are revealed, Orelia, Arran, Vesper, and Cormak, along with others at the Quatra Fleet Academy, face significant changes and new challenges.
Identifiers: LCCN 2019001739| ISBN 9780316510516 (hardcover) |
ISBN 9780316510493 (ebook) | ISBN 9780316510509 (library edition ebook)
Subjects: | CYAC: Space stations—Fiction. | Military education—Fiction. |
Schools—Fiction. | Secrets—Fiction. | Science fiction.
Classification: LCC PZ7.M8249 Sup 2019 | DDC [Fic]—dc23
LC record available at https://lccn.loc.gov/2019001739

ISBNs: 978-0-316-51051-6 (hardcover), 978-0-316-51049-3 (ebook)

Printed in the United States of America

LSC-C

10 9 8 7 6 5 4 3 2 1

In memory of my friend David Crist:
writer, teacher, adventurer, and sci-fi evangelist.
Thank you for sending me in search of wondrous
new worlds.

CHAPTER 1

ORELIA

Orelia lay on her back on the narrow, rigid bench—the only piece of furniture in the tiny cell. The gravity controls here were separate from the rest of the Academy, and the force was so intense, she could hardly lift her arm to scratch her nose, let alone try to escape. Standing was out of the question, and even sitting proved too arduous for more than a few minutes at a time. She could almost feel her heart struggling to pump blood through her heavy, immobile body.

No one had spoken a word to her since yesterday, when she'd been seized by the guards and dragged from Zafir's office. She wasn't even entirely sure what she'd been accused of. Had the Quatra Fleet realized she was a Specter? Or were they merely suspicious of her knowledge of the

Specters' spread spectrum, a fact Orelia had exploited to help her squadron mates destroy the ship headed for the Academy? If it was the former, then there was no doubt that Orelia's labored breaths would be her last. She'd be tortured and interrogated by the fleet's top intelligence officers, perhaps even by Zafir himself. Orelia shuddered as she imagined the face that'd once made her heart flutter gazing at her impassively as she writhed in pain.

She closed her eyes and forced her overtaxed lungs to take a few deep breaths as she fought against the panic expanding inside her like toxic gas. She'd spent her entire life training for this mission, and despite the immense danger, she'd succeeded. She'd managed to infiltrate the Quatra Fleet Academy, triangulate its top-secret location, and transmit the coordinates to her commanding officer on Sylvan. Because of Orelia, the Sylvans could finally launch the campaign they'd been planning for years—a crippling strike at the heart of the Quatra Federation's military operations, the Quatra Fleet Academy. But at the last minute, Orelia had found herself unable to watch the Sylvans kill the first real friends she'd ever had, and she'd made the wrenching decision to sabotage the attack by telling her squadron mates to fry the Sylvan ship's communication system by sending a directed pulse across multiple frequencies. The plan worked, but success had come at a devastating cost. Every Sylvan on the battlecraft had been killed, and the Quatrans had grown immediately suspicious about Orelia's knowledge of Specter technology.

The door hissed open and Orelia flinched. Her head felt too heavy to move, forcing her to lie tense and still.

"Hello, Orelia," a deep, familiar voice said. She managed to turn her head just enough to see Zafir and Admiral Haze standing in the doorway.

"Can you sit up, please?" Zafir pressed his link and the weight pinning Orelia to the bench vanished. She moved her fingers tentatively and flexed her feet a few times before she rolled onto her side and tried to push herself into a seated position. She'd been in the best physical condition of her life when she'd arrived at the Academy—a state she'd maintained through grueling daily training sessions—but the long hours she'd spent in the cell had weakened her muscles enough to make even this small act difficult.

She glanced at Zafir, who'd stepped into the cell and was now watching her with an inscrutable expression. Just a few days ago, it would've seemed like the most natural thing in the world for him to reach for her hand and help Orelia sit up. She could still feel the lingering traces of the warmth that had spread through her body the last time he'd touched her. But this time, Zafir's arms remained at his sides as he watched Orelia struggle into a seated position with her back against the wall.

She knew she shouldn't be surprised by his detachment; although they were about the same age, he was one of the most accomplished intelligence officers in the Quatra Fleet. Like Orelia, he'd been trained to maintain his professionalism in any situation, even if that meant interrogating the girl who'd kissed him in the ocean simulator. Unless—a new wave of fear crashed over her—unless he'd known her secret all along and feigned attraction to get close to her. Could he really have faked the look in his eyes that night? The tenderness and intensity with which he'd kissed her back?

"What's going on? What am I doing here? There has to be some mistake…" It didn't take much effort to make herself sound confused and terrified instead of guilty and terrified.

"You can skip the theatrics," Admiral Haze said. "Tell us your name."

"Orelia."

"Your *real* name."

"That *is* my real name." It was true. There'd been no need to devise a fake name. To the best of their knowledge, the Quatrans had never even laid eyes on a so-called Specter, let alone compiled a database of known secret agents.

Admiral Haze glowered at Orelia, then gave a small nod toward Zafir. The nearly imperceptible gesture was enough to send an ominous shiver down Orelia's spine as she wondered how many times they'd performed this routine: Haze stepping aside to let her counterintelligence expert and master interrogator do what he did best—extract information from unwilling participants.

"How did you know about the spread spectrum?" Zafir asked, his tone surprisingly light, as if they were back in his classroom instead of a high-security prison cell.

"I told you. It was a lucky guess."

Next to him, Admiral Haze crossed her arms and glowered, but Zafir merely raised an eyebrow. "You have an impressively analytic mind, Orelia. I highly doubt you ever resort to lucky guesses." He sounded more amused than accusatory, but that only made the situation feel even more chilling. It didn't matter that her life was on the line; this was just a game for him. *It's all just a game.*

"Right," Orelia said. "We tried a number of options, but none of them worked. The spread spectrum was unlikely, but it was still worth trying."

"We know you sent that encrypted transmission with the coordinates," Admiral Haze said, ignoring Zafir's subtle look of warning as she abandoned whatever plan they'd devised. "The security cameras caught you prowling through restricted areas. *You* were responsible for the attack. So either you're spying for the Specters, or else—" She cut herself off with a frown, as if the second option were too disturbing to say aloud.

"Or else you *are* a Specter," Zafir continued calmly.

Her years of training kicked in, allowing Orelia to keep her voice and breath steady despite her frantically thudding heart. "A *Specter*?" she repeated with as much incredulity as she could muster.

"Enough," Admiral Haze snapped. "We have sufficient evidence to lock you up on Chetire for the rest of your life. If you even make it that far. The Quatra Federation knows we captured a spy who put the entire solar system at risk, and we have the legal authority to extract information from you by any means necessary. If you refuse to tell us the truth, then Lieutenant Prateek will be forced to resort to less pleasant methods."

Orelia looked at Zafir, desperately searching his face for a sign of sympathy, some indication that he'd do his best to protect her. But his expression remained as inscrutable as ever.

She'd been trained to resist interrogation. It'd been the most frightening, grueling portion of her intense preparations, but she'd learned to stay calm and withstand pain. *This one will never crack*, her gruff instructor had told General Greet while Orelia sat slumped in a nearby chair, struggling to breathe normally after being deprived of oxygen. She'd find out soon enough if he'd been right.

"I don't think that'll be necessary, Admiral," Zafir said, turning to Orelia. Instead of the sadistic gleam she'd always associated with interrogators, Zafir's eyes seemed full of something akin to wonder. "You *are* a Specter."

"That's ridiculous," she said quickly. Under no circumstances was she to admit the truth. Better to die a terrible, violent death than endanger her people.

Zafir's face hardened slightly as he reached into his jacket and produced a metal device Orelia didn't recognize. "Fine.

If you don't feel like cooperating, there are other ways to discover the truth."

Orelia took a deep breath and let it out slowly, trying to steel herself for what was about to happen. Part of her had always known she'd be forced to withstand torture, but she'd never imagined that the first person she'd ever cared for would be the one to do it.

"I'll ask you one more time," Zafir said with unsettling composure as he stepped up next to the bench. "Are you a Specter?"

"Of course not. I don't know what you're talking about."

Zafir leaned toward her with the metal device and she twisted away, but he still managed to brush it against her arm. She felt a mild stinging sensation and braced for the agonizing shock of pain that was sure to follow, but to her confusion and relief, Zafir drew back. He held the tool in the air and squinted as he examined it, brow furrowing as he stared at a small screen Orelia hadn't noticed. It wasn't a torture device, she realized as her relief drained away. It was something far more dangerous.

"What does it say?" Admiral Haze asked.

"Her DNA matches the structure of the samples we collected from the Specter ship." Orelia could tell it was taking considerable effort to keep his voice steady as he turned to her and said, "This is remarkable. You *are* a Specter. Though you certainly wouldn't call yourself that, would you?"

Her brain raced to come up with a plausible explanation: The DNA scanner had malfunctioned or been contaminated. Yet the denials fizzled in her mouth as she took in the expression on Zafir's face. He knew the truth, and for the first time since she'd left her home planet, the fact filled her with more relief than terror.

"No." Orelia met his eyes. "I'm a Sylvan." It was the first time she'd spoken the word aloud since arriving in the Quatra System.

"Sylvan," Zafir repeated, frowning. "How many of you are at the Academy?"

"Just me," Orelia said quickly.

"How many of you are there in the Quatra System?" The edge had returned to his voice, and all traces of wonder had disappeared from his penetrating gaze.

"Just me," she repeated. "I'm the only one."

"That's ridiculous," Admiral Haze said with a dismissive sniff. "Why would they send you on your own? It'd be a suicide mission. If you're actually a Specter, then there must be more of you embedded throughout the Quatra System."

"I'm telling you the truth. I'm the only one."

Admiral Haze narrowed her eyes as she took a few steps toward Orelia. "What do the Specters want from us?"

Orelia stared at her, wondering if this was a trick. She glanced at Zafir for clarity, but the counterintelligence officer's gaze had become searching and urgent. "We don't want anything from you," Orelia said. "We just want you to stop killing us."

"Then perhaps you shouldn't have attacked us unprovoked," Admiral Haze said dryly.

They really don't know, Orelia thought as her confusion turned to disbelief. During her first week at the Academy, she'd discovered that the cadets and instructors were under the false impression that the *Sylvans*, not the Quatrans, had attacked first. But she hadn't realized just how far the lie had spread. Not even the highest-ranking officers in the Quatra Fleet seemed to know the truth.

"We didn't," Orelia said, careful to keep her voice firm without being accusatory. "Fifteen Tridian years ago, the Quatra Fleet sent a probe to collect soil samples from Sylvan. A few months later, three battlecraft arrived and dropped a bomb on our capital city."

"That's impossible," Admiral Haze snapped. "No Quatran battlecraft has ever made it all the way to your home planet."

"That's what you've been told. But it's a lie."

"This is becoming ridiculous. Lieutenant Prateek, you have ten minutes to extract the truth from this girl, or else I'll bring in someone who'll get the job done. There's an attendant that's been programmed to interrogate enemies of the state. It has a one hundred percent success rate and even cleans up after itself, no matter how much blood it leaves on the floor."

"Just wait a moment, Admiral," Zafir said before turning back to Orelia. "What kind of soil samples? Do you know what the probe was looking for?"

"Fyron," Orelia said, using the Quatran word for the mineral.

Zafir and Admiral Haze exchanged startled looks. "Are you sure?" Zafir asked.

"Yes. After the first bombing, it was clear that the Quatrans would be willing to kill every Sylvan on the planet to get to the fyron. That's why we launched a retaliatory attempt." She took a deep breath and closed her eyes. "And that's why I was sent to transmit the coordinates of the Academy."

"That's the most absurd story I've ever heard," Haze said as she shifted her weight uneasily, glancing at Zafir out of the corner of her eye. "There's no record of any such mission."

"That doesn't mean it didn't happen." Orelia's voice grew louder, her exhaustion momentarily pushed aside by desperation.

Haze gave Orelia a long, searching look that made her glad the admiral was Vesper's mother and not hers. Then she jerked her head to the side to focus her penetrating gaze on Zafir instead. "Can we trust her?"

Zafir's eyes traveled over Orelia, and for a moment, she felt some of her anxiety drain away as she thought about their kiss, when he had looked at her with an expression she'd never seen directed at her before. Like he'd glimpsed the real her, and it'd been enough to make him want to kiss her back.

Zafir would believe her. He'd understand that she'd done the best she could, given the terrible position she'd been put in.

When he spoke, his voice was so light, it took a moment for her to process the meaning of his words. He sounded almost amused when he said, "She's the last person I'd ever trust."

CHAPTER 2

ARRAN

"Are you okay?" Vesper asked, glancing at Arran with concern as they hurried through the crowded corridor toward the launchport, where they'd been ordered to report for patrol duty. Since the Specter attack, the Quatra Fleet had tripled the security around the Academy, requiring so much additional manpower that even first-year cadets were given shifts on patrol ships.

"I'm not sure how to answer that," Arran said with a rueful smile. Just days ago, their squadron had managed to foil a Specter attack on the Academy; they were still recovering from their near brush with death while preparing for the larger assault that now seemed inevitable. But it was impossible to focus on the task ahead with their squadron mate Orelia missing. Arran hadn't seen or heard from Orelia in nearly two days, despite sending her eight messages and making multiple trips to her room.

Vesper let out a dry laugh. "I don't mean in the larger, existential sense, obviously. You just looked particularly tense back there."

Arran glanced over his shoulder at the guards they'd just passed. There were about a dozen lined up on each side of the long corridor, their helmet shields pulled down over their faces. They'd arrived a few hours after Arran's squadron had blown up the Specter ship, and while they were ostensibly here to protect the cadets, that knowledge couldn't overwrite the fear stored in his pounding heart. "I didn't expect to see so many guards," he said with a shrug.

"After facing down the Specters, it's the *guards* that make you nervous?" Vesper asked with a teasing smile. "Afraid you're going to get a speeding ticket?"

"That's not what we worry about on Chetire," Arran said quietly. On his ice-covered home planet, the most remote in the solar system, the guards served as a constant visual reminder of who was really in charge—the wealthy Quatran mine owners whom the government allowed to act with impunity. They used the government-paid guards as their own private security service, breaking up strikes and silencing anyone brave, desperate, or foolish enough to protest the cruel treatment of the miners.

Vesper pressed her lips together and looked chastened. "Sorry. I keep forgetting how different things are other places."

"It's fine. I need to remember that the guards are here to keep me from getting blown up by the Specters, not to bash my face in." He lowered his voice. "Have you heard anything about Orelia?"

Vesper shook her head grimly, then glanced down at her link and scrolled through a message, blushing slightly.

"So I assume things are back on with Rex?" Arran said, smiling despite the anxiety roiling his stomach.

"I don't know. Maybe. I guess." She sounded uncharacteristically flustered, and the flush on her cheeks deepened. "It seems a little silly to worry about something like that, given everything that's going on."

"It's not silly at all. If we don't allow ourselves to be happy, then what are we really fighting for?" Despite his best efforts, he couldn't quite keep a wistful note out of his voice, prompting a sympathetic smile from Vesper, one of the only people he'd told about his breakup with Dash.

Arran had spent the first few weeks of the term in a frenzy over Dash, analyzing the minutia of every interaction as his brain struggled to reconcile the outward signs of flirtation with the irrefutable truth—that no one as handsome, smart, and charming as Dash would ever fall for an awkward Chetrian. His skepticism was compounded by the fact that Dash was the son of Admiral Larz Muscatine, the most outspoken opponent of admitting Settlers to the Quatra Fleet Academy. However, the persistent, disarming Dash had eventually convinced Arran to trust him, and for a few blissful weeks, Arran had his first experience of true happiness.

Then, a few days ago, Dash told him that word of their relationship had reached his father, and that if Dash didn't break up with Arran, he'd be forced to leave the Academy. Dash—the first boy Arran had ever loved, the first boy he'd ever kissed, the first person to make Arran feel like he'd mattered, like he deserved the future he'd dreamed of—had dumped him a few weeks ago. The jagged pieces of Arran's broken heart were still embedded in his chest like shrapnel.

"Hey," Sula said, falling in step with Vesper and Arran. "Are you two also on patrol duty this afternoon?"

"Yup," Arran said as Vesper nodded, her attention once again fixed on her link. "Is this your first shift?"

"I had my first one yesterday," Sula said, rubbing her eyes. "Five straight hours of staring at a radar screen."

Arran frowned. "They shouldn't assign you back-to-back shifts like that."

"I don't really mind," she said with a weary smile. "It's nice to feel like we're actually doing something, you know? I like to think that my little sister sleeps better knowing that I'm up here, helping to keep her safe."

Arran's heart cramped as he thought about his mother parsecs away on Chetire, alone in their sparsely furnished, spotless cabin. "I do know," he said. But before he could say anything more, his monitor trilled in his ear. *Report to the superintendent's office immediately. Based on your current location, your estimated travel time is eight minutes.* From the look on Vesper's face, it was clear that she'd just received the same notification.

They excused themselves, telling Sula they'd see her on the launchport, then hurried to the administrative wing. "Any idea what this is about?" Arran asked as a knot of dread formed in his stomach.

"Nope," Vesper said, imbuing her voice with forced cheer. More than anyone at the Academy, the superintendent's daughter knew that a summons rarely boded well.

As they turned into the corridor that led to Admiral Haze's office, Arran saw Rex approaching from the other direction. His grim expression softened when he saw them, and he raised his hand in greeting. "I assume we're being invited for a surprise party, right?"

Vesper rolled her eyes and gave Rex an affectionate smile that made Arran's chest twinge with a mixture of happiness and sorrow. The sensors outside Vesper's mother's office detected their presence, and the door slid open before any of them had time to lift their links to the scanner. To Arran's surprise, Admiral Haze wasn't alone. Commander Stepney, the head of the Quatra Fleet, was standing next to her desk, looking graver than Arran had ever seen him.

Admiral Haze wasted no time getting to the point. "Thank you three for coming. What I'm about to tell you is highly classified. So classified, in fact, that none of you should even know the *name* of this level of security clearance, let alone the actual intelligence. But given the extraordinary circumstances, I've been permitted to brief you. Orelia has been arrested under suspicion of treason."

She paused and scanned the cadets' faces, searching for a glimmer of recognition—a sign that they'd somehow known or suspected. But from the stunned silence, it was clear that Vesper and Rex were as aghast as Arran.

"We believe that Orelia was passing information to the Specters," Admiral Haze continued. "Her knowledge of the spread spectrum roused our suspicion, and after further investigation, we discovered that, a few weeks ago, someone broke into the command center and sent an outgoing transmission with the Academy's coordinates. Now, I'm only going to ask you once: Did you ever notice anything unusual about her behavior? If you know anything, speak up now, and there will be no disciplinary consequences. But that deal lasts only until you leave my office, so consider your actions carefully."

Arran's head had begun to spin; he felt dizzier and more disoriented than he had during his first ride on the shuttle, watching the ground fall away beneath him. Orelia had grown up on Loos. She'd been eleven years old when the Specters destroyed her capital city. How could she ever work for the callous, cold-blooded killers who'd murdered half a million people?

"With respect, that doesn't make any sense," Arran said. "Why would she have wanted to help the Specters? And how would the Specters have even contacted her to begin with? I don't understand how…" He trailed off as the commander of the Quatra Fleet fixed him with a steely glare.

"She wasn't helping the Specters. She *is* a Specter."

Arran stared at Commander Stepney, his already overtaxed brain unable to make sense of the words.

"Sorry, what?" Rex said, echoing Arran's own mess of confused thoughts.

"Your squadron mate is a Specter spy who infiltrated the Academy by posing as a cadet. She admitted it during questioning."

The real meaning of the word *questioning* unfolded in Arran's mind—*interrogation*. The Quatra Fleet's technical ban on torture didn't extend to anyone accused of treason, a loosely defined term that could be applied to a variety of scenarios. "Where is she?" Arran asked, surprised by his own vehemence. "What are you doing to her?"

Commander Stepney shot him a cold look. "I'm troubled by the fact that you seem more concerned about the welfare of a Specter *spy* than that of the Quatra System. Moreover, I find it *staggering* that none of you realized something was wrong with that girl. You spent how many hours together?"

Arran winced as the words unleashed a tide of shame.

He should've never spoken like that to the commander of the Quatra Fleet, regardless of the circumstances.

"But Orelia didn't *do* anything suspicious," Vesper said carefully, looking from Arran to Rex, who nodded his agreement. "She was quiet, that's it. And she's the one who figured out how to blow up the ship. She saved all of our lives."

"She wouldn't have had to save anyone's life if she hadn't sent those coordinates to the Specters." Commander Stepney was nearly shouting by this point. "And now our enemy knows our exact location."

Admiral Haze stepped forward until she was standing between Commander Stepney and the cadets. "They say they didn't notice anything suspicious, and I believe them."

When Stepney spoke again, his voice was icy. "I think we should continue this discussion in private." He turned to Arran, Vesper, and Rex. "You three are dismissed."

They saluted and hurried out, none of them speaking until they'd left the administration wing. Finally, Arran broke the silence. "It has to be a mistake, right? How could Orelia possibly be a..." He pressed his lips together, unable to produce the word.

"I don't know," Rex said, shaking his head. "Someone had

to transmit those coordinates, and even without the security footage, you have to admit, it's strange that Orelia knew about the spread spectrum."

"Really?" Arran snapped. A flame of anger flickered amid the cloud of confusion. "Or maybe there was some major intelligence screwup and it's easier for them to blame a cadet than admit their own mistake."

"Maybe," Rex said, unfazed by Arran's outburst. "But I really don't think that's what's going on here. As much as it hurts to admit it, we have to face the truth—Orelia wasn't who she claimed to be."

CHAPTER 3

VESPER

This was a real patrol flight, not a training session in the simulcraft or the short mission Squadron 20 had been sent on as a reward for winning the tournament. The crafts would be flown by fully qualified fleet officers—first-year cadets like Vesper and Arran were only there to analyze the radar screens. But as Vesper climbed up the steps of the battlecraft, she felt a pang of longing as she turned right toward the tech bay instead of left toward the pilot's seat. It didn't matter that she'd never flown anything nearly as large as a battlecraft; her yearning to grasp the controls was like a physical ache. She missed everything about flying, but today she especially missed how it demanded her complete focus, ridding her head of all nonessential thoughts. Her brain had been spinning out of control ever since they'd left her mother's office. How could Orelia be a *Specter*?

An eon didn't feel like enough time for Vesper to wrap her head around the moonshaking, extraordinary revelation. No one had ever actually *seen* the elusive, violent beings that'd been launching deadly attacks on the Quatra System for decades. Any enemy ships the fleet managed to destroy were blown up in space at long range, making it impossible to catch a glimpse of the bloodthirsty killers inside. That's why they were called Specters. No one knew whether they resembled Quatrans or whether they belonged to an entirely different genus. But based on their callous ability to kill millions without ever making contact, most people assumed that the Specters were an alien life-form—certainly not a quiet blond girl who, when she finally opened up, demonstrated surprising empathy. It was hard enough to understand why Orelia would pass information to the Specters, let alone believe that she was one herself.

Yet that hadn't been sufficient defense for Stepney. Vesper's stomach twisted as she recalled the look of disgust on the commander's face as he shouted at them. She'd devoted the past five years of her life to earning a spot at the Academy, and then worked tirelessly to distinguish herself during the first term. Against all odds, her squadron had won the tournament *and* destroyed a Specter ship heading toward the Academy. But now the commander of the Quatra Fleet was furious with them, and all her hard work was in vain.

Unlike the fightercraft, which only had one cabin, the much larger battlecraft had multiple levels. Arran and Vesper would be stationed on the main deck, scanning the radar for signs of enemy activity, while Sula would report for duty in the control room on the lower level near the weapons bay. *"Remain seated for launch,"* the copilot's voice rang in Vesper's ear; once they'd boarded the battlecraft, their monitors had automatically synced up with the ship's network.

The announcement was followed by a series of low beeps that signaled the ship was moving along the tracks of the launchport toward the airlock and would soon depart the Academy. She felt a slight tremor as the port side of the battlecraft knocked against the side of the hangar. Normally, this would cause her to sigh dramatically, prompting an affectionate eye roll from Arran. But at the moment, she had much bigger things on her mind than witnessing a poorly executed launch. She couldn't stop herself from picking over every piece of information she knew about Orelia. It wasn't much. For the first few weeks, Orelia had barely spoken during their practice sessions in the simulator. No one was *that* shy. Looking back, maybe it should've been clear that Orelia had been keeping some kind of secret.

She glanced over at Arran, who seemed similarly lost in his thoughts, staring listlessly at the monitor, something he'd been doing with increasing regularity ever since his falling-out with Dash. She wished there was something she could do about it, to talk sense into her misguided childhood friend, especially now that Arran needed Dash's support more than ever. Of all of them, he'd been the closest to Orelia, and this news would affect him the most. Now wasn't the moment to let pride or misunderstanding separate two people who were clearly in love. But it'd taken the better part of a term to earn the intensely private Arran's trust, and she sensed that he'd never forgive her for meddling.

She was grateful that she and Rex had moved on from their blowup at the end-of-term celebration, where she'd learned that he'd purposely thrown their first battle to win a bet, a loss that had sent the hypercompetitive Vesper into a downward spiral. She'd forgiven him for misleading her, and he in turn had forgiven her for the cruel things she'd said to him in anger—barbs that still made her wince thinking about them. But for some reason, Rex wasn't bothered by Vesper's occasional outbursts. Unlike her ex-boyfriend, Ward, who always told Vesper to "relax" and "stop getting so worked up," Rex seemed to appreciate her intensity. She suppressed a smile, thinking about the message he'd sent her before her patrol shift: *Come help with my tie before dinner? I can't remember the trick you showed me . . .*

Dash had lent Rex an extra set of evening clothes for the Academy's formal dinners, and the first time he'd worn it a few nights ago, he'd messaged Vesper for help with the tie— a visit that'd ended with them wearing far fewer clothing items than they'd started with. She had no doubt that the highly competent Rex, who'd received the highest score on the aptitude exam of any first-year cadet, could figure out the mechanics of tying a tie on his own. But she was happy for him to keep up the charade for a bit longer.

"Cruising speed reached. Resume normal operations." Vesper unhooked her harness, and she and Arran began to scroll through the radar screens, checking for any unusual movement on the edges of the solar system. It was both tedious and nerve-wracking work. The Specter ships were

undetectable while traveling at light speed, which meant they could appear on the outskirts of the Quatra System without warning.

"Any movement?" Vesper spun around to see Captain Arrezo striding across the deck toward the navigation bay, looking both elegant and powerful in her white uniform with its gleaming brass buttons.

"Nothing, Captain," Arran said while Vesper shook her head.

Arrezo frowned, her attention diverted by her link. "Sula's reporting some inconsistent readings on the electrical system. Korbet, will you check it out?"

"Right away." Arran saluted and hurried off. Although, officially, first-year cadets didn't specialize, Arran's technical aptitude had already been noticed by the faculty.

Just as Arran stepped into the hall that led from the main deck to the stairway, a bone-shaking rumble filled the air and the ship pitched to the side. As a pilot, Vesper was normally unfazed by sudden, stomach-dropping movements, but that was in an agile fightercraft, not a massive battlecraft. Unable to secure herself in time, she skidded out of her seat and crashed against the wall with a painful thud.

"We've been hit!" the pilot shouted. Even from a distance,

Vesper could see his knuckles turning white as he used all his strength to steady the swaying ship. "Is everyone okay?"

Captain Arrezo was still upright, bracing herself against the wall with one hand as she spoke into her link. "It's the Specters. Attack positions." Her calm, steady voice poured from the speakers. Then she lowered her wrist and swiped through various configurations of the radar screen. "Where the hell did they come from?" she muttered. "Did you see anything before the blast?"

"No, there was nothing," Vesper said as she stared at the radar screen in a daze. "I'll show you the playback from the last few minutes." The shaking had subsided enough for Vesper to stagger back to her seat, but when she reached her chair, she found she couldn't sit down. Her feet wouldn't even stay on the ground. The ship's gravity had gone out.

"Shit," Arrezo grunted as she scrambled along the wall, trying to find something to hold on to. "They must have used some kind of electromagnetic pulse to scramble the gravity and Antares knows what else. Mills, reverse course!" she called to the pilot before turning to Vesper. "Find the ship that attacked us *now*. I have to alert the Academy."

"I'm on it." Vesper pushed off the wall and managed to wrap her legs around the base of the chair long enough to hook her harness. She expanded and collapsed the radar screens, examining the surrounding area from all angles, but there was no sign of movement anywhere. *Where the hell did they go?*

"Arran, do you see anything?" There was no answer. "Arran?"

The harness dug into her shoulder as she twisted around, trying to get a glimpse of Arran's chair. Surely he would've returned to his post after hearing Arrezo's command. But to her confusion, his seat was empty. "Arran?" she called again, then twisted in the other direction. Out of the corner of her eye, she could just make out the shape of a still body floating outside the entrance to the bridge. "Arran!"

Vesper unhooked her harness, grabbed on to the chair for leverage, and then brought her feet against the back of the seat and pushed off as hard as she could. The momentum was enough to cover nearly half the distance between her and Arran, but she didn't want to get stuck floating in the middle of the cabin, so using a technique she'd learned from her hours playing around in the zero-gravity room, she landed in a crouch and pushed off again, touching down lightly next to Arran. Wedging her foot in the doorway that led to the stairs, she was just able to hold herself in place.

Arran was floating only a few inches above the ground, pinned under a piece of metal that'd been jarred loose from the ceiling. "Arran," Vesper whispered as she gently squeezed his shoulder. His eyes were closed and his skin had a grayish cast. "Are you okay?" The words had barely made it out of her mouth when she saw the blood blooming on Arran's leg. Vesper swallowed a gasp as her gaze followed the blood to its source—a piece of jagged metal sticking out of Arran's thigh.

"No…" Vesper brought her fingers to Arran's neck. His pulse was still strong. She just needed to stop the bleeding. "I need help back here!" she shouted.

"What's going on?" Captain Arrezo called as she bounded toward them, performing a maneuver similar to Vesper's.

"Arran's hurt. I'm not sure what to do."

Captain Arrezo knelt down to check his pulse. "Medical attention required for Cadet Korbet," she said into her link before cursing under her breath. "The medical attendant is stuck in the infirmary. The door's been jammed. You'll have to follow the instructions and do your best."

"What?" Vesper said, staring at Captain Arrezo in horror. "I have no idea what I'm doing."

"Mission control is asking for you, Captain," the pilot called hoarsely.

"I have to get back over there," Arrezo said. "Ask your monitor for instructions. I'll be right over there if something goes wrong." She launched herself back toward the command center, leaving Vesper alone with Arran.

"Help me, please," Vesper said into her monitor.

"Emergency mode activated. Please await instructions."

"Oh, Antares, Arran," Vesper whispered, squeezing his hand. "Please, hold on. Please."

"Scans show that your skin contains negligible hazardous microbes. You may remove the foreign object from the patient's leg."

Vesper's stomach clenched as she stared down at the piece of metal sticking out of Arran's thigh. "Will it hurt him?"

"The pain will not last long."

Her heart was pounding, and she felt sweat beginning to form on her palms. She almost wiped them on her jacket but caught herself just in time. She couldn't risk contaminating them any further. "Okay, Arran, I'm going to do this as quickly as possible, and then it'll be over. Everything's going to be okay, I promise."

Gingerly, she placed her hand on the object, which looked like a piece of the filtration system, adjusting the angle of her grip a few times before she tightened her hold. She anchored herself to the wall with one foot, then took a deep breath, gritted her teeth, and tugged. It came out easily, and Arran's eyelids fluttered but didn't open. She dropped the metal object and left it floating in the air. "Okay, what's next?"

Vesper's monitor talked her through creating a makeshift tourniquet, which she tied around Arran's leg, just above the wound.

"Vesper," he said groggily as his eyes opened. The color had returned to his cheeks, thank Antares. "What's going on?"

"There was an attack and the gravity's out. I'll help you back to your chair."

"No." He shook his head with a wince. "I need to find Sula."

"Absolutely not. You just almost bled to death!"

"*Low oxygen warning*," a calm, automated voice announced from the speakers as the lights began to flash. "*Life-support system has been compromised.*"

"What the hell?" Arrezo said from the captain's chair.

"That's impossible. We can't run out of oxygen that quickly. Not on a ship this size. Sula, check the readings."

She paused, but there was nothing but static. "Sula, we need a report on the damage." The silence that followed sent a ripple of fear down Vesper's spine.

"Low oxygen warning," the voice said again. *"You have... eleven minutes of life support remaining."*

"That's impossible," Arrezo said again, though this time she sounded less convinced.

"That's not enough time to make it back to the Academy!" the pilot shouted.

"Cadet Korbet," Arrezo called over her shoulder. "Do you think you can make it down to the control room to help Sula? Even if the oxygen converter was damaged, there should be enough to get us back to the Academy. Find out what's going on."

"I can try."

Vesper started to protest but then bit her lip. If anyone could figure this out, it was Arran. She double-checked that his bandage was secure, then told him to wait while she peeked down the stairs. The ceiling had collapsed, revealing a web of singed wires that sparked dangerously. "It's blocked!" she called over her shoulder. The words came out more like a gasp than a shout, reminding her how foolish it was to waste oxygen right now. By the time she managed to pull herself along the wall to investigate the blockage, she was already light-headed. She took a deep breath to steady herself, then immediately regretted it. Surely the efficient thing was to keep her breathing steady and even.

"Warning," her monitor rang in her ear. *"Blood oxygen is below optimum levels."*

"No shit," Vesper muttered. Whatever was going on, it wasn't a mistake with the readings. The oxygen was truly running low.

The web of exposed wires was wide enough to block the stairs, and it would be impossible to pass safely through the sparking and sizzling circuitry.

Cursing to herself, she turned around and, by pushing herself along the wall, managed to make it back to Arran. "The stairs are blocked. You'll have to walk Sula through the repairs over your link," she said calmly, as if this were a routine exercise instead of a matter of life or death.

"She hasn't responded yet," Arran said. "I think she must be hurt."

"*Warning*," Vesper's monitor rang in her ear. "*Blood oxygen is dangerously low. For information on asphyxiation, say* tell me more."

From the look on Arran's face, it was clear he'd received the same update from his own monitor. "I'll have to find another way to the control room," he said as he looked around the cabin with a grimace. "There. Look." He nodded at an air vent near the ceiling. "Based on the schematics I've studied, that vent should lead to the control room."

Vesper tried to shake her head but found that she couldn't quite muster the energy. "You can't. Not with your injury." But Arran was already on his way, floating through the air with his injured leg sticking straight out, motionless, as he used the rest of his body to propel himself toward the ceiling. He reached the vent, which he opened with a deft flick of his wrist, and then, holding on to the edge, repositioned his body so his back was against the opening.

"Be careful," Vesper croaked, her lungs suddenly too tired to produce the force required for a shout. She watched anxiously as Arran guided himself into the air vent, wincing as his injured leg bumped against the side.

Vesper forced herself to wait a few minutes before speaking into her link. "How you doing in there?"

"Fine." Arran's voice sounded faint but composed. "I'm going as quickly as I can. There's smoke coming up from somewhere."

"Take your time," Vesper said just as her monitor pinged. *"Blood oxygen is dangerously low. You have...six minutes left before risking permanent brain damage."*

"How's it going with Korbet?" Arrezo called hoarsely from the front of the ship, where she was directing the pilot, preparing for the next Specter attack.

"He's trying to get to the control room. Through the air vent."

Arrezo made a sound Vesper couldn't quite identify, but she decided to take it as a grunt of approval.

"I'm almost there," Arran said with a wheeze. "I just need to..." He took a shallow, whistling breath. "I just need to open the grate." Vesper heard a faint clatter followed by a gasp.

"Everything okay?"

"The control room is full of smoke. There's a fire somewhere—that's what is eating up all the oxygen." Arran coughed, then began to shout hoarsely. "Sula...Sula, are you okay?"

"Can you see her?" Vesper asked.

"Sula!" Arran called again. "Oh, god, no…no, no, no."

"What?" Vesper said, though her frantically pounding heart seemed to know the answer already. "Arran, tell me…" She trailed off as a wave of dizziness engulfed her. Her head was spinning, but every time she tried to take a deep breath to steady herself, the room only spun faster.

"She's not moving…I don't think she's breathing."

"Warning…Blood oxygen is dangerously low. You have… four minutes left before risking permanent brain damage."

"I…I don't know what to do. How do I help her?" Arran's voice cracked.

"You have to try to repair the life-support system first. Then we'll do everything we can for Sula."

"I don't think there's anything I can do," Arran said faintly. "It…looks like the pulse fried the converter, and the fire next door is eating up all our available oxygen. It seems too big for the sprinklers to contain."

"Warning…Blood oxygen is dangerously low. You have… three minutes left before risking permanent brain damage."

"You have to do something," Vesper said, her voice growing ever hoarser. "Arran, please…"

"Okay, okay…hold on. This is really strange…" Arran's faint voice trailed off, and it was unclear whether something had distracted him, or whether he'd succumbed to weakness and fatigue.

"What's strange?"

"It looks like the vents are closed. I think there must've been a hydrogen buildup. That's what caused the explosion. No wonder the sprinklers aren't putting it out—it must be an inferno."

The fear in his voice made Vesper's heart constrict. "So there's nothing we can do?"

"We need to expel the hydrogen. If I manually open the vent, the emergency systems should be able to contain the fire."

"Try it. Just hurry."

"Wait, hold on, I might be able to..."

"*Warning...Blood oxygen is dangerously low. You have... one minute left before risking permanent brain damage.*"

This is it, Vesper thought. *This is how I'm going to die.* She closed her eyes. *Goodbye, Rex*, she thought, wishing with all her might that she could send the words through the dark void of space into the mind she'd spent so long trying to understand.

The alarms went quiet.

"Arran? What happe—"

"I flipped the manual valve," he said hoarsely. "The hydrogen is venting and the sprinkler system is putting out the fire."

"*Systems normal*," the automated voice announced.

"Arran, you're a genius," Vesper said as she closed her eyes in exhaustion and relief. "Stay where you are. I'm coming for you. We need to get you secured in case we sustain another hit."

"There's still no sign of them," the shaken-sounding pilot said over the comm system.

"What? They just disappeared?" Vesper asked, startled.

"They don't call them Specters for nothing."

When Vesper half led, half carried Arran out of the battle-craft, a crowd was already waiting on the Academy launch-port, including a team of medics who deftly settled Arran onto a stretcher suspended between two attendants and then whisked him away. Vesper started to follow, but someone grabbed her arm. "Vesper, thank Antares." Before she could respond, she was pulled into a tight hug she would've recognized if she could count on more than one hand the number of times her mother had embraced her.

"I should go with him," Vesper said as she took a few shaky steps toward the swiftly retreating attendants.

"He'll be fine," Admiral Haze said in her closest approximation of a comforting tone. "You saved his life. Now, I know you just experienced quite a shock, but I need you and the rest of the crew to come with me for debriefing. We need you to tell us what happened during the attack."

Vesper nodded, too exhausted to do anything more than allow her head to succumb to gravity, then she slowly turned to investigate the source of the commotion behind her. Another stretcher was emerging from the battlecraft, but this time the attendants' movements seemed more cautious than urgent.

Unlike Arran, whose pale face and bloodstained shirt had been plainly visible, this figure was covered by a white sheet. But as the attendants glided by, the sheet shifted enough to reveal Sula's cold, still fingertips—fingertips that would never again clutch the controls of a fightercraft, or clasp the hand of someone she loved. Vesper's head began to spin, overwhelmed by the force of her grief and horror. *Get it together, Haze*, she commanded, but her insubordinate body refused to follow orders, her cowardly knees threatening to give out.

She struggled in vain against the dizziness, trying to blink away the blurry edges of her vision, but her efforts weren't enough to keep the floor from rushing toward her.

"It's okay," a deep voice murmured softly. "I've got you."

The last thing she felt was the warmth and support of Rex's arms around her, and then everything went dark.

CHAPTER 4

CORMAK

The first-year common room was usually bustling at this time of day—packed with cadets gossiping with friends, cramming for an exam, or ordering snacks from the attendants to tide them over until dinner. This evening, however, the common room was as quiet as the Devak Barrens before a sandstorm.

In the wake of the second Specter attack, the one that'd killed Sula and nearly destroyed Vesper and Arran's patrol ship, the Academy had been placed on the highest alert. Commander Stepney had extended the range of the patrol ships to create a perimeter around the entire solar system, since no one knew where or how the Specters would strike next.

Almost no one, Cormak corrected himself grimly. If Orelia was truly a Specter spy, if she'd indeed been the one to transmit the Academy's coordinates to the enemy, then there was a good chance she knew all about the Specters' strategy. *She could have stopped this*, he thought, as he clenched and unclenched his fist. But then again, she had stopped the last attack—telling Cormak and the others about the spread spectrum and allowing them to blow up the Specter ship moments before it launched a missile at the Academy. His head spun as he tried to make sense of it all. If Orelia was really a Specter sent to destroy the Quatrans, why would she turn around and help them kill her own people?

He glanced down at his link and frowned. Only thirteen minutes had passed since he'd left the medical center, where he'd spent the afternoon going back and forth between Vesper's and Arran's rooms. Visitors weren't normally permitted, but Cormak was given special dispensation as the patients' squadron mate, a relationship that trumped all others at the Quatra Fleet Academy. He'd heard that Vesper's ex-boyfriend, Ward, had also tried to see her, only to be turned away. The fact that he'd even *tried* to visit Vesper revealed the endless depths of Ward's stupidity. There was no way she'd take him back after learning he was the one who'd defaced the corridor with the hateful message *Go Home Edgers.*

Ward had resented the Settlers—people born on Loos, Chetire, and Deva—before he'd even arrived at the Academy, and his ire had only grown worse throughout the term; he blamed his "Edger" squadron mates for his subpar performance in the tournament, and his animosity had reached a fever pitch when he realized that Vesper had fallen for her Devak captain. Yet despite being outed as a bigot, Ward continued to move through life with the grating good cheer of someone who'd never met an obstacle that couldn't be removed with a favor or a bribe. That's why, despite all evidence to the contrary, he seemed to believe he had a shot at winning Vesper back.

"Hey, Rex," a weary voice said. He looked up to see Mhairi, a Chetrian first-year. He didn't know her that well—Arran didn't mix his Chetrian crew with his squadron mates all that often—but one glimpse was enough to tell that something was wrong. Her hair was lank and straggly, and faint shadows hovered under her normally bright eyes.

"Hey," Cormak said, scooting over to make room for her on the couch. "I guess you heard?"

She gave a small nod as she sat down next to him. "I think

I'm in shock," she said, her voice trembling. "I'm not sure why. I mean, we all know what we signed up for. We understood that not all of us would live to see the end of the war, but I guess I didn't expect us to lose someone quite so soon. And I know it's crazy, because who can control these things, but I never would've pictured Sula as the first casualty."

"I know what you mean. You could almost imagine her fending off the Specters with one of her disapproving frowns."

"Only if she added one of those slow headshakes," Mhairi said with a sad smile. "Forget my instructors or my squadron mates. Sula was the one I was most afraid of letting down. The other day, I suggested skipping our workout in order to get a good seat in the screening room, and I swear I've never seen anyone look so disappointed in me. But it wasn't because she didn't like to have fun, you know? She just believed in her friends so much, she wanted us all to live up to our potential." She paused, cringing slightly as a look of pain flashed across her face. "I hate talking about her in the past tense like that."

"I get it," Cormak said quietly. After his older brother died, he'd found himself avoiding talking about Rex altogether rather than use the past tense. *My brother* was *always so funny. My brother always* looked *out for me. My brother* sacrificed *everything to make sure I got off Deva.*

"How are Arran and Vesper doing?" Mhairi asked.

"Arran's probably going to spend a few nights in the medical center, but Vesper's meant to be released today. They just wanted to keep her under observation for a few hours, because of the oxygen deprivation."

"Thank Antares," Mhairi said, letting out a long breath. "Will you let me know when they're out and feeling up to visitors?"

"Definitely." Cormak's link buzzed, and he looked down to see a new message from Vesper: *I am being held against my will. Commence rescue operations.* Cormak grinned. Clearly, she was feeling better.

"Is that Vesper? Are they letting her out?"

"Yes, but I can meet up with her later," Cormak said quickly, looking up from his link. As anxious as he was to see Vesper, he didn't want to abandon Mhairi. With Arran in the medical center and most of her friends on patrol duty, there weren't many people left at the Academy for her to talk to.

"I'm fine," Mhairi said kindly. "You should go find her."

"Okay, if you're sure." He rose from the couch and placed

a hand on Mhairi's shoulder. "Hang in there. You know Sula would want you to carry on."

"I know," Mhairi said with a smile. "I'm going to do my best."

By the time he reached the medical center, Vesper was standing in the reception area, arguing with the doctor. "This is ridiculous, I'm *fine*," she said curtly. "If I can't manage to walk from the medical center to the residential wing, then you should probably just discharge me from the Quatra Fleet right now."

"It's policy," the medic said with the tight, weary smile of someone long used to dealing with strong-willed cadets. Though perhaps not as strong-willed as Vesper Haze. "A medical attendant will take you back to your room, at which point you'll be free to do whatever you think is best."

"He'll make sure I make it back to my room." Vesper nodded at Cormak.

The doctor sighed. "I'm not the one who writes the rules. Now, if you'd like to lodge a formal complaint with the superintendent, you're welcome to do so while I attend to my other patients."

Cormak suppressed a smile at Vesper's scowl. They both knew she'd rather remove her own kidney on the operating table next door than bother her mother with something like this. He took her hand and squeezed it. "Come on, Vee. Let's just get this over with." As much as he enjoyed watching the fire return to Vesper's eyes, he didn't want to spend any more time in the medical center than necessary.

Until very recently, Cormak had spent his days in a state of constant low-grade terror. For despite being made captain, leading his squadron to victory in the tournament, and helping thwart a deadly attack on the Academy, the truth was that Cormak hadn't even been accepted to the Academy. In fact, he'd never even applied. Rex had been the one who'd won a spot, but he'd never gotten the chance to attend. He'd died in a mining accident trying to earn enough money to send Cormak off planet, refusing to leave his younger brother behind. Rex had known the risks and had left Cormak a note instructing him to take Rex's spot at the Academy if the worst happened.

Against all odds, Cormak had managed to make it to the Academy, but within days, it became clear that the charade wouldn't last unless he somehow replaced Rex's biometric data with his own. After a series of close calls, Cormak had finally managed to pay his old boss, Sol, an infamous hacker and black-market arms dealer, to update the Academy's files, but he was still in a precarious position. If the Quatra Fleet discovered that Cormak was posing as his dead brother, he'd be thrown in prison on icy Chetire...or worse. So while he was in the clear for now, being around the medics with their needles and DNA scanners made him uneasy.

After Vesper gave a short, impassioned speech about "wasted resources," she finally convinced the doctor to let her go, and after checking in on the sleeping Arran, Vesper and Cormak made their way into the corridor.

The normally quiet administrative wing was a flurry of activity. Guards patrolled the corridors, and although Cormak knew they'd been sent to the Academy for the cadets' protection, the loaded guns served as a constant reminder that Cormak was also an intruder. He might pose less of a threat, but that wouldn't make the Quatra Fleet any more lenient. They were at war, and that seemed like a spectacularly bad time to be revealed as an imposter.

The color had returned to Vesper's face, but she still seemed a bit unsteady, and it took all of Cormak's self-control not to take her hand, a gesture she'd no doubt interpret as insultingly overprotective or embarrassingly affectionate. Vesper Haze had joined the Quatra Fleet for one purpose—to become a warrior—and here at the Academy, she was all business. That was one of the things Cormak loved most about her: She was fiercely ambitious, held everyone around her to incredibly high standards, and held herself to even higher ones. That was partly why he was so afraid of Vesper discovering his secret. What would she think when she learned that Cormak was nothing more than a school dropout with a criminal record?

"Are you okay?" Vesper asked, looking at him with an expression that always made his heart race, one of tender concern that appeared only rarely, away from the hypercompetitive atmosphere of the classrooms and the simulcrafts.

"I'm fine. It's you I'm worried about."

"Because I passed out?"

"Because you nearly *died*."

"Oh." Vesper paused to consider this. "I guess I haven't really thought about it that way."

"Well, I didn't have that luxury," he said, his light tone belying the knot of residual fear twisting in his stomach. "When I heard that your ship had been attacked..." His voice cracked and he looked away, unsure how Vesper would react to the show of emotion. *You have to get used to it*, he could imagine her saying with a scoff. *If you're going to date someone in the Quatra Fleet, you have to accept a certain degree of risk.*

But instead, Vesper took his hand and squeezed. "I'm sorry," she said.

Cormak wrapped his arm around her and pulled her against him, relishing the warmth of her body against his. "You don't need to apologize for being a hero."

"Don't be ridiculous," she said, although he could hear the smile in her voice. "I never thanked you for catching me."

He tilted his head down to kiss her hair. "I'll always be there to catch you, Vee."

"Thank you," she said with a look as comforting as a caress, and for a moment, he imagined how good it'd feel to tell her everything, to lift the weight that'd been pressing down on him ever since he'd arrived at the Academy. But even more than that, he wanted to tell her about Rex, to share the memories of his brother that were slowly fading from the universe. *You can't do that*, he reminded himself. It's not that he didn't trust Vesper—if she promised not to tell anyone, he knew she'd keep her word. But his secret was just too big, a literal matter of life and death. He couldn't risk it, and it'd be unfair to burden her with it.

They reached Vesper's suite, which, thankfully, was empty. He knew the last thing she wanted was to make polite conversation with her roommates. In the aftermath of severe oxygen deprivation, the walk to her dorm was enough to leave Vesper exhausted. He faced a surprising lack of resistance as he helped her into bed, even taking her shoes off for her. "I'm sorry," she said weakly, her eyes already closed. "I don't think I'm going to make it to dinner."

"It's fine," Cormak said as he sat on the edge of her bed and rubbed her leg through the blanket. "I'll go to the canteen and bring something back for us."

"Are you sure?"

He nodded. "I can't really imagine sitting in the dining hall right now." He wasn't ready to face the empty chair at the table where Sula normally sat with the other Chetrians. He waited for her to respond, but from the sound of her breath, she'd already fallen asleep. Cormak leaned over to kiss the top of her head. "I'll be back soon."

He decided to change out of his uniform before heading to the canteen, but it took him longer than usual to make it back to his own room. Every few feet, he was stopped by worried-looking cadets anxious to grill him about the recent attack, assuming that he, as Vesper's boyfriend, was privy to better information than the rumors that had spread like wildfire through the Academy.

Up ahead, someone stood in front of the door to his suite. Cormak shortened his stride; he wasn't in the mood to chat with any of his roommates, let alone Basil's asshole Tridian friends. But to Cormak's annoyance, the figure didn't move. "Shit," Cormak muttered under his breath as he got close enough to take in his visitor's light brown hair, ruddy skin, broad shoulders, and smug grin. It was Ward.

"What do you want?" Cormak called once he was within earshot.

"Phobos, just the man I was looking for," Ward said in the carefree, confident tone particular to Tridians. Cormak always found it grating, but tonight it made his stomach roil with disgust. One of Ward's classmates had *died* today, and here he was, acting like he was back at the Tridian country club.

"You were looking for me? I thought leaving anonymous, cowardly messages was more your style."

"That was just a joke. Seriously, you need to lighten up."

"Apparently you and I have different opinions about what constitutes a joke."

Ward's smile tightened. "I suppose that explains why Vesper always looks so miserable around you. I never had any trouble making her laugh."

"Too bad that couldn't make up for you being an asshole." Cormak scrunched his forehead and feigned puzzlement. "Though, if I remember correctly, Vesper grew tired of you *before* she found out that you were a vile bigot. That part only made her decision to dump you easier."

The mask of affability fell from Ward's face, revealing something colder. "Talk all you want, Phobos, but you and I both know the truth. Vesper's only dating you to piss off her mother and make herself feel virtuous. It's just a matter of time before the fun of parading around her Devak boyfriend wears off and she realizes what I've known all along: that you're a cocky piece of space trash who doesn't belong here."

"Cool," Cormak said as he raised his wrist to scan into his suite. He'd been dealing with rich idiots his whole life and knew that nothing pissed them off like being dismissed. "Good talk, Ward."

Ward grabbed Cormak's wrist and held it in midair. "I'm warning you, Phobos. Leave Vesper alone or you're going to be in real trouble."

"Not as much as you're going to be in if you don't take your fucking hand off me," Cormak said calmly. They locked eyes, and Cormak could see Ward wavering as he weighed his options, so he decided to make it easy for him. Cormak wrenched his arm free and then shoved Ward back a few steps. "And just for the record, *I'm* not the reason you're not with Vesper. *She* decides who she dates. Even if she and I break up—which I don't see happening anytime soon—there's no way in hell she'd ever get back together with an idiot like you."

"You'd better watch the way you talk to me, *Edger*," Ward spat, his face growing even redder. "I know your secret, you lying, cheating piece of shit."

A jolt of panic shot through Cormak's chest, but he managed to keep his voice steady. Growing up on Deva required creative and often illegal means of survival, and he had years of experience maintaining his composure even while his heart pounded an alarm. "I have no idea what you're talking about. Now get the fuck away from my door."

"You know, you're a surprisingly bad liar for a criminal,"

Ward said with a sneer. "I was in your suite, hanging out with Basil, and I decided to take advantage of the opportunity to get to the bottom of your undeniably shady behavior. It's almost as if you *wanted* to get caught, leaving your link lying around like that. It took me less than ten minutes to cross-reference your contacts with the military police database, which led me to your impressive friend, Sol. We had a very...illuminating chat."

"You called Sol?" Cormak said, forcing himself to sound more bemused than terrified.

"Such a charming guy. Really colorful language. I wish I could remember exactly what he said, but it was something along the lines of 'I'm not doing anything else for you, shithead, unless you're prepared to pay double this time.' What was he talking about?"

Cormak fought desperately against the panic threatening to take control. "I ran a few errands for him once, back on Deva. It's not a big deal. No one's going to find that information useful or interesting."

"Oh, really? Would it seem more useful if I started calling you *Cormak*?"

A tidal wave of cold terror enveloped his spine. "Cormak?" he repeated, feigning puzzlement.

Ward's slightly beady eyes narrowed. "I knew there was no way someone like you could ever get into the Academy on your own. You're a fucking fraud, and if you don't break up with Vesper by tomorrow, I'm going to turn you in."

Cormak's heart was beating so fast, it was growing difficult to speak. "Do you need an escort to the medical center?" he said, managing to imbue the words with bored disdain. "Because it seems like you're having some kind of psychotic breakdown. Though, you know what?" Cormak glanced at his link. "I don't really want to be late for dinner. Good luck with that, Ward."

Without another word, Cormak scanned into his suite and slipped inside. The moment he heard the door hiss shut behind him, he collapsed onto the couch, head spinning. *Cormak.* Hearing it on Ward's lips made him hate his own name, as if the Tridian had poisoned it somehow. How had someone as dense as Ward figured out what the Quatra Fleet had failed to recognize?

You're a fucking fraud, and if you don't break up with Vesper by tomorrow, I'm going to turn you in.

Ward's words rattled in Cormak's skull as he sat on the edge of his bed, his head buried in his hands. He knew it wasn't an empty threat. Ward might have the fewest admirable qualities of anyone Cormak had ever met, but once he set his twisted mind on something, he followed through. If Cormak didn't break up with Vesper tonight, he'd wake up in the prison cell next to Orelia.

"That fucking bastard," Cormak said with a growl as he sprang to his feet and slammed his hand against the wall. Back on Deva, where nothing was built to last—not walls, relationships, or vital organs—this would've been enough to shatter the cheap plaster. But the Academy walls would never offer that kind of satisfaction, remaining resolutely undented as Cormak clutched his hand in pain. Vesper was the best thing that'd ever happened to him; he'd never known that kind of happiness was even possible. The thought of giving in to that shithead Ward's blackmail made his blood curdle with disgust and rage. But he didn't have a choice. It was that or be charged with high treason, the punishment for which was death.

He closed his eyes and pictured Vesper as he'd left her, her smooth black hair fanning out across the pillow. Even in sleep, her expression looked slightly defiant, her lips pursed together in resolve. If she knew what Ward had done, she'd lose her mind. But even Vesper's fury would be no match for the information Ward had at his disposal. The fleet wouldn't turn a blind eye to identity theft, trespassing, and conspiracy just because the superintendent's daughter asked them to.

As much as he hated to admit it, Cormak knew he didn't have a choice. If he didn't break Vesper's heart, and his own in the process, he'd be writing his death sentence.

CHAPTER 5

ORELIA

She might have been in solitary confinement, but Orelia's head felt like the noisiest place in the solar system. A cacophony of voices echoed through her skull, a demented chorus of her darkest thoughts and the accusations that'd been hurled at her since her arrest. She should've been relieved when Zafir and Haze left without dragging her off for interrogation, yet unlike a physical blow, the memory of his parting words grew more painful as time passed.

She's the last person I'd ever trust.

On the surface, it was the most obvious, expected reaction possible. She was a *spy* who'd infiltrated the most top-secret base in the Quatra Fleet. Only a fool would trust her. Yet there'd still been a small part of her that believed

Zafir might be able to see past that, to separate the enemy operative from the girl he'd stared at in wonder that night in the ocean simulator.

Perhaps she'd been the biggest fool of all.

The gravity was set to normal levels today, and she paced her cell, trying to get her thoughts in order. She'd be punished for her crime at some point—the only question was whether they'd try to extract more information from her before they executed her.

The door slid open, startling Orelia enough that she leapt to the side. Without time to steel herself, it was impossible not to look frightened as Zafir entered the cell, and she thought she saw a flash of pain on his face as he took in her appearance. Or perhaps she'd only imagined it, for by the time he said, "Let's go," his detached expression had returned.

"Where?" she asked, her voice thick and scratchy as if she'd just woken up, although Orelia couldn't remember the last time she'd actually slept.

"Stop asking questions and come with me." She followed him out of the tiny cell into the corridor, where Zafir nodded at the guards flanking the door. He didn't even bother restraining her; they both knew there was nowhere for her to run. She was on a military base in an asteroid belt light years from home. There would be no escape, no way to avoid her fate. She'd known when she accepted this mission that it would likely end this way, but while her training gave her the strength and courage to hold her head high as she walked alongside Zafir, it wasn't enough to keep the terror from flooding her veins. This was it. At some point soon, either a Quatra Fleet bullet would shatter her skull, or a Taser would stop her heart.

After what felt like an eternity, Orelia broke the silence. "If you're going to torture me for more information, I suppose this wing of the Academy is as good as any."

"I thought I told you to stop talking."

Orelia could barely conceal her surprise when she realized they were heading toward Admiral Haze's office. Surely they wouldn't interrogate her in the Academy's administration wing in between the bursar's suite and the uniform storage room. Unless Haze's office opened up into a secret, soundproof space for torturing spies? From what Orelia knew about the admiral, she wouldn't be surprised.

Without a word to Orelia, Zafir brought his link up to the sensor next to the door and it slid open. Before Orelia had time to orient herself and take in her surroundings, Haze rose from her desk and strode toward her.

"A patrol ship was attacked a few days ago," she said without preamble, "and the president of the Quatra Federation declared a state of emergency, which means that the rules concerning the treatment of accused criminals have been suspended."

No. The word echoed through Orelia as an ominous shiver crawled down her spine. She looked at Zafir, desperately searching his face for a sign of sympathy, some indication that he'd do his best to protect her. Yet his expression remained as inscrutable as ever.

"Vesper, Arran, and Sula were on board the patrol ship," Haze continued, her voice taking on an even sharper edge. Another wave of dread surged through Orelia's chest as she tried to brace herself for perhaps the worst news of her life—that her treachery had led to the death of her friends and squadron mates. "It was attacked by an electromagnetic pulse that created an explosion. Arran sustained a serious injury and Sula was killed."

Sula was killed. Orelia's heart cramped as she thought about the no-nonsense Chetrian girl with the serious ambition and kind smile. The girl who'd always moved over to make room for Orelia on the common-room couch, who took care to never make anyone feel excluded or unwelcome. Sula was dead and it was all Orelia's fault.

"Needless to say, the death of a cadet isn't something we take lightly," Haze said. "But Sula is just one of thousands whose deaths might've been prevented if we'd done things differently. This war has come at far too high a cost, and it's time to think about ways to stop the bloodshed. We want you to help negotiate a truce."

Orelia stared at Haze blankly, convinced she'd misheard. Perhaps the time she'd spent in quadruple gravity had damaged her eardrums. "I'm sorry...what?"

"We'd like to send an envoy to Sylvan to propose a cease-fire," Admiral Haze continued. "With the aim of holding a peace summit and negotiating the end of the war. Do you think you'll be able to convince your leadership to consider the proposal?"

"I...I can try," Orelia said, her head spinning.

"I'm glad to hear it," Haze said with a nod. "Because your life depends on it. If the Specters—or Sylvans, as you claim you call yourself—refuse to attend the peace summit, refuse the cease-fire, then you'll be brought back to the Quatra System and tried for your crimes."

"You think the Sylvan army will let you extradite me from my own planet?"

Admiral Haze raised one eyebrow and surveyed Orelia for a moment before responding. "Once they discover that you were the one responsible for blowing up that ship, there's no telling what they'll do."

The words were no crueler than those Orelia had hurled at herself—*traitor, liar, murderer*—but there was something about hearing them aloud that made her stomach twist with a painful mix of guilt and shame. "Why bother sending me all the way to Sylvan, then? I have a device that allows me to communicate with my commanding officer. I could explain about the cease-fire that way."

"The crew's already been assembled, and you'll be accompanied by a small team overseen by Lieutenant Prateek."

Her heart lurched as she turned to look at him, too startled to determine whether her pulse had sped up with fear, excitement, or a strange combination of both. A few days ago, the prospect of taking a transgalactic journey with Zafir would've made every cell in her body fizz with giddy joy. Yet as she met his eyes, there was no sign of the tenderness that, after many long, lonely weeks, had finally made the Academy feel like home. That boy had disappeared, been swallowed up by the stone-faced counterintelligence officer staring back at her now.

"I've sent an attendant to gather your things from your room. We're leaving tonight. You'll go straight from here to the launchport."

"Tonight," Orelia repeated, trying to wrap her head around the fact that she was moments away from leaving the Academy forever. If she successfully convinced the Sylvans to attend the peace summit, then she'd be freed and would remain on her own planet. If she failed, she'd be brought back for trial on Tri, the judicial capital of the Quatra System. Either way, she'd never see her squadron mates again. "Please, can I just have a few minutes? I need to say goodbye."

"To whom?" Admiral Haze said coldly. "The people you're thinking of are currently attending a memorial for Sula. I don't think you'll be missed."

She's right, Orelia thought grimly as a trio of guards escorted her to the launchport. It was ridiculous to think that her friends would want to see her, that they'd even consider themselves her friends after what she'd done. But she couldn't bear the thought of leaving without a chance to explain, to try to make them understand how much she cared about them.

By the time they reached the launchport, her heart was pounding so quickly it was becoming hard to breathe. Orelia had to do something before she left, before she was out of range forever.

Zafir was standing next to their transport ship, watching a line of attendants load supplies into the hull. Next to him were two officers she didn't recognize, a young brown-skinned woman in a colonel's uniform and an older, stocky gray-haired man in civilian clothes. The remaining members of the peace envoy, Orelia presumed.

"Time to go," Zafir said when he saw her. "You can head inside."

"Can I just check to make sure they packed everything? I'll be quick."

At first, it looked like he was going to refuse, but then he disappeared inside the hull and returned a few moments later with her bag. "Be quick," he said, handing it to her.

She nodded, then placed it on the ground and pretended to riffle through its contents as she fiddled with her link. "Record new message," she whispered to her monitor. "It's me, Orelia..."

CHAPTER 6

ARRAN

Orelia's a Specter. The words had been playing in a loop in Arran's head since he, Vesper, and Rex had left Admiral Haze's office before the doomed patrol shift. And while there were times when the words had grown quieter—like during the attack itself, and when he thought about Sula— they'd never truly disappeared.

He'd been discharged from the medical center a few hours earlier and had been preparing to return to class when he'd received a message summoning him back to Haze's office. He hoped it was to give them additional information about Orelia, but when he arrived at the admiral's office door, breathing heavily from the exertion of walking for the first time in days, he found that he'd been summoned alone.

Arran hesitated, unsure how to announce his presence. But before he could raise his link to the scanner, the door slid open. "Arran," Admiral Haze said warmly—warmly for her, at least—as she rose from her desk and strode across the room to shake his hand. "It's wonderful to see you up and about. How are you feeling?"

"I'm fine, Admiral," he said, resisting the urge to pat the electronic bandage on his thigh, under which his skin was still being knit back together. It didn't hurt, but there was a strange tugging sensation that kept him from fully forgetting about his injury. Though none of that compared to the pain in his chest—the constant dull ache that'd been present ever since his breakup with Dash, and the flashes of searing heat that shot through him whenever he thought about Sula.

"I'm very glad to hear it," Haze said in the tone of someone unused to—or perhaps uninterested in—making pleasant small talk. She motioned for Arran to take a seat and then settled back into her own chair on the other side of her massive desk. "I shouldn't be telling you this quite yet, as the paperwork hasn't gone through, but I'm happy to let you know that you've been awarded the Medallion of Valor. It'll be presented to you at a ceremony on Tri at some point, though I'm afraid all nonessential scheduling has been put on hold while we deal with the Specter crisis. Still, it's something to look forward to. We'll cover transportation costs for your family, if you'd like them to attend."

For a fleeting moment, Arran's heart swelled as he imagined the ceremony, him standing in his dress uniform in front of a distinguished crowd. His mother beaming in the front row, sitting next to a handsome young officer whose face was also aglow with pride. Then the pain returned, pulling him back to reality. Of course Dash wouldn't be at his Medallion of Valor ceremony.

"Thank you, Admiral," Arran said. He hoped the warmth in his cheeks didn't mean he was blushing. "It's an honor."

"The honor is ours, cadet. If it wasn't for your bravery and quick thinking, we would've lost that ship and everyone on it." They both fell silent for a moment, each of them picturing the body that'd been carried off the battlecraft. How had Sula's parents been notified? Her home sector on Chetire was slightly less remote than Arran's, but he doubted her parents had a link at home. Had the Academy deputized a local official to visit them and break the terrible news in person? Or had Haze sent a message that Sula's parents wouldn't read until their next visit to the public link in town? The idea that they might not know their daughter was dead was somehow both a source of comfort and heart-wrenching sorrow.

"There's something else I wanted to talk to you about," Haze said, clearly relieved to have an appropriate reason to break the silence. "We recently created a new division—an experimental program devoted to analyzing Specter technology. It's all very preliminary at the moment, but given the urgency of the situation, we want to get started as soon as possible. After the recent attack, we have to accept the disturbing possibility that the Specters may have found a way to damage our ships from a great distance. That means we have a short amount of time to upgrade our systems before it's too late."

"That sounds like a good plan," Arran said hesitantly, unsure what this had to do with him.

"We could really use someone like you on the team."

"Like me?" Arran said before he could stop himself; he knew this was exactly the wrong tack to take with someone like Admiral Haze.

"Yes, exactly like you," she said with unusual patience. Apparently, earning the Medallion of Valor afforded you a certain amount of goodwill. "You've demonstrated considerable talent in this field, so I hope we can count on you. It'll mean a great deal of extra work, on top of your academic responsibilities," she said with a hint of a challenge.

"It would be a privilege," Arran said quickly.

"Excellent." Haze rose to her feet. "Best of luck, cadet."

"Thank you, Admiral." Arran performed a crisp salute and spun around as quickly as his injured leg would allow, lest Haze see the un-soldierlike smile on his face.

By the time Arran arrived in the dining hall for dinner, however, his pride over the unexpected honor had given way to exhaustion as his overtaxed brain struggled to process the events of the past few days: his breakup with Dash, the truth about Orelia, and the Specter attack on his patrol ship. It felt like he couldn't go more than a few minutes without seeing Sula in his head, the frozen look of surprise that'd been on her face when he'd found her in the control room. Was it just the shock of the explosion? Or had she seen something strange before she...He winced, unable to complete the grim thought.

He wasn't hungry—and he definitely wasn't in the mood to socialize—but years of food insecurity had taught him never to skip a free meal.

It was normally impossible to sit on your own at dinner. There were just enough seats for the two hundred and forty cadets, so if you didn't sit with your own friends, you ended up at a table surrounded by people who might awkwardly try to include you in their conversation or, more likely, ignore you and carry on talking as if you weren't there. But tonight, enough of the cadets were off on patrol duty that the dining room was only half-full, giving him the rare luxury of his own table.

Arran looked around the elegant room: the chandeliers that glinted in the starlight, the portraits glowering from the walls, the delicate glassware sparkling on the tables. His first week at the Academy, he'd been overwhelmed by the grandeur, convinced that he'd never feel like he belonged. But then he started to find his place, befriending his squadron mates and, to his rapturous delight, catching the eye of the adorable Tridian he'd met on the shuttle from Chetire. The dining hall began to symbolize the glittering future that had opened up for Arran when he'd been accepted to the Academy—a future unlike anything he'd ever dared imagine.

Yet now, the portraits and the antique wooden tables seemed like remnants of a shattered dream. The Specters had sent a massive fleet to destroy the Quatra System, and even if Arran survived the next few weeks, a future without Dash, Orelia, and Sula seemed like a bleak one.

As Arran picked listlessly at his appetizer—some tiny neon-pink fish imported from Loos—he replayed every interaction with Orelia he could remember. But the more he thought about it, the more it made his head spin. He wished he could talk about it with someone, but the only person Arran could imagine discussing it with was Dash.

Arran winced as a new wave of pain threatened to tear his heart into even smaller pieces. He'd never again watch Dash's eyes fill with sympathy and understanding as he gently encouraged Arran to share the feelings he'd hidden away for years. He'd never feel Dash's warm breath on his skin as he whispered, "It's okay. Everything's going to be fine."

"Is this seat taken?" a familiar joking voice said, sending Arran's heart plummeting toward his stomach. His head jerked up to see Dash addressing a table full of Tridians, including Dash's friends Frey and Brill. Heat rose to Arran's cheeks and he immediately regretted sitting alone. He was looking around the dining hall, wondering whether it was too late to join a group of Chetrians on the other side of the room, when he realized that Dash had turned around and was looking at

Arran with a strange expression. The distant, polite smile that Dash had taken to plastering on his face when he saw Arran slipped away and was replaced by a wistful look tinged with something else.

A moment later, Dash turned from the table and began to make his way toward Arran, whose chest tightened until it started to feel too small to contain his rapidly beating heart. "How are you doing?" Dash asked as he came to an awkward stop next to Arran's chair.

"Why does it suddenly matter to you?" Arran tried not to care that he sounded like an asshole. It was unfair and unkind for Dash to suddenly feign interest in his feelings after how he'd treated him.

Dash winced. "I never stopped caring about you. I just didn't have a choice."

"So what are you doing, Dash? I'm not trying to be difficult. I just want to understand why you're making this harder than it has to be."

"I thought we could be friends," Dash said in a small, tentative voice that sent a jolt of pain through Arran's rib cage.

"And *that* would be okay with your father?"

Dash shrugged wearily. "Sure. Yes. I don't care. He can't

control who I sit with at dinner. I know it sounds ridiculous, but can we at least *try* to be friends?"

The word *no* tore through him. Arran couldn't have pleasant, meaningless chats with the boy he loved, who had once been the person he felt closest to in the galaxy. If Dash was too much of a coward to stand up to his father, if he didn't care enough about Arran to fight for him, then it was time to move on. Arran had enough to worry about without adding a self-centered, spoiled Tridian to the list.

Before Arran could respond, his link buzzed with a new message—likely from Vesper, who'd been checking in every few hours to see how he was feeling. But when he looked down, his breath caught in his chest, and he stood up so quickly that he knocked his chair over.

"Sorry, I have to go," Arran said as he fumbled to straighten the chair. Dash had also reached for it, and their hands accidentally brushed. "Sorry," he said again, blushing as he turned away.

Arran could feel the eyes of everyone in the dining hall turning to him, but for the first time in his life, the attention didn't bother him. Without looking up from his wrist, he hurried out of the room to find his squadron mates.

CHAPTER 7

VESPER

I'll always be there to catch you, Vee. Vesper grinned at the warm, tingling feeling these words produced when she replayed them in her head, though part of her was afraid to replay them too often lest they lose some of their potency. She wanted to savor them for as long as possible.

Rex was the first person who'd caught a glimpse of the real Vesper—the girl she kept hidden away behind her screen of brash confidence and ambition. Rex was the only person who'd seen her break down, who'd heard her explain why she'd never felt good enough, why there was part of her that always felt like a fraud. He'd seen her, and instead of running away, he'd pulled that girl closer. For the first time in her life, Vesper knew what it was like to be seen—and maybe even *loved*—for the real her.

Her link buzzed on her wrist. *"New message from ... sender unknown,"* her monitor announced. That was strange. The only time she'd received a similar message, it'd turned out to be from her mom, who'd been stationed at a top-secret base on one of Chetire's moons.

She opened the message and, to her surprise, saw that it was a video transmission. When the face appeared on her link, Vesper's knees gave way, and she sat on her bed with a heavy thump.

"It's me, Orelia," Orelia said unnecessarily. For the past four months, Vesper had spent two hours a day six inches from her squadron's intelligence officer. She knew the side of Orelia's face as intimately as she knew the contours of the simulcraft's control panels.

Vesper froze as a barrage of emotions battled for dominance. After the initial pang of shock, a wave of hot anger rose up. This was the spy who'd infiltrated the Academy, earning the trust of everyone around her so she could send the school's coordinates to the Specters.

Yet even the tide of anger wasn't enough to drown the

relief she felt at seeing Orelia alive and well. Or, at least, alive. She looked somehow exhausted and exhilarated. Dark shadows hung beneath her eyes, and sweaty strands of blond hair clung to her flushed face.

"I'm so sorry," Orelia said, shaking her head. "I know I let you down. I know I betrayed you. But...it's more complicated than that. I..." She closed her eyes and took a deep breath. "I guess by now you've heard that I'm not from Loos. I'm from Sylvan, though I know that's a name you've never heard before. I'm what you call a Specter."

Orelia paused as if waiting for Vesper to process what she'd just said.

"I know you have no reason to trust me, but there's something I need to tell you."

An unsettling mix of nausea and numbness spread through Vesper's body as she watched a breathless Orelia explain how the Quatra Fleet had attacked the Specters' planet first and then launched a massive cover-up to conceal the truth. It was like listening to the rantings of a mad person. It couldn't possibly be true, could it?

"I'm on my way to Sylvan," the message continued. "I'm going with Zaf—Lieutenant Prateek to broker a cease-fire and propose a peace summit. I don't know when I'm going to see any of you again, so I wanted the chance to say..." Orelia closed her eyes and pressed her lips together. "I don't know, really. To say I'm sorry...and thank you." She opened her eyes and smiled sadly. "You're the best friends I've ever had. The only friends I've ever had, really. And whatever happens, I need for you to know that." Orelia opened her mouth as if to say something else, but the message ended abruptly.

Vesper paced the room, running her fingers through her hair and muttering, "There's no way."

"Elevated heart rate detected. Consider taking a few deep breaths and imagining a calming scenario. For more relaxation tips, say—"

"Dismiss and fuck off!" Vesper shouted at her monitor, which, mercifully, fell silent.

There was frantic pounding on her door, and before she had time to answer, Arran burst in. "Did you see this?" he asked, thrusting his link toward her.

"I just watched it." She shook her head, but the small action was hardly enough to clear it. "I don't know—"

She cut herself off as Rex stepped into the room, his brow furrowed. "Did you get it too?" he asked, sounding slightly dazed. Both Vesper and Arran nodded. "They're sending Orelia to organize a peace summit?"

"Apparently," Vesper said. "Though I have trouble believing that they'd really trust someone who, very recently, tried to get all of us killed."

A look of pain flashed across Arran's face. "She also saved our lives, if you'll remember."

"After revealing the location of the Academy and making us vulnerable to attack. I know she was our friend, but, Arran, I watched you almost *die* on that patrol ship."

"That wasn't Orelia's fault," Arran said quietly.

"What are you talking about? She's the reason the Specters knew where to find us!"

"I don't know...I just think it might be more complicated than that." He shook his head and let out a long sigh. "I know I'm not making any sense. I think I'm too tired to put words together. I'd better lie down for a bit."

"Are you sure?" Rex asked, looking at Arran with concern.

"I'm fine. I'll see you guys later."

Once the door closed behind Arran, Vesper turned to Rex. "Do you think we should go after him?"

Rex didn't respond and lowered himself onto the edge of her bed, looking grave. She sat next to him and placed her hand lightly on his knee. To her surprise, he moved his leg to the side, avoiding her touch. "What's wrong?"

She waited for him to say "nothing" and take her hand in a gesture of apology. To smile and tell her that he needed to study tonight. But he leaned forward, put his head in his hands. "Listen, Vesper...I think maybe we should cool it for a while." He sounded strangely wooden, like he was reciting from a script someone else had written.

The words landed like a lash on her skin. "What are you talking about?"

He let out a long sigh, then turned to face her, still without meeting her eyes. "There's just so much going on right now, it seems like we should really be focusing on what matters. Classes, patrol, preparing for the next Specter attack."

"What *matters*?" Vesper said, as if repeating the mysterious words would unlock their hidden meaning. What could matter more than finding someone who brought out the best in you? Who made you believe in yourself? Who pushed you and challenged you?

"I mean, maybe if we hadn't been so distracted by our own drama, we would've noticed that something weird was going on with Orelia."

The hurt and confusion in Vesper's stomach began to bubble into anger. "So, let me get this right. You're breaking up with me for national security reasons? Wow, that's really noble of you."

Rex stood up and ran his hands over his buzzed hair. "I'm sorry, Vesper," he said with infuriating composure, refusing to rise to her bait. "But I really think this is for the best."

"Then why won't you look at me?"

"I *am* looking at you," he said with a weariness that made her heart sink. Just a few days ago, he'd looked at her like she was the only girl in the solar system. And now he was treating her like an irritant, a burden. Something he was better off without. But when she forced herself to look into his eyes, she saw none of the callousness she'd braced herself for. Instead she glimpsed something akin to pain.

"Why are you doing this?" she asked softly, stepping toward him to place her hand on his arm.

"I'm just trying to do what's best...for both of us," he said. Though this time, he waited a few moments before shaking her hand off. "I'm sorry, Vesper."

She watched him go, frozen in place as he turned and left her room. *I'll always be there to catch you, Vee.* Of all the lies

Rex had told her over the past few months, this one hurt the most.

The multi-environment track was blissfully empty, so there was no one to stop Vesper from cranking up the gravity. Before she even finished her first lap, her lungs were burning and her legs had started to tremble. But after her bewildering conversation with Rex, the pain felt almost comforting. It was a relief to empty her mind and focus on nothing except her breath and her stride.

She knew she was better off without him, yet she couldn't look at her red badge—the same as his—without feeling a stab of pain that had nothing to do with her burning leg muscles.

With a groan, she yanked her foot off the track, but before she could set it down again, she'd started floating. Instead of double gravity, it felt like she was bouncing in half gravity. "Hey!" Vesper shouted. "I was *training* here."

A figure emerged from the control room and half jogged, half floated toward her. "I thought you needed a break," her mother called. "I was worried you'd hurt yourself."

"You've never worried about that before," Vesper shouted, trying to hide the relief she felt as she landed lightly on the track, then took off again, launching into the air for nearly five seconds.

Admiral Haze fell into place next to her, matching her giant, bounding strides. "Why aren't you at dinner?"

"Wasn't hungry."

"Usually, skipping a meal for an unnecessarily grueling workout is seen as a cry for help. Is everything okay?"

"*You're* skipping dinner too, aren't you?"

"I'm eating after this," Admiral Haze said. "So why aren't you with your friends?"

Vesper hesitated, unsure how much to confide. Admiral Haze wasn't the type of mother who had the time or inclination to follow the ups and downs of her daughter's love life. Nor was she particularly fond of Rex, whose cockiness and Devak manners seemed to count for more than his brilliance in the simulcraft. But Vesper felt that she had to tell *someone* about what had happened, and at least she could count on her mother's discretion. "I just had a strange conversation with Rex. I think...I think he just broke up with me."

To her credit, Admiral Haze managed to arrange her

features into a vague approximation of concern. "What'd he say?"

Vesper gave her mother the short version, partly because she didn't want to relive the painful details, and partly because she knew her mother would only be able to feign interest for so long.

To her surprise, instead of responding with something like *Don't waste your time worrying about him; you can do better*, her mother simply nodded thoughtfully and said, "That must've been hard to hear."

"It was," Vesper said cautiously, not quite sure what to make of this unprecedented amount of sympathy. "Especially since everything seemed to be going so well."

"It's a stressful moment...for everyone," Admiral Haze said. "And people react to pressure in different ways. Perhaps Rex just needs a little time to process everything."

"Maybe," Vesper said. "We had just gotten some pretty shocking news." She told her mother about the message she, Arran, and Rex had received from Orelia.

Admiral Haze came to a sudden stop. "She told you about the mission?"

"Is...is that okay?" Vesper asked as she tried to catch her breath.

"No, it's certainly not okay that an admitted *spy* relayed sensitive intelligence."

"We haven't told anyone," Vesper said quickly. "I promise."

Admiral Haze muttered something under her breath, and Vesper braced for a prickly retort, but her mother merely let out a long breath.

"So it's true? About sending a peace envoy to the Specters?"

Admiral Haze's eyes brightened. "Yes, although we're trying to keep it under the radar for now."

Vesper stretched her arms out to find her balance in the low gravity as she stared at her mother in wonder. For her whole life, all she'd ever heard was that the Specters were bloodthirsty killers who couldn't be reasoned with—who wouldn't stop until every Quatran in the solar system was dead. "Do you think peace is really possible?"

"I hope so. The fighting has gone on long enough. It's time to find a diplomatic solution."

"Do you actually believe what Orelia said? About us attacking them first?"

Admiral Haze glanced over her shoulder, then lowered her voice. "I'm starting to. I've done some digging, and there's a disturbing lack of documentation from that period, which is certainly suspicious."

"But surely people *want* to know the truth, don't they? What does Commander Stepney think about this?"

Her mother pressed her lips together, and when she spoke again, her voice was slightly strained. "Commander Stepney is having a little difficulty adjusting to the new circumstances."

"But he must be coming around if he signed off on the peace envoy." Admiral Haze looked away, and Vesper felt her stomach sink. "Mom... he knows, right?"

"I'm doing what I need to do to protect the solar system, Vesper. If there's a chance of stopping this war, then nothing else matters."

CHAPTER 8

ARRAN

Arran hesitated in front of the door that led to the Research and Development wing. That mysterious portion of the Academy required a much higher security clearance than Arran's—a fact he'd learned the hard way once after making a wrong turn, setting off an alarm, and receiving a security escort back to his proper domain. But today was different. He'd received orders that, after his classes ended, he should report to Lab Four in D Wing where, presumably, the new technology team was meeting. However, there was no guarantee that anyone had updated his security clearance, and Arran didn't want to risk triggering the alarm.

How did Orelia do it? he wondered. How had she managed to bypass every security measure in the Quatra Fleet?

How had she arrived in the Quatra System to begin with? Who'd helped her forge all the necessary documents to gain admission to the Academy? That alone was an extraordinary accomplishment, never mind what she'd managed to achieve once she'd arrived.

As Arran stood in the hall, trying to decide what to do, three young officers approached—two men and a woman who looked just a few years older than Arran. They weren't cadets, nor did they look like the senior officers who periodically traveled to the Academy to meet with Admiral Haze. They were heading for D Wing, Arran realized, which meant that they must've also been recruited for the new tech team. As they passed, two of the three shot Arran curious looks, which he understood. In a place as bustling and regimented as the Quatra Fleet Academy, it was unusual to see a cadet standing around, looking anxious—let alone one from Chetire, since these officers would've graduated before the Academy began accepting Settlers.

Heat rose to Arran's cheeks as he imagined what he must look like—an awkward, lost first-year cadet standing in the way of officers here on real business. For a brief moment, Arran fantasized about turning around and going straight to his room, the one place where no one could make fun of his accent, his clothes, or the fact that he'd never been off-planet until he boarded the Academy shuttle.

You're not that person anymore, he reminded himself. *Your squadron* won *the tournament. You saved the Academy from a Specter attack* and *won the Medallion of Valor. You were hand-picked for this new division. This is where you belong.* Arran took a deep breath to steady his racing heart. He was going to show the solar system—Dash, his father, everyone—what Chetrians were made of.

Arran strode purposefully into D Wing, wincing slightly as he crossed the barrier. But the alarm never sounded; his clearance had been upgraded.

It didn't take long to find Lab Four, a large room that contained workstations on one end and a conference area on the other. At the moment, everyone in the room was gathered in the conference area. The lights were dim and the chairs had been arranged to face a glowing screen. A cursory glance didn't reveal anyone Arran recognized, so he sat down in the closest empty seat. A few minutes later, a tall, slim boy with purple-streaked black hair slid into the seat next to him. It was Rees—a quiet first-year Loosian who mostly kept to himself. Arran had always found him intriguing. Unlike other cadets who existed on the fringes of the Academy social scene, Rees didn't seem shy and awkward. Instead, he projected a detached curiosity, as if he preferred to watch and observe from a distance. It was a little intimidating, actually. Arran wasn't sure what to make of someone who wasn't anxious to fit in and make himself liked. Even Vesper, the most confident person he knew, clearly cared about winning respect and admiration, although it seemed enviably easy for her to dismiss anyone who *didn't* admire her as an idiot.

Unsure whether or not Rees was expecting him to make conversation, Arran pretended to fiddle with his link, which was easier said than done, given that links didn't function in this highly secure wing of the Academy. Luckily, he didn't have to keep up the ruse for long. A moment later, Commander Stepney strode to the front of the room and everyone scrambled out of their seats to salute and stand at attention.

He was accompanied by a young woman Arran didn't recognize. She had short, unruly, curly black hair and was casually dressed in a combination of civilian clothes and military attire—an unbuttoned captain's jacket over a T-shirt and loose gray trousers. Her outfit violated nearly every tenet of the Quatra Fleet dress code, but instead of seeming sloppy or rebellious, she gave the impression of a scientist too busy with important research to bother shining a pair of regulation shoes every day. "Welcome, everyone," she said. "I'm Captain Alexis Mott. I'm heading up this newly formed research group, and I'm delighted that you were all able to make it today. I know many of you weren't given much notice, but we don't have any time to waste."

She turned to Commander Stepney and nodded as he said, "As you know, the location of the Academy has been compromised. Ten days ago, a squadron of first-year cadets managed to prevent what would've been a devastating attack. Four days ago, a second Specter craft managed to enter our solar system undetected. This time, they succeeded in detonating an electromagnetic pulse that damaged one of our patrol ships. Cadet Sula Trembo was killed in the blast, and had it not been for the bravery and quick thinking of her fellow cadets, more lives would've been lost. Evidently, since the last round of attacks, the Specters have made certain technological advancements. For years, we were able to detect the enemy the moment they slowed from light speed, which allowed us sufficient time to prepare for an attack. We cannot afford to lose that advantage. That's why I asked

Captain Mott to head up this new initiative. You're here because you've been identified as the brightest engineers and theoretical physicists in the fleet. We need you to determine how the Specters are evading our radar and upgrade our systems to protect our fleet from similar attacks. It's a tall order, but this room is full of people who've achieved the impossible, and I have no doubt you'll rise to this challenge as well. For now, I leave you in Captain Mott's capable hands."

The assembled cadets saluted him and then turned their attention to Captain Mott, who was already pointing to the images that'd just appeared on the screen.

"So that's what counts as the *brightest*?" a disdainful male voice said quietly. Arran turned his head to find the source. The speaker was a man in his midtwenties in the third row, leaning all the way back in his chair with one foot resting on his knee. Even in the dim light, Arran could make out the shape of a smirk as he gestured toward Arran and Rees. "Those two look like something someone dug out of a mine."

Arran froze as shock and embarrassment coursed through him. Even after receiving a Medallion of Valor, there were still people in the fleet who'd never see Arran as one of them.

It was a lesson he'd learned long ago and one he'd been foolish to try to forget.

"The acceleration of the center of mass of a system is related to the net force exerted where A equals... where A equals... where A equals..."

Arran stood from his desk, walked to the front of the classroom, and banged his fist against the side of his physics instructor's head. Fifty percent of the time, this was enough to stop the stammering.

"Where A equals... where A equals..."

With a sigh, Arran returned to his desk and began to read the textdoc on his own. This was what happened when your physics instructor was an attendant so old that it was impossible to repair since no one made the requisite parts anymore. Arran didn't really mind teaching himself physics. It was far better than being stuck in a classroom with the other nine-year-olds, who were still learning multiplication and division. It was a little lonely here in the storage unit with the buggy attendant who was only programmed to deliver lectures, not answer questions or grade assignments, but lonely was better than boring. Arran loved losing himself in a math problem, when the crowded jumble of thoughts and worries disappeared, replaced by elegant equations that always led to a clear answer. He didn't have to wonder whether his mother was skipping lunch so he'd have more to eat at dinner that night. He didn't have to worry whether his father would come home after his shift, or if today they'd get the news that every mining family on Chetire most feared. News delivered by a tired, jaded spokesperson who'd have to glance down at his link to make sure he got the name right. I'm so sorry for your loss, Mrs. Korbet.

Ignoring the still-stuttering attendant, Arran began to fill out an exercise on momentum. He'd ask his real teacher, Ms. Fen, to look it over later.

"Arran?" a pleasant voice called. He glanced over his shoulder to see Ms. Fen herself standing in the doorway. "It's time to go." Arran's head was so full of equations that it took him a moment to remember what Ms. Fen was talking about. There was a Quatra Fleet exhibition in town this afternoon, and everyone in Sector F was "highly encouraged" to attend.

Arran joined the rest of his classmates in the hall, where they were bundling themselves into their matted, oversized fur coats— most of them hand-me-downs that'd been worn by countless relatives. Arran's own coat had once belonged to an older cousin who'd been killed in a mining explosion at seventeen.

It was freezing outside, as usual, and within a few minutes the slivers of exposed skin on Arran's face began to burn. But it was *sunny and Arran was happy for the chance to be out in the day-light. This time of year, the sun appeared for only three hours on Chetire, which meant he walked to and from school in icy darkness.*

"Everyone, stay together," Ms. Fen said as they approached the central square. Although her mouth was covered with a scarf, Arran could tell from her voice that she wasn't smiling, which was unusual for her. Why is Ms. Fen nervous? *he wondered. This wasn't the type of problem he could solve with an equation, which always frustrated him.*

But as they entered the square, Arran forgot all about his question. Crowds of people gathered along the sides of the enormous square—Settlers in fur coats and a few Tridian mine owners and managers in warmer, sleeker thermalskin—while troops of Quatra Fleet soldiers performed drills in the center.

Arran and his classmates watched as best they could, though it was difficult to see over the heads of the adults in front of them. At one point, two girls grew bored and started to play a hand-clapping game before Ms. Fen rebuked them. She wasn't quick enough, though, and a tall man in a long black thermalskin coat turned to glare at them. "These men and women risk their lives to keep you safe. Show some respect."

"They're just children," Ms. Fen said, placing a protective hand on each of the girls' shoulders.

"They're old enough to know better." His words were clear, for instead of a scarf wrapped around the lower half of his face, he wore a mesh shield designed to keep in heat without obstructing speech. "It's up to you to teach them to behave properly. Antares knows their parents won't. No sense of respect or personal responsibility."

Arran looked from the man to his teacher, waiting for her to respond, but then something caught his eye that made him forget about everything else. Someone had landed a real fightercraft nearby, and it looked like people were allowed to touch it! Without thinking, Arran broke away from his classmates and hurried over. He'd never seen a fightercraft up close like this before and was surprised to see that it was even larger than he'd imagined.

Arran ducked through the crowd until he made it to the very front. Tentatively, he reached out and pressed his gloved hand against the smooth metal. This ship had traveled through space! It might even have traces of meteor dust on it!

"She's a beauty, isn't she?" Arran looked up to see a fleet officer smiling down at him.

Arran nodded. "Is it capable of faster-than-light travel?"

"Not this model. Only the battlecraft have that capability. But we can dock ships like this to a battlecraft and travel at light speed that way."

"When I'm older, I'm going to design fightercraft." Arran had

never said the words aloud before, but he'd thought them so many times, they felt as true as anything else he knew.

The officer laughed. "You have quite an imagination. Listen, these are complicated machines, and it takes a very special kind of person to fully understand them. Those people are rare, and they don't come from places like this. Don't set yourself up for disappointment."

Back at home that night, Arran told his mother about his exchange with the officer and was surprised to see her face cloud with anger. "What did he mean when he said 'places like this'?" he asked.

"Don't give it a second thought," she said, eyes flashing. "That man is living in the past and doesn't recognize that children like you are the future. You'll do great things one day, Arran. And no one is going to stand in your way."

Arran stared straight ahead, at the screen. Perhaps if he focused on Captain Mott's presentation hard enough, he'd be able to ignore the quiet, cutting laughter directed at him. But each muffled chuckle landed like a jagged chunk of ice on the back of his neck. Part of him hoped Captain Mott would notice the disruption and put a stop to it, but a larger part of him was mortified by the prospect of her coming to his defense, of revealing his vulnerability to everyone in the room.

His cheeks burned as he willed himself not to react. The less he appeared to notice them, the better. It wouldn't make them stop—he'd had far too much experience with bullies over the years to believe in such simple tricks—but at least he'd maintain some semblance of dignity. And a moment later, the laughter *did* stop, and despite his better judgment, he glanced over his shoulder, an act that would surely only provoke them further. But to his surprise, the young Tridian officers had gone quiet and were sitting stiffly, exchanging slightly startled looks.

Rees slid silently into the seat next to Arran, who hadn't even realized he'd left. With his long legs and lanky frame, he reminded Arran of the ghost leopards he'd occasionally spot back on Chetire, padding noiselessly through the drifts. One of the Tridians seemed to be watching Rees warily, but when Rees turned to meet his eye, the boy looked away quickly. "Did you say something to them?" Arran whispered.

"We might've had a quick chat," Rees said without looking away from the screen at the front of the room.

"What did you say?" he asked quietly.

Rees said nothing, and for a moment, Arran thought perhaps he hadn't heard him. But then a small smile crept across Rees's face, prompting an unexpected blush from Arran, who was glad that Rees was still staring straight ahead.

At the end of the lecture, Rees rose from his seat and began to walk away without saying a word to Arran. With a final glance at the Tridians, who were conspicuously avoiding looking at Arran, he hurried into the corridor to catch up with Rees.

"Thanks for that," he said, falling into step next to him.

"Don't mention it," Rees said in a tone that made it difficult to tell whether he meant *you're welcome* or *don't mention it again*.

"Do you think they're all staying at the Academy?" Arran asked, glancing over his shoulder.

"Probably. It'd be too expensive to ferry everyone back and forth on the shuttle multiple times a week."

"Super," Arran said as they passed a group of Tridian officers.

"I don't think they're going to mess with us again," Rees said, the smile returning.

"But you're not going to tell me what you said?"

"I doubt you really want to know."

Arran smiled. "Well, that explains why I was always too intimidated to talk to you."

"Intimidated? Or...otherwise occupied?"

Arran shrugged. "You just seemed happy to keep to yourself."

"I guess it depends on my mood. Sometimes, I *am* happy on my own, but then when I'm in the mood to be social, I guess I don't always know how to, you know, switch gears."

Arran glanced at his link. "It's almost time for dinner. What kind of mood are you in right now?"

"I suppose I could tolerate company," Rees said with a smile. "If you're not meeting anyone else."

"I'm not," Arran said. And for the first time in weeks, the thought felt more freeing than painful.

After agreeing to meet in front of the dining hall, they returned to their own rooms to change. Arran walked quickly, buoyed by a combination of nerves and fizzy excitement, which drained away the moment his eyes settled on the figure standing in front of the door to his suite.

It was Dash.

Arran took a deep breath and then fixed a smile on his

face. He would do his best to remain polite, poised, and detached. The last thing he needed was another confrontation that'd leave him hurt and worked up before his dinner with Rees. "Hi," Arran said, then lifted his hand to wave awkwardly. "Are you looking for me?"

"No, Lissa," Dash said with a smile, referring to Arran's nice but slightly eccentric roommate who'd become the source of numerous inside jokes between them. "I was going to ask her for some fashion tips."

Arran pretended to survey Dash's suit jacket. "I'm sure Lissa will be able to spice that up with some sequins. Or glow-in-the-dark beads."

Dash laughed, but the sound did little to loosen the knot in Arran's stomach. It seemed forced, as if the two of them were performing a hollow imitation of the old Dash and Arran. "I just dropped by to give you these, in case you were looking for them. You must've left them in my room at some point." Dash reached into his pocket and produced a pair of dark blue socks.

"Those are yours."

"Are you sure?" Dash asked, brow furrowing.

Arran reached for the feather-soft socks. "You know they are. They're made from glacier ram's wool." The rare, silky-coated beasts were found only on Chetire, but of course, items made from their wool were far too expensive for Settlers and were exported to Tri.

"Oh…whenever I look at them, I picture them on your feet."

"That's because you lent them to me that night I was cold and then wouldn't let me return them. I put them back in your drawer when you weren't paying attention." With a sigh, Arran handed the socks to Dash. "But you know that, of course."

"Okay, fine, so I made up an excuse to see you. Is that so awful?"

"Yeah, it kind of is. I need time and space to get over you, and you're making it a little difficult for me."

Dash's face fell, and his shoulders slumped. "What if I don't want you to get over me?" he asked quietly.

For a moment, Arran couldn't do more than stare as he struggled to hold back the tide of warmth Dash's words threatened to unleash. He'd spent the past week desperate to hear something like this, yet he knew that he had to be careful, lest he suffer even greater pain than the agony he'd recently endured. "Does that mean your father suddenly came around to the idea of you dating a Settler?"

"He will eventually, I'm sure of it," Dash said, sounding anything but sure.

"What are you saying, Dash? That you want to get back together? That you're suddenly brave enough to face the consequences when word reaches your father?"

"Just...give me time to figure it out. Please. I don't want to lose you."

"So, what? You want me to wait? That's not how this works, Dash. You can't put me on hold like some item in a fancy Tridian boutique. I have my own life to live. Now, if you'll excuse me, I need to change. I'm meeting someone for dinner and I don't want to be late."

Arran brushed past him and hurried inside, but not fast enough to avoid seeing the expression on Dash's face. As the door shut behind him, Arran winced and closed his eyes as a wave of pain crashed over him. No matter the circumstances, no matter how badly your pride had been bruised, there was no agony like hurting someone you loved.

CHAPTER 9

CORMAK

This is it. I'm officially in hell, Cormak thought as he approached the simulcraft where he was due for his first practice session.

Yesterday, Admiral Haze had summoned the first-year cadets to the auditorium to announce that they'd all been assigned to additional practice sessions in the simulator. "We hope to be able to avoid a catastrophic battle, but if it proves inevitable, we need to use every tool at our disposal, and that includes our most promising cadets. It's crucial that you have the training and experience you need to serve the Quatra Federation and protect the solar system."

And of course, since the gods he'd never believed in anyway appeared to hate him, he'd been assigned to a simulcraft with Ward and Vesper. Vesper was already inside when he arrived, along with the fourth member of their new crew, a Loosian first-year named Belsa who was friends with Orelia's roommate Zuzu.

It was the first time Cormak had seen Vesper since their terrible breakup—four of the worst days of his life. Saying those awful, clichéd words, *I think maybe we should cool it for a while*, had felt like plunging a knife into her chest. The pain in her eyes had nearly destroyed him, and it'd taken every ounce of self-control not to shout, "I don't have a choice. Your ex-boyfriend is blackmailing me, and he has the power to get me arrested."

Vesper didn't even turn in Cormak's direction as he entered the simulcraft, but he could tell from her rigid posture that his presence was causing her similar anguish. That's what she did—the more pain she felt, the more desperately she tried to mask it.

He tried to distract himself by making small talk with Belsa, but it didn't take her more than a minute to realize that she'd stumbled into something fraught and awkward, and the conversation soon trailed off.

After a seemingly endless period of uncomfortable

silence, Ward ambled into the simulcraft, and the oxygen in the small space seemed to vanish, as if someone had opened an airlock. *Get it together, Phobos,* Cormak told himself as Ward settled into the captain's chair without waiting for instructions. *He wants to annoy you as much as he wants to get back together with Vesper. Don't make this any easier for him.*

Yet while Cormak managed to remain aloof and disinterested, Belsa fixed Ward with a glare. "Maybe we should wait until we know the assignment before deciding our roles?"

"Relax, Beka. I just didn't feel like standing," Ward said as he draped his arms over the sides of the chair in a decidedly proprietary manner. "Maybe you should take a seat yourself. You seem a little wound up."

"Her name's *Belsa,*" Cormak snapped before he could stop himself. "And we're all 'wound up' because we're at fucking war."

"Are you sure that's why you're so wound up, Phobos?" Ward asked with an infuriatingly knowing smile. He glanced at Vesper, who seemed to be making it a point to ignore both of them.

The simulcraft screen flashed to life and the now-familiar voice came through the speaker. "*Welcome, cadets. Today's exercise is being monitored, and you'll be assessed on your speed, accuracy, and ability to work as a team. You have two minutes to agree on your assignments and then your mission will commence."*

"How do we want to do this?" Vesper asked, speaking for the first time since they'd entered the simulcraft, her ardent desire to avoid contact with Ward and Cormak overpowered by her even more ardent desire to succeed in the exercise. "Anyone mind if I pilot? Okay, great," she said, sliding into the pilot's seat without waiting for an answer.

"Just like the olden days," Ward said with a grin as he leaned back in the captain's chair, hands clasped behind his head. "Right, Vee?" She didn't respond, but Ward's words alone were enough to turn Cormak's stomach. He knew they'd been on the same squadron back at their Tridian prep school.

"Who wants to be captain?" Cormak asked lightly, as if he couldn't see Ward settling into the captain's chair. "Belsa?"

She glanced at Ward, then sighed. "I'm fine with tech officer," she said with the weary air of someone too tired to fight.

"Are you sure? Because now that Ward's had time to rest,

I'm sure he wouldn't mind moving into one of the other seats."

"You heard her, Phobos." An edge had crept into Ward's voice. "She wants to do tech, which means you're the counterintelligence officer. Don't let the name intimidate you, though. It doesn't require *that* much more brainpower than you seem to possess."

"Is that so?" Cormak pretended to scratch his head thoughtfully. "Remind me again whose squadron won the tournament and whose came in fourteenth?"

"Will you two cut it out?" Vesper snapped without turning around. "We're running out of time."

"*I'm* not the only one still standing. It's Phobos here who seems to be gunning for a fight. Not exactly captain temperament, is it?" Ward lowered his voice slightly. "I'd choose your battles very carefully if I were you."

The lights in the simulcraft cabin darkened and images began to flash on the screen. "Fine," Cormak said as he lowered himself into the counterintelligence officer's chair. *It's never going to stop*, he realized. *That shithead is going to keep blackmailing me to get whatever the hell he wants.*

A map of the solar system appeared on the screen, then

zoomed in on Deva. *"A fleet of Specter ships is approaching the solar system, and the southern hemisphere of Deva appears to be their target. Your mission: Evacuate a group of stranded miners from the Shotwell Barrens before the first missile hits. You have twelve minutes to complete your objective. Commence mission."*

"Stranded *miners*?" Ward scoffed. "Seems like an awful lot of effort to rescue some people no one would miss."

Belsa scowled at him over her shoulder. "I know you think you're being funny, but you really just sound like an idiot."

"What? I'm being serious."

"First off, their lives matter just as much as yours. And what do you mean no one would miss them? What about their families?"

"I *meant* that if the Specters were really twelve minutes away from attacking Deva, we'd have to make some hard choices about who we evacuate. Any Quatran death is a tragedy, of course. But if, Antares forbid, there *is* a series of massive strikes, we have to think about who'll be most essential when we rebuild, and frankly, miners aren't going to be at the top of the list."

"So the fyron we need will just magically appear out of the ground?" Belsa said.

"I'm not saying we won't need miners. I'm just saying that we don't necessarily need *those* miners in particular. It's a job anyone can be trained to do. Listen, it'd be awful to have the Specters blow up a bunch of miners, but the truth is, they're replaceable."

Rage was bubbling so fiercely in Cormak's chest, he felt his whole body trembling. But he willed himself not to take the bait. Ward was only saying this shit in an attempt to make him snap, and Cormak sure as hell wasn't going to give him that satisfaction. He refused to let himself look foolish in front of a Tridian ever again, no matter what.

"Why are you just standing here?" Cormak was so sure the girl had to be talking to someone else, he actually looked over his shoulder.

"I'm talking to you," she said with a laugh that, while not entirely kind, wasn't exactly unkind. She looked to be about eight, so maybe a year younger than he was, but she had the assurance of someone much older. They always did, these Tridian girls. Even if she hadn't spoken, he would've known she wasn't a Settler. Her long, glossy hair suggested frequent washing, which required access to more water than anyone he knew had. Even more telling,

her fingers were free of the red dust that gathered under the nails of even the most fastidious Devaks. That's why he was so surprised that she seemed to be addressing him. Most Tridians acted as if looking at a Devak would be enough to contaminate them. "Are you waiting for your parents?"

Cormak shook his head. His mother had died when he was a baby and his father wouldn't be able to leave the mine for hours. "I'm here by myself."

She cocked her head to the side and surveyed him curiously. "Then why aren't you going inside?" They were in the metrocenter—an enormous building in the middle of the sector that contained trading stalls, an amphitheater, and a large multipurpose hall that housed a number of events throughout the year. At the moment, it contained the traveling zoo that arrived on Deva every so often. There was no way Cormak could afford a ticket, but he'd come anyway, hoping that a careless visitor might accidentally drop one.

"I don't have a ticket," he said.

"They're selling them right there." The girl pointed. "You can just go get one."

"I don't have the money," he said simply, without shame. He didn't know many people who could afford such a luxury.

She narrowed her eyes and scrutinized him as if convinced he was playing some trick on her. "Why didn't you ask your parents for money before you came here?"

Now it was Cormak's turn to stare at her disbelievingly. "My father doesn't have ten credits just lying around. And if he did, he'd have more important things to spend them on."

"So you're poor?" the girl asked.

Cormak shrugged. He'd never really thought about it that way. On Deva, there were a few people who lived in nice houses full of plants and books. And then there was everyone else, people like him who lived in the towers and were never quite sure how they'd pay the next month's rent.

"I can buy your ticket, if you'd like."

"Really?" Cormak said as excitement bubbled inside him. "Your parents won't mind?"

"They're not here. I came with Roos." She pointed at an attendant waiting in the ticket line. "I'll tell her to buy you one," the girl said as she pressed a button on her link.

"Thanks! I'm Cormak, by the way."

"I'm Ada." She extended her arm, then let it fall to her side. She'd either remembered that Devaks didn't normally shake hands, or else she had second thoughts about touching Cormak. He didn't *care which it was. How could he be upset when he was about to go to the zoo? He'd only ever seen a few animals in real life: sand lizards—one of the only species native to Deva and capable of breathing its toxic air—and a cat he'd once seen a Tridian carrying through the launchport.*

Roos glided over to them with the tickets. "Here's one for you, Ada, and one for your little friend."

Cormak stared at her in wonder. He'd seen attendants before, of course, but never one who spoke like a real person. "Thank you very much," he said, hoping that was the right thing to do.

Ada shot him a strange look but didn't comment on the fact that he'd thanked the attendant. He followed her to the entrance, doing his best to walk normally instead of bouncing up and down with excitement. The guard smiled at Ada, didn't acknowledge Roos, and frowned slightly at Cormak, which was pretty typical, in Cormak's experience. If he'd had the money for a ticket and tried to enter the zoo on his own, the guard still would've interrogated him—asking him where he'd gotten the money, scrutinizing the ticket to ensure that it wasn't counterfeit, then keeping a close eye on Cormak...if he let him in at all. But with Ada, it was different. Easy.

"Whoa..." Cormak whispered as they stepped inside. The air was cooler in here, no doubt for the animals, who weren't

accustomed to the climate on Deva. It was also humid, something he'd never felt before, growing up on a planet where it never rained. He took a deep breath, relishing the way the air felt going down into his lungs.

He let Ada lead the way and followed her to the first enclosure, where an enormous pink bird was wading through a turquoise pool. Every few seconds, it'd lower its curved orange beak to scoop a gleaming silver fish out of the water. Cormak watched, mesmerized, transfixed by the bird's elegant movements, its shockingly bright feathers, and the squirm of the wriggling fish. "This is boring. Let's find something else," Ada said, tugging on Cormak's sleeve. He didn't look to see if she wiped her hands on her pants afterward.

"Do you think he's lonely?" Cormak asked as they walked away.

"Who?"

"The bird. He was all by himself. But the books I've read say that birds travel in flocks."

Ada ignored his question and pulled him over to a tank where an enormous red-feathered snake was coiling itself along a tree branch, but even this didn't hold her attention for long. Yet despite the frantic pace set by his companion, Cormak had the best afternoon of his life. At one point, Ada told him to stop smiling so much because it made him look weird, but he found he couldn't. Not when there were so many amazing animals to see!

As they finished the ice pops Ada bought them, Roos said: "I've received a message from your mother, Ada. She wants us to go home now."

Ada rolled her eyes but obligingly tossed her half-eaten ice pop into the garbage. Cormak winced and wished she'd offered it to him first. "You can stay longer, if you want," she said.

"Okay." He hoped this was true, and that the guard wouldn't come find him when Ada left. "Should I give you my ping code?"

She looked slightly affronted. "Why?"

"So we can play together sometime," Cormak said.

Ada laughed. "We can't play together."

"Why?"

"Because," she said in the same tone Cormak's teacher used when she wanted to make him feel stupid—which was most of the time. "My mother would never let someone like you into our house, and I'd never want to visit yours."

"I don't understand. We had fun today, didn't we?"

"Oh, definitely." She gave him what she probably imagined to be a kind smile. "But that doesn't mean we could ever be friends. Goodbye, Cormak."

And with that, she left without another word. Looking back,

Cormak always thought he could picture Roos giving him a slightly pitying look as she passed, but that was impossible.

Robots didn't care for Settlers any more than Tridians did.

"Will everyone shut up and pay attention?" Vesper called without turning around. "We're going in."

Cormak glanced up to see his rust-colored home planet filling the screen. He knew he should be scanning the atmosphere for storms and other obstacles that would impede their descent, but the closer they got to Deva, the more his fury grew. His brilliant, kind, funny, caring older brother *had* died in a Devak mine. And not because of a Specter attack. After learning that he'd been accepted to the Quatra Fleet Academy, Rex had signed up for a short-term job in a notoriously dangerous mine to earn enough to get Cormak off planet as well. He'd refused to leave his little brother behind and had paid the ultimate price—he'd been killed in an explosion a few days before the end of his contract. But Cormak knew he wasn't alone in his grief. That mine had been full of people who'd risked their lives to provide for their families, and for Ward to call them all *replaceable* made Cormak's stomach curdle with disgust.

"How's the flight path looking?" Vesper called, her tone all business.

Cormak glanced at the radar screen. "There's a sizable storm in the mesosphere," he said flatly. He'd have given anything to be back with Arran and Orelia, the four of them operating as a single unit, using the shorthand they'd developed during the countless hours they'd spent in the simulcraft.

"How long will it take to go around?"

Cormak started to perform the calculations, but before he could respond, Ward spoke up. "You don't need to go around. You could get through this storm in your sleep, Vee," he said in an encouraging voice Cormak had never heard him use before. "I've seen you do it a million times."

Cormak waited eagerly for Vesper to tell him to knock it off. Ward would have to do better than *that* to get back into her good graces. But to his disappointment, she said nothing, and her shoulders even seemed to relax slightly.

Sticking to the most direct route, Vesper deftly navigated her way through the storm, which grew fiercer as they descended toward Deva's surface. The simulcraft began to rattle, but Vesper never wavered, and while she barely spoke, Cormak could feel her and Ward settling into a rhythm—the same kind of rhythm he'd always felt when it was him in the captain's seat.

"We're almost there," Ward said. "It's just like that time we won the tournament back at school. Though this time, we'll find a better way to celebrate." He forced a laugh and shook his head. "I can't believe we thought that hosting a dinner party for our squadron was a good idea. Remember when the fire alarm went off and my brother came running down in his underwear?"

Vesper still didn't respond, but a small smile seemed to be forming on her face.

"I never thought that smoked magma boar was a good idea," Vesper said. "You insisted on making it and wouldn't take no for an answer." She still wasn't looking at Ward, but there was a hint of amusement in her voice.

"One of the many times I should've listened to you," Ward said in a wistful tone that made every muscle in Cormak's body twitch with an urge to punch him in the face. As if Vesper would ever fall for such an obvious ploy.

But to Cormak's dismay, she didn't call him out on it. She didn't even roll her eyes. Spotting his opportunity, Ward continued softly, "I'm never going to make that mistake again. I don't like the person I become when I'm not around you."

Bullshit, Cormak thought, biting his tongue to keep from hurling the word. What the hell was Ward talking about? He and Vesper had still been dating when he'd decided to write *Go home Edgers* on the wall. But he couldn't say anything. Not when Ward held Cormak's secret in his hand like a grenade, his fingers ready to pull the pin at any moment.

The rest of the mission went smoothly, although Cormak found it impossible to take pride in their success. Not with Ward in the captain's seat, whispering sweet nothings to Vesper like they were together in bed instead of a simulcraft. As soon as the words *Mission completed* flashed across the screen, Cormak jumped out of his seat, refusing to subject himself to this torture any longer than necessary.

But Vesper had already stood up as well, and Cormak slowed down, letting her pass him as he waited for the barbed-wire noose around his stomach to loosen. But it was a futile exercise. No amount of time would lessen the pain of hurting the first girl he'd ever truly loved.

CHAPTER 10

ORELIA

Orelia's extensive training had prepared her for a variety of challenges. She'd traveled four parsecs from her home planet, posed as a Loosian, gained entry to the Quatra Fleet Academy—the most secure location in her enemy's solar system—and then transmitted its top-secret coordinates to her commanding officer. Even her arrest hadn't really come as a surprise. When she'd agreed to this mission, she'd known she'd likely end up in a Quatran execution chamber.

But none of the lectures, exercises, or briefing manuals could've prepared her for this. In the span of a few hours, she'd gone from a maximum-security prison cell to the stateroom of a Quatran battlecraft bound for Sylvan, her home planet. She wasn't even going to be kept under guard during the journey. "We've offered you the deal of a lifetime," Admiral Haze had explained as she'd seen them off on the launchport. "If you try to escape, it'll mean that you're far too stupid to be useful to us, so there's no point in forcing someone to follow you around."

During the quick initial briefing on board, Zafir had introduced Orelia to the two other fleet officers who'd be accompanying them—a young female linguist named Captain Avar, and an older, slightly grizzled negotiator named Colonel Beaune who'd conspicuously refused to shake Orelia's hand when they'd met.

Orelia had been ordered to brief the others during the journey, preparing them for the most important, delicate, dangerous meeting in the history of the Quatra System. And so, shortly after the ship had entered light speed, the small group met in the ship's dining room for their first session. Round, star-filled windows lined one long wall, while across from it hung antique maps of the Quatra System. Dark red leather chairs surrounded the polished wooden table—a strange choice for a military transport ship, Orelia thought. The Sylvans would've never used materials that required so much upkeep.

Colonel Beaune and Captain Avar were already seated

and talking quietly when she'd arrived. They were both dressed in civilian clothes, which was permitted for this stage of the journey, but that small concession did little to make the gathering feel any more casual. They both glanced at Orelia as she entered, and while Captain Avar was able to maintain some semblance of normalcy, Colonel Beaune didn't bother to hide his disdain as he glared at Orelia with open hostility.

Let him judge me, Orelia thought, raising her chin. She'd been working on behalf of her own government, just like everyone in this room was doing right now. She had no more blood on her hands than they did. Everyone here had supported the war against the Specters, even when the strategy included murdering millions of civilians. There were no innocent parties on this ship. Yet just as Orelia began to regain her confidence, the final member of the team entered the dining room, and her frantically beating heart dove for shelter in her stomach.

She'd never seen Zafir in civilian clothes, his bathing suit notwithstanding, but he looked no less impressive in a white shirt and gray trousers than he did in his uniform. He moved with purpose but seemed unhurried, and unlike the others, he didn't stare at Orelia with either curiosity or aggression. In fact, he didn't glance her way at all. As he took the last remaining seat, he appeared as relaxed and professional as always save for the hint of dark stubble on his cheeks. Yet rather than making him look tired or unkempt, it merely emphasized his sharp cheekbones and dark, nearly black eyes.

The others were looking at her expectantly, but when Orelia opened her mouth to speak, no words came out—a surprising setback for a secret agent who'd been trained in subterfuge. She wished she could see what was going on in Zafir's head, whether he'd ever see her as anything more than a fragile ally, a tool.

"Perhaps we should start out by asking you a few questions," Captain Avar suggested, almost kindly. "Who will we be meeting with when we arrive? What does Specter, excuse me, Sylvan leadership look like?"

Somehow, Orelia managed to provide an informative answer without stammering.

She spoke about the extreme seasons on Sylvan—a winter equivalent to an ice age, and a summer during which the oceans swelled to cover most of the land—and explained how for centuries, the people of each region did their best to survive on their own, often suffering significant casualties. She gave a brief overview of modern Sylvan history and discussed how ten years ago, they joined together to create an international governing council and a joint military force that still held power today. "General Greet, the head of the military alliance, is in charge of planetary defense. She's the one who'll either approve or reject the cease-fire, and decide whether to participate in the peace summit."

"Is she also the one who approved the attack that killed that girl? Or the bombing that killed fifty thousand people on Chetire?" Colonel Beaune asked gruffly.

Zafir shot him a sharp look. "I believe you were briefed on our newest intelligence regarding who actually started the war, weren't you, Colonel?"

"Intelligence?" he repeated with a bitter laugh. "Yes, I heard what this girl told you, but until I see actual evidence, you'll forgive me for not begging for the Specters' forgiveness with tears in my eyes." Orelia wished she could ask why, exactly, he'd been chosen for such a delicate, diplomatic mission when, as if reading her mind, he said, "But if Stepney's against this fool's errand, then I'm happy to count myself among the fools."

"We don't know that he's against it," Captain Avar said quickly. "I believe Admiral Haze was on her way to brief him when we left. There just wasn't time to wait for his official approval."

Zafir cleared his throat. "That's Admiral Haze's business. Our job is to do whatever is necessary to arrange the cease-fire and peace summit."

At that moment, two attendants glided in with trays containing their refreshments—predinner drinks and a few snacks, a time-wasting, expensive custom, especially on a battlecraft. The disruption was enough to bring the conversation to a halt. When she'd first arrived at the Academy, Orelia had been struck by how people of different ages interacted with the attendants. The instructors and staff members generally stopped talking mid-conversation whenever an attendant passed, whereas the cadets carried on talking, unbothered. When Orelia had asked Arran about this, he'd explained how, until somewhat recently, a party with authoritarian tendencies had controlled the Quatra Federation. During the darkest periods, the government secretly collected data from attendants to monitor "unpatriotic" behavior across the solar system. It didn't happen anymore, but people who remembered the old days were still hesitant to speak in front of the machines.

"So, Orelia," Zafir said, turning to her. "What else do we need to know about the Sylvans?"

Orelia continued with a basic overview of Sylvan history and culture, stressing the Sylvans' emphasis on directness, honesty, and practicality. Yet while Zafir and Captain Avar hung on her every word, Colonel Beaune's skepticism seemed to grow until he broke in during one of her pauses. "We discussed the logistics but not our most pressing security threat."

"And what is that, exactly?" Zafir asked.

Colonel Beaune jerked his head in Orelia's direction. "Her."

Captain Avar looked startled, but Orelia maintained her composure as she said, "What threat do I pose? With the pilot and the crew, you outnumber me eight to one."

"For about twelve more hours," Colonel Beaune said gruffly. "Then you're going to outnumber us by four *billion*."

"That's the population of the Quatra System. The population of Sylvan is only six hundred million." Orelia paused and affected a thoughtful expression. "Though I suppose there's no way for you to know that, given the shocking dearth of intelligence you've managed to gather over the past fifteen years."

"You think this is all a joke, don't you?" Beaune turned to lock eyes with Zafir. "This girl could be leading us into a trap. There's probably a fleet of Specters waiting for us. They'll extract her and kill the rest of us. Or, knowing the Specters, they'll probably blow up our ship with her inside. They don't seem like the types to mind a little extra blood-shed, do they?"

"Orelia is on our side," Zafir said, an edge creeping into his voice. "She agreed to help us negotiate for peace. Having her with us lends credibility and increases the likelihood that the Sylvans allow us to speak instead of blowing up our ship on sight."

"Interesting," Beaune said, crossing his arms over his chest. "You seem very quick to defend the traitor's honor. Going soft, are you, Prateek?"

"I'm trying to defend the solar system, Colonel. And right now, listening to Orelia is the key to our survival. So if you don't mind, I'd like to hear what she has to say."

Despite his sharp tone, his words made Orelia's heart flutter like the wings of a thawing frostfly coming back to life after its long hibernation. She knew it was unlikely that

Zafir would ever trust her enough to care for her again, but perhaps it wouldn't be entirely foolish to hope.

By the time the meeting ended, Orelia's head was swimming. She would've given anything for a breath of fresh air—it'd been months since she'd inhaled anything but endlessly refiltered oxygen or felt sunlight on her skin. She was too antsy to stay in her room, so she headed to the viewing deck at the front of the ship. Yet as she approached, she saw that the bench was already occupied. She froze and was about to turn around when the figure stood abruptly.

"Did you want to sit? Go ahead. I was just leaving." Zafir spoke with such polite detachment that it made her heart cramp. "Thank you for the briefing. It was incredibly helpful," he said pleasantly, as if she were a colleague he was passing in the corridor.

"It was nice of you to defend me back there. Though Colonel Beaune has a right to be suspicious. I *am* a spy."

"Maybe. But he doesn't have a right to speak to you like that."

Orelia recalled what she'd learned about Quatran martial law. "I think, technically, he does, actually."

"Not while I'm around." Zafir looked her in the eyes for the first time since they'd started their journey and, for a brief moment, Orelia caught a glimpse of the boy she'd kissed that night in the ocean simulator. But then he vanished as quickly as he'd appeared, dissolving within the professional reserve of Lieutenant Prateek the counterintelligence officer. "Please excuse me. I have some messages I need to send."

"Wait a second. Will you talk to me, please?"

"I believe we're talking now."

"About something other than the mission, I mean."

"I think ending the war and saving millions of lives deserves our full attention, don't you?"

She winced and lowered herself onto the bench he'd just vacated.

He stared at her with what she could tell was feigned confusion, but then he sighed, and the pain he must've been holding back began to show in his weary face. "You lied to me," he said quietly.

"I didn't have a choice. I was sent on a mission to protect my planet. Of all people, you should understand what that means."

"It's one thing to carry out a mission. It's quite another to play with someone's feelings for sport. You didn't need any information from me. There was no reason for you to trick me into caring for you."

Even saturated with sadness, the words still produced a flutter in Orelia's stomach. He had cared for her. "I didn't trick you," she said softly. "That was real."

"Orelia, come on," he said, forcing a smile. "We're on the same side now. I appreciate your commitment, but it's time to stop the charade. I know getting...close to me was part of your assignment."

"It wasn't!" she insisted. "Zafir, I swear."

"You expect me to believe that you, a spy sent to infiltrate the Quatra Fleet Academy, just *happened* to befriend the highest-ranking counterintelligence officer at the base?"

"You think befriending you was part of my plan? It was the riskiest thing I could've done. The moment I met you, I realized that my survival depended on staying as far away from you as possible."

"You didn't do a particularly good job with that part."

"No, I didn't," she said, unable to keep herself from smiling at the memories. "And soon I realized that I didn't *want* to. Here I was, alone on the other side of the galaxy, surrounded by people who'd wish me dead if they knew who I really was, and yet when I was with you, none of that seemed to matter. It was impossible to think of you as the most dangerous person at the Academy when you were the only person who understood me."

"How well could I have understood you if I didn't realize you were a Specter?" he asked, shaking his head with embarrassment and bitter amusement.

"You were looking for someone—some*thing*—totally alien. Not an awkward girl who didn't know what to do with herself at parties."

"I can't believe you sat there during all my ridiculous lectures, listening to me drone on and on about things I apparently knew nothing about."

"You didn't get everything wrong. I was pretty impressed with some of your inferences, considering how little data you had."

"And yet, all along, I had the most valuable data source in the solar system right there in front of me," he said with the faintest hint of a smile.

"Data source?" she repeated, trying to ignore the sting. "Is that how you would've thought of me if you'd known the truth?"

"No, of course not." He took a deep breath, then lowered

himself back onto the bench next to her. "Though valuable, certainly."

"In what way?"

"For reminding me what it was like to care that deeply about another person. That's…that's why I felt so betrayed. When I realized you were a…Sylvan, I assumed that you'd gotten close to me in order to extract information. It confirmed all my worst fears."

"Do you still feel that way?" she asked softly.

He turned to meet her eyes. "I'm not sure. I'm still figuring it out. Is that enough for now?"

The guilt that'd been crystallizing in her stomach finally broke apart. "I think so. As long as you promise to let me help you figure it out."

He smiled. "I promise."

CHAPTER 11

ARRAN

"Are you sure you know what you're doing?" Rees asked, raising an eyebrow as the metal panel in their test pod began to melt and twist in on itself. Today was the second meeting of the new technology task force, and Captain Mott had split them up into teams to try to re-create the event that had damaged the patrol ship. Rees had originally been assigned to work with a Tridian, but after he'd gotten into a heated argument over an equation that'd yielded different results for each of them, Captain Mott had reshuffled the groups so that Arran and Rees were working together.

They were experimenting with different types of electromagnetic pulses in an attempt to figure out what the

Specters had used to fry the oxygen converter and close the hydrogen vents.

"Do I know what I'm doing? Not really," Arran said cheerfully, as flames began to creep along the edge of the twisted metal. "Fire's not exactly a concern on Chetire. Nothing to burn."

Rees merely looked at Arran with mild amusement, his lips twitching into a not-quite smile Arran was just beginning to recognize. They'd had fun at dinner the other night—at least, Arran had had fun. But Rees was tricky to read, and it'd been hard to tell whether he'd actually *enjoyed* Arran's company or merely tolerated it.

"Do you want me to take over?" Rees asked. They'd divided the tasks so that Arran was in charge of directing the pulse, while Rees monitored the effect on the simplified oxygen converter and dummy hydrogen vents.

"It's fine. Everything's under control. How are the readings looking?"

"They're going haywire." Rees paused thoughtfully. "But didn't you say that the ship's readings were normal before the explosion?"

"Sula didn't report anything, and it'd be very unlike her

not to notice." It was the first time he'd managed to say her name aloud in a normal tone of voice.

"That's strange," Rees said. He wrinkled his nose in a way that seemed at odds with his cool, detached demeanor, reminding Arran of a little kid. "What's that *smell*? Is that something burning?"

"Yeah, it's the insulation in the vent," Arran said with a nod, then hesitated. "You know what's strange? I don't remember smelling this on the ship. Whatever caused the hydrogen vents to close and cause that buildup, I don't think it was an external pulse."

"You mean you think it was an internal malfunction?"

"Maybe…but there was no warning or alarm before the explosion. And I've never heard of the monitory system *and* the backup system failing at the same time, have you?"

"No, I haven't," Rees said in a voice Arran couldn't quite read.

"Everything okay over here?" Captain Mott asked as she passed by their workstation and peered over to look at the melting vent.

Rees and Arran locked eyes for a moment, and Rees nodded slightly. "Everything's fine," Arran said. "I just realized, though, that I didn't smell burning insulation when

I went to manually open the vents. And I wonder…does that mean something else caused them to close? Something other than an electromagnetic pulse?" Despite the effort he made to keep his voice from sounding accusatory, he still braced for a look of annoyance to flash across Captain Mott's normally cheery, youthful face. Even his nicest teachers on Chetire would chastise Arran for "asking disrespectful questions," i.e., those that questioned their knowledge and authority.

But to his relief, Captain Mott nodded seriously. "Something like what?" she asked, curious, without any hint of a challenge in her voice.

"I don't know…maybe it was an internal malfunction."

She pressed her lips together. "All the evidence points to an attack with a concentrated pulse directed at the oxygen converter and the hydrogen vents."

"But then I would've smelled the burning insulation, right?"

"The fire in the weapons bay was pretty large, wasn't it? Couldn't the smoke have obscured the smell?"

"*This* smell?" Rees said, wrinkling his nose for effect.

"Listen," she said with a sigh. "If you're not convinced, you two can go down to the launchport and examine the damaged ship. There'll be burnt circuitry all along the hydrogen vents. Hold on, I'll update your security clearances." She fiddled with her link for a moment, then looked up at them. "Okay, you're all set."

"Thank you," Arran said. "We'll be quick."

Mott glanced down at her link again. "Take your time. Our session is nearly over anyway. Go examine the ship and then report back to me tomorrow."

Arran saluted, while Rees raised his arm in a close-enough approximation of a salute, and they headed toward the door. On his way out, Rees locked eyes with his former Tridian partner, and while Arran couldn't see the expression on Rees's face, from the look on the Tridian's, he could only assume that Rees's glare was fearsome to behold.

"Sorry for making you run errands with me," Arran said as they turned into the corridor.

Rees made a noise somewhere between a snort and a laugh. "Yeah, because I was clearly having so much fun in the lab. If I'd known that this 'prestigious opportunity' would involve teaching remedial math to the winner of the nepotism award, I would've told them to shove the opportunity up their asses."

Arran furrowed his brow in mock confusion. "I'm not

sure how that would work, given that there's only one opportunity and multiple asses." Rees raised an eyebrow and surveyed Arran with amusement but said nothing. "Maybe you're the one who needs remedial math," Arran continued.

This time, the noise Rees made was much closer to a laugh, and Arran felt a thrill of pride. "What do you mean by nepotism award?" Arran asked.

"That dipshit Tridian cadet, Marcel. His mother is the president of the Orion Corporation, that massive fyron distributor."

"So what? You think she paid his way into the Academy?" Arran asked skeptically. Even before they began admitting Settler cadets, the acceptance rate had been incredibly low. It would've been difficult for an unqualified candidate to make it, regardless of his family's wealth.

"She wouldn't have had to. Do you have any idea how much money Stepney gets for being on the Orion advisory council? There's no way he'd let the Academy reject Marcel."

"There's no way Stepney could be on the Orion advisory council. That would be a massive conflict of interest."

"Oh, Arran," Rees said, shaking his head. "So sweet, so innocent."

Arran bristled slightly. "How do you know he's on the

council? I've never read anything about Stepney being involved."

"I make it a point to know stuff like this. Everyone acts like letting Settlers into the Academy is this huge step toward equality, but that's bullshit. There are very rich, very powerful people who'll do anything to maintain the status quo. Those are the ones we need to pay attention to, so I make a point to do just that. For a long time, we were too poor, too broken, too sick to pay attention to what was really going on. But now we're in a position to ask questions, and that's exactly what I'm planning to do."

Rees spoke with such intensity that his eyes seemed almost to glow, fueled by a fire deep within him. Arran's skin tingled as his mild irritation gave way to admiration. It'd been a long time since he'd heard someone speak so passionately about something unrelated to life at the Academy. When Arran didn't respond, Rees shook his head and looked away. "Never mind. I know it's not what everyone wants to think about."

"No, you're right," Arran said firmly. "I'm glad you told me about Marcel's mom and Stepney. I'm just embarrassed I didn't figure it out on my own."

They walked the rest of the way in silence, but it was

a companionable, thoughtful silence, as if Rees was purposefully giving Arran time to process his thoughts. They reached the launchport and, using their upgraded clearance to enter the restricted area, made their way to the head mechanic's office.

Arran explained their task to the harried-looking blond woman, who let out a long, weary sigh. "The ship's already been taken apart and sent to different labs for analysis. What did you want to look at?"

"The vents for the hydrogen. The ones that were damaged by the Specter pulse," Arran said patiently.

The head mechanic grunted. "Looks like today's your lucky day. The crew forgot to pack up one of the vents. I put it right over here in case anyone came back to get it. The people they sent to fetch them seemed pretty anxious to make sure they had all the pieces, but it's not my fault they couldn't be bothered to count."

"Definitely not your fault," Rees said, amused. It was clear he'd taken a shine to this disgruntled woman.

She gave him an appraising look without saying anything, then walked over to the cabinet against the wall. She pressed her thumb against the scanner, and a drawer slid open with a hiss. She reached inside and removed a large, vacuum-sealed plastic bag and handed it to Arran. "Here you go. You'll need additional clearance to open the bag," she said. "We can't introduce any contaminants."

"I don't need to open it," Arran said without taking his eyes off the bag. "This is all I need to see." He held it up in front of Rees. "Look, there's no damage. No sign of burnt circuitry or melted insulation. That's why I didn't smell anything."

Rees nodded once, implying that he agreed but that they shouldn't talk about it here. Arran took a photo of the vent with his link and thanked the head mechanic for her help, and then the two boys left her office. When they were a safe distance away, Rees broke his silence. "So what do you think is going on?"

"I'm not sure. But whatever caused that explosion, it wasn't an electrical pulse. Maybe it was some kind of malware?"

"But how could the Specters have installed malware in one of our ships?"

"Who knows? They did install a spy, after all. They might have more access than we realize."

"That's a good point. Do you think she might've had something to do with it?"

"Orelia?" Arran shook his head. "No, she wouldn't have done something like that."

"Why not? Wasn't that her whole mission?"

"Her mission was to transmit the coordinates of the Academy. Not install malware to blow up a ship. Trust me, she wouldn't have wanted anyone to get hurt."

Rees looked at him quizzically. "Okay, sure."

Arran knew he sounded ridiculous. By sending the coordinates to the Specters, Orelia had jeopardized the life of every person here. A few days after her transmission, a Specter ship had come within seconds of blowing up the Academy. Yet, at the very last moment, Orelia had given her squadron mates the information they needed to destroy the Specter craft, killing a crew of her own people in the process. So while it was impossible to know exactly what Orelia was capable of, Arran couldn't imagine her causing the explosion that'd killed Sula.

"So who do you think did it, then?" Rees asked as they turned back into the central corridor.

"I have no idea. That's why I'm slightly nervous about telling Captain Mott—it makes me sound a little paranoid."

"Paranoid? Or awake?" Rees asked.

"You know, that's the exact question I've been asking myself about you and your theories."

"Just you wait, Korbet. Stick with me long enough, and I'll tell you things that'll blow your mind."

"Is that a promise or a threat?"

Rees gave him another one of his intense, searching looks, then he smiled. "I guess it depends on how much you like getting your mind blown."

By the time they made it back to the main wing of the Academy, there were only ten minutes left. "Do you really think Captain Mott won't mind if we don't go back?" Arran asked, glancing nervously at the time on his link.

"I'm pretty sure that's why she said *report back to me tomorrow*. If you go back now, she'll think you don't know how to follow orders."

"So what should we do, then?" Arran asked, then cringed slightly, wishing he hadn't been quite so presumptuous. The fact that they'd had dinner together once didn't make them friends.

To his relief, Rees didn't seem fazed. "Come with me. I have an idea."

Arran followed Rees down the main corridor and then into a narrow passageway he'd always assumed led to a maintenance closet. At the end was a large metal door that, although unlocked, might as well have been emblazoned with the words DO NOT ENTER. After four months at the Academy, Arran had gotten very good at identifying places he wasn't meant to enter. Yet Rees merely raised his link to the scanner and, a moment later, the heavy door creaked open.

"How'd you do that?" Arran asked.

"I figured out the master code they use on the locks and programmed it into my link. Here, I'll send it to yours too," Rees said as he tapped on his wrist.

"No, it's okay," Arran said quickly.

"Too late. It's already done. Welcome to the dark side."

"So where are we going, exactly?" Arran asked in a voice he hoped was more curious than anxious.

"It's a surprise."

"A surprise that's going to get me arrested?"

"Relax, Korbet," Rees said with a smirk. "Our upgraded security clearance hasn't expired yet. Everything's going to be fine."

"I don't think Captain Mott upgraded us so we could go gallivanting around the Academy."

"You think this counts as gallivanting?"

Arran fought back the heat threatening to color his cheeks. "I guess I'll reserve my judgment until I see where you're taking me."

Rees nodded. "That's a good idea," he said seriously. "You don't want to burn out on gallivanting by starting too early."

This remark would've earned one of Arran's friends a playful smack on the arm, but he didn't feel comfortable doing something like that with Rees. He was intense in a way Arran had never really encountered before. His whole body seemed to be made of tightly coiled energy, and even when he smiled, his sharp, searching gaze never really softened. Yet instead of being off-putting, it somehow seemed to draw Arran in, and he found himself with a strange desire to earn Rees's approval.

He followed Rees up a staircase that led to a set of large glass doors that, to Arran's surprise, were streaked with condensation, an odd sight in a space station. "Where are we?" he asked, no longer able to feign nonchalance.

Rees waved his link in front of another scanner; the doors slid open, and they stepped inside. The first thing Arran noticed was the air, which was warm and strangely soft. Almost wet. *Humid.* He'd only read the word in books, never said it aloud. But he knew this was the word he was looking for. The second thing he noticed was the explosion of color, more than he'd ever seen in one place in his entire life. Plants of all shapes and sizes spilled out of clear containers. Some were so tall, they nearly brushed against the transparent ceiling, while others had low branches dropping with the weight of brightly colored fruit and vibrant blossoms.

"The Academy has its own *greenhouse*," Arran said, looking around in amazement.

"Where do you think all the fruit comes from?"

"I don't know. I figured they imported it from Loos or something."

"That would be an even more unconscionable waste of money and resources." Rees shook his head as he surveyed the lush tangle of vines, stems, and blossoms. "Can you imagine how much this must cost?"

"Nope," Arran said with a smile. "But at this particular moment, I don't really care." He took a few steps forward to run his finger along the edge of a pale purple flower, relishing the sensation of the smooth petal against his skin.

"I thought you might like it," Rees said, his voice softening slightly.

"How'd you find it?" Arran asked without turning his

head, his gaze still transfixed by the flower. "It seems like they're trying pretty hard to keep people out."

"I don't like the idea of living in a place with secrets."

"At least this is a good secret," Arran said as he turned to face Rees. "This is the first flower I've ever seen in real life."

"Really? I don't know if that's sweet or tragic."

"Well, you've probably never seen snow."

"Definitely not a fair comparison. Snow is decoration. Plants are life."

"Deep thoughts from Rees."

To Arran's surprise, Rees laughed. "Yeah, I know I tend to take myself a little seriously sometimes."

"That's okay. That's one of the things I like about you."

Rees raised an eyebrow. "So there are multiple things about me you like?"

"At least three. Possibly four," Arran said lightly, trying to mask his embarrassment.

"I'll take it. That's more than most people do." There was a wistful note in his voice, but before Arran had time to examine his expression, Rees had turned to examine the large, waxy leaves of an enormous spineberry plant.

Arran began to wander down the narrow, cramped aisles, murmuring in amazement every time he reached out to touch a stem or wipe a drop of condensation from a leaf. He closed his eyes and took a deep breath, relishing the sensation of the warm air in his throat. Was this what it was like to live on a planet where the temperature wasn't always thirty centis below freezing? Where the air outside felt like a caress instead of a slap?

"I guess that means you've never seen the ocean either," Rees said, suddenly appearing next to him.

"Nope."

"That's such bullshit," Rees said, surprising Arran with his sudden intensity. "They keep us prisoners on our own planets, working ourselves to death so they can gallivant all over the solar system like it's their own private playground."

Arran didn't need to ask who "they" were. It didn't matter that he and Rees had grown up at opposite ends of the solar system. Every Settler grew up knowing that "they" referred to the Tridians. Despite Rees's anger, there was something comforting about being able to use this kind of shorthand. It was something Dash had never understood, of course, and sometimes his apologies for not understanding had been more irritating than his naïveté.

"Well, we're the ones gallivanting right now, remember?"

Rees smiled, though it wasn't quite enough to extinguish

the fire in his eyes. "I've heard that word more in the past ten minutes than I have in my whole life. Is that a Chetrian thing?"

"Just a weird Arran thing."

"Is referring to yourself in the third person a Chetrian thing?"

This time, Arran couldn't stop himself from hitting Rees's arm playfully. But before he had time to retract his hand, Rees grabbed his wrist and grinned. "That was a poorly thought-out attack, Korbet."

"I hardly think that constitutes an *attack*," Arran said, rolling his eyes. He tried to pull away, but Rees tightened his grip and pulled him closer. Arran's heart began to pound as the pressure of Rees's fingers sent a current of electricity up his arm.

"Oh, really? I look forward to seeing you in action, then." He let go of Arran's arm, but the tingling sensation didn't fade.

At that moment, every thought, every feeling left Arran's body except for how much he wanted to kiss Rees. To feel the electricity he could sense surging beneath the other boy's skin. But he couldn't do that. He'd never kissed anyone but Dash, and that had happened only after weeks of hanging out. Arran had always assumed he was the type of person who grew on you, for whom you developed a gradual attraction.

But then he looked at Rees, who was staring at him with an expression Arran had never seen on anyone's face, not directed at him, at least. Rees's eyes burned with their usual intensity, but this time they seemed fueled by something other than anger or suspicion. Something akin to longing.

Before he could lose his nerve, Arran leaned in and let his lips brush lightly against Rees's, who shivered slightly, sending a thrill through Arran's own body. He kissed him again, a little harder this time, and brought his hand to the back of Rees's head. His lips tingled with the electricity he'd known he'd feel, but even that wasn't enough to banish the image taking shape in Arran's mind—the face of the boy he was trying his hardest to forget.

CHAPTER 12

VESPER

"The gang's all back together!" Ward said cheerily as he walked toward Belsa, who looked annoyed, and Rex, whose features were contorted by so much fury and disdain it was almost comical. Yet before Vesper could smile—or worse, do something to help put Rex at ease—she reminded herself how they'd gotten into this mess in the first place. Rex had broken up with her, using some bullshit excuse about needing to *focus on what matters* because he was too cowardly to tell her the truth. And while she found it a little distasteful that Ward had taken advantage of her recent breakup to start cozying back up to her, if Rex couldn't handle watching it, that was his problem, not hers.

"Everyone excited to save the solar system by restocking

toilet paper?" Ward asked with a grin. Instead of practicing in the simulators, today their group had been assigned the slightly less glamorous task of performing inventory checks on the battlecraft that'd recently docked at the Academy.

"You're in a good mood today," Belsa said, eyeing him suspiciously.

Ward shrugged. "I'm always in a good mood."

"Except when you're vandalizing hallways, I assume."

Belsa's words made Vesper cringe. She'd still been dating Ward when he'd written *Go home Edgers* in the corridor, and while her shame paled in comparison to the hurt and anger the Settler cadets had felt, she hated that she was somehow associated with his cruelty.

Yet instead of growing defensive or brushing it off with a joke, Ward nodded, looking grieved. "That was the stupidest thing I've ever done, and I'm sorry about it. I know words aren't enough to make up for my actions, but I've done a lot of soul-searching since then, and I'm doing my best to learn from the pain I've caused and be a better person."

"That's…nice to hear," Belsa said, looking slightly startled as she tried to catch Vesper's and Rex's eyes. But Rex was staring off in the distance, his face hard and unreadable.

"Thank you," Ward said seriously. "I want to prove myself

worthy of the Quatra Fleet Academy and"—he looked sig-nificantly at Vesper—"worthy of all the people whose trust I've unfortunately lost."

He sounded so sincere that, for a moment, she wondered whether she'd been too hard on him. Did one moment of stupidity really negate all the years of loyalty and love he'd shown her? Ward had never kept secrets from her, never callously broken her heart.

"You're here to do inventory, right?" a brisk voice said. Vesper turned to see a young woman in a corporal's uni-form striding toward them.

The four cadets nodded and saluted.

"I need two of you in the infirmary and two of you in the galley."

"Vee and I can do the infirmary," Ward said, shooting Vesper a quick smile. "We don't have the best record in the kitchen."

Out of the corner of her eye, she saw Rex's jaw clench, and she felt a satisfying surge of anger that burned away the mistlike sadness that had been seeping through her for days. If she wanted to talk to Ward, or if he wanted to drop references to their past intimacy, that was their business. Rex had forfeited his right to an opinion.

However, the corporal did not appear amused either. "You're here to help prepare this ship for battle, cadet. Not to canoodle with your girlfriend. You and Cadet"—she looked at the badge on Belsa's chest—"Borgone will report to the galley, and the other two will report to the infirmary."

The cadets saluted, Ward a little less enthusiastically than he had before, and boarded the battlecraft. Vesper felt the same tingle of excitement she always did upon entering the massive ship. She'd spent so much of her childhood fantasizing about joining the Quatra Fleet that it was impossible not to feel awed. But this time, the thrill didn't last quite as long as usual, and it was soon replaced by a prickle of dread as she imagined an afternoon spent shut up in the ship's tiny infirmary with the boy who'd just broken her heart.

"See you later, Vee?" Ward said. "Maybe we can meet up for dinner or something?"

"Maybe," she said hesitantly.

He grinned. "Great," he said, apparently unbothered by her noncommittal response.

Ward and Belsa split off toward the galley, leaving Vesper and Rex to walk in silence through the narrow corridor and down the spiraling metal staircase that led to the infirmary on one of the lower levels of the ship.

They still hadn't exchanged a word, or even made direct eye contact, since Rex had left her room the other day, and she tried to imagine what was going through his head. Every time she caught a glimpse of Rex's face, she could see the pain in his eyes, but she wasn't sure what it meant. If he still cared about her, then why had he reached into her chest and dug his nails into her heart?

They both stood awkwardly while the infirmary supervisor explained their task—taking inventory of various medical supplies and ordering whatever needed to be refilled. In any other situation, Vesper might've resented this kind of grunt work, but today she was grateful to have a mindless task that didn't require her to talk to Rex.

Unfortunately, the medical-supply room was so small that the silence felt heavier than the highest gravity setting on the multi-environment track, and it was impossible not to be aware of every movement, every quiet sigh, every breath.

As she watched Rex out of the corner of her eye, she noticed him staring at a shelf of medications without recording them on the inventory chart, as they'd been instructed, and she felt a flash of irritation. He'd told her that their relationship was too much, and yet here he was, staring off into space like a petulant child avoiding a chore.

He flinched slightly, as if he could feel the weight of her gaze, then without turning around, he said, "The names on the bottles don't match the names on the chart. It's like they gave us the wrong list."

For a moment, Vesper's spite threatened to get the better of her, and she considered ignoring him. If she were such a liability, then surely he could get along without her. But then she let out a weary sigh and stepped toward him to look at his chart. "What are you talking about?" She picked up a bottle of Ziosnene from the shelf in front of him and pointed to the corresponding entry on his chart. "There."

"That says Triocide, not Ziosnene," he said gruffly, as if he resented having to talk to her.

"Ziosnene is a form of Triocide," she said, unable to keep herself from injecting a note of condescension into her voice. "Haven't you ever had a headache?"

He shot her a look, as if unsure whether or not she was joking. "I had a headache for sixteen years straight. That's what happens on Deva when you live in old housing and can only afford a cheap gas mask. You grow up with low-grade carbon monoxide poisoning…and that's if you're lucky."

"Oh," Vesper said, cheeks flushing. There was so much

about Rex's life that was completely foreign to her. Had he hidden the truth about his childhood so she wouldn't pity him? Or had she simply been afraid to ask? Walking into Rex's room for the first time had broken Vesper's heart a little. There were no personal belongings at all: No knick-knacks from home on the dresser. No holopics of friends and family on the wall. She didn't even see any non-Academy-issued clothes peeking out of the drawers. Yet despite the lack of personal touches, it was clear that Rex took great pride in the room. The bed was perfectly made, Rex's uniforms all hung neatly in the closet. But the detail that pinged against Vesper's heart was the bottle of shoe polish and the small brush on the shelf above the desk. She'd thought that everyone had the attendants polish their shoes for them.

For the first time, she found herself wishing she hadn't always let Rex off the hook so easily every time she'd tried to ask him about his life on Deva only to have him deftly change the subject.

"I guess Ziosnene wouldn't have been that helpful, then."

He shrugged. "I have no idea. There wasn't any Ziosnene."

"Do you use a different form of Triocide on Deva?"

He let out a short, bitter laugh. "We don't have painkill-ers. At least, the poor people don't. And everyone I knew was poor. If you had a headache, or cracked your head stumbling through the dark during a power outage, or got your face smashed in by thugs on your way home from work, you waited for it to pass. That's all we could do."

Vesper reached for a bottle of antibiotics. "I guess you didn't have these either."

Rex shook his head. "Nope."

Vesper thought about the elaborate lengths her father had gone to when she was sick growing up. Asking the attendant to make pricklefish soup, insisting that the doctor see Vesper in person instead of sending a medical bot to collect her vitals.

"Listen," Rex said, shifting his weight from one foot to the other. "I know it's none of my business, but I think you should be careful around Ward."

He sounded more concerned than jealous or possessive, which Vesper found vaguely touching. "You're right. It isn't any of your business," she said, more curtly than she actually felt.

"I know, I'm sorry. I just…" He trailed off, apparently unsure how to continue.

Before she could respond, her link buzzed, startling her. She normally set it to sleep mode when she was on duty, but she'd been so distracted by Ward and Rex that she'd apparently forgotten. She looked down and saw a new message from Arran. She skimmed it quickly, then frowned and read it again more slowly, trying to process everything he'd told her.

"What's going on?" Rex asked.

The almost tender concern in his voice momentarily made Vesper's hackles rise—he didn't have the right to use that tone with her anymore. But her need to share what Arran had told her overpowered her fleeting desire to put Rex in his place.

Vesper glanced at the door and listened for a moment to make sure no one was moving around in the main area of the infirmary. "Arran thinks that the explosion was caused by malware planted *inside* the ship. That's why we didn't see anything on the radar—it wasn't from a Specter pulse."

"Really?" Rex said, his eyes widening. "So it was an inside job?"

"I guess so. I mean, that's what it looks like."

"Do you think it was Orelia?" Rex asked quietly.

"No," Vesper said quickly, surprising herself with her firmness. "I can't believe she would've sent that confession without mentioning the malware."

She readied herself for a contradiction or at least a hint of skepticism on his face. But to her relief, he nodded. "I think you're right." He paused for a moment, looking puzzled. "It's a little strange that we haven't heard anything else about the peace envoy, isn't it? Everyone else seems to act like it's all business as usual."

Vesper hesitated, unsure how much to tell him. If Rex seemed to refuse to trust her, why should she trust him? But then again, if anyone was capable of keeping a secret, it was Rex. "Okay, well... it turns out that my mom arranged this peace summit without consulting anyone."

"What?" Rex stared at her, startled. "The Federation hasn't been involved?"

"Nope. Even Stepney didn't know what she was planning."

Rex shook his head and laughed, a sound so comfortingly familiar that it unleashed a wave of warmth through Vesper's body. "Your mother is something else."

"I'm not sure it's *funny*," she said, although she wasn't quite able to suppress a smile.

"No, you're right. It's more impressive than funny. Your mother doesn't let much stand in her way, does she?"

"Not really, no."

"Like someone else I know."

Vesper raised an eyebrow. "Are you calling me reckless?"

"No. Recklessness is certainly not one of your many notable qualities."

There was a hint of amusement in Rex's voice, just enough to make Vesper bold enough to ask, "And what are those notable qualities?"

"Intelligence, stubbornness, drive," Rex said, counting off on his fingers. "Kindness, stubbornness...hold on, did I mention stubbornness?"

"Is that why you broke up with me?" Vesper asked quietly, feeling a sudden prickle of dread. "Because I'm too stubborn?"

"Vesper, no..." Rex said as his face fell. "Of course not. That's one of the reasons I lo—" He cut himself off and looked away, suddenly intently focused on the medicine bottles.

Then why did you break up with me? The words spilled out of her heart, pooling in her chest, where she could only feel them, not speak them. *What are you hiding from me, Rex Phobos?*

CHAPTER 13

ORELIA

"So that's it," Zafir said quietly, his eyes fixed on the small, deep blue sphere in the distance: a single planet alone in its otherwise empty solar system. He leaned in even closer to the window.

The journey to Sylvan had taken six days. They could only travel at light speed until they hit Sylvan airspace, lest they create the impression of an attack instead of a diplomatic mission, and as they traveled closer to Sylvan, the tension grew so thick Orelia could feel it rubbing against her skin.

Orelia certainly didn't blame the Quatrans—they were going to face an unknown enemy that, until very recently, they'd believed had attacked their solar system unprovoked. The Sylvans were surely grappling with similar emotions right now.

After they'd set off, Orelia had contacted General Greet through the secret communication device she'd brought with her to the Academy. The first conversation had been nothing short of a disaster, as once the general heard that Orelia was traveling with the Quatrans, she'd assumed that her secret agent had been turned or was being forced to lure the Sylvans into a trap. Eventually, however, General Greet had agreed to listen to the Quatrans' proposal but only under certain terms. She'd meet with Orelia and one of the Quatrans; the others would have to stay behind on the battlecraft. And instead of landing on the planet, Orelia and the Quatran delegate—Zafir—would meet General Greet on one of her ships.

"Did you ever think you'd actually see it?" Orelia asked.

"No, not really. I certainly never imagined traveling there as part of a peace envoy." He shook his head, then met her eyes. "And yet, somehow, that's not even the strangest thing that's happened to me recently."

"Strange?" she repeated, a playful challenge in her voice.

"Unexpected. In a good way," he said with a smile before

turning his attention back to the window. "I can't see any landmasses. How many continents are there on Sylvan?"

"Just one. About twice the size of Galgo," she said, naming the largest continent on Zafir's home planet, Tri.

"So it must be facing away from us now."

Orelia shrugged. "I'm not sure. You can't see it from this distance."

"That doesn't make sense," Zafir said, brow furrowing. "We're only 200,000 mitons away. You said it's twice as large as Galgo?"

"That's right." It was amusing to see Zafir so desperately out of his depth. Although Zafir's research had led to significant discoveries about the Sylvans, it was still only a microscopic fraction of what the Sylvans knew about the Quatrans. "During summer on Sylvan, the oceans cover ninety-five percent of the planet."

"Right, of course." Zafir let out a low whistle as he looked out the window, then turned back to Orelia. "But it's only summer on one hemisphere."

"Sylvan's orbit is elliptical, as you know. The distance from the sun matters more than the tilt of the axis."

"How long does summer last?"

"About twelve Tridian years."

"That gives you lots of time to work on your tan," he said, his glib tone belying the alertness and intensity of his expression. He'd spent years analyzing the minerals in Sylvan bomb fragments, and now he was hours away from meeting actual Sylvans. "I wish we were actually visiting the planet."

"If our peace talks are successful, you'll go down in history as the man who ended the war," Orelia said. "I'm sure you'll be back."

"Lieutenant?" They both turned to see the pilot shifting his weight from side to side nervously.

"Yes?"

"We've received a message from the Sylvans. The transport ship is on its way."

An hour later, Zafir and Orelia headed to the airlock where Colonel Beaune, Captain Avar, and the rest of the crew were waiting to send them off. Captain Avar's dark eyes glowed with excitement as she wished them luck, and even Colonel Beaune seemed slightly awed by the proceedings. He shook Zafir's hand warmly and even issued a gruff "good luck" to Orelia that seemed truly sincere.

A panel on the wall began to beep, and everyone turned their attention to the monitor. One of the crew members, a young woman, gasped as the Sylvan ship came into view. Orelia didn't blame her. The shape of the craft was the stuff of Quatran nightmares. A few briefings could only do so much to counter decades of propaganda and fearmongering, to say nothing of the carnage caused by the Sylvan bombs. The Quatrans had no evidence that the Sylvans wouldn't kill them all on sight.

Orelia knew how that felt. She wondered if her commanding officers knew that she had disobeyed orders when she refused to stop her squadron mates from firing on the Specter ship bound for the Academy. Or even worse— whether they knew that Orelia had provided the secret to destroying the ship, that she had Sylvan blood on her hands.

The monitor beeped again and an automated voice rang through their monitors. *"Permission to dock at airlock has been granted. Please hold. Estimated time to completion is…one minute."*

"How are you feeling?" Orelia asked Zafir. To a casual observer, he would've looked impressively calm and composed for someone in his circumstances, but to Orelia, his movements seemed unusually stiff, as if it were requiring a massive amount of energy to appear unruffled.

He gave her a tight smile. "It's fascinating. I didn't realize it was possible to feel dizzying excitement and petrifying fear all at once."

"Docking complete. Airlock is opening. Please step aside."

As the door opened with a loud hiss, Zafir's smile slipped away, his expression all focus and determination. He and Orelia stepped into the airlock, and the door to the Quatran battlecraft shut behind them. Next to her, Zafir flinched just slightly before regaining his composure.

The walk through the airlock tunnel to the Sylvan ship felt like both the longest and shortest journey of Orelia's life. She'd spent so much of her life preparing for her mission to the Academy—a mission she'd known she was unlikely to survive—that she hadn't thought much about what it'd be like to come home. And had she thought of it, she would've treated herself to the pleasure of imagining a hero's welcome instead of a traitor's return.

As they approached the entrance to the Sylvan craft, the outline of the triangular door began to glow red. Zafir came to a sudden halt and looked at Orelia with concern. "Does that mean we should stop?"

Orelia shook her head and forced a smile. "Red has the opposite meaning on Sylvan. Everything's fine."

"Ah, all systems normal, then." He caught her eye, and she almost laughed. Nothing about this endeavor could be further from normal.

A series of low beeps sounded. Zafir inhaled sharply as the door turned transparent, revealing the silhouettes of five Sylvan soldiers, then opened completely. Orelia bowed in greeting, and Zafir did the same, as he'd been instructed.

None of the Sylvans bowed back. *"We will search you before you come on board,"* one of them said in Sylvan, a boy about Orelia's age who looked vaguely familiar. *"Step under the scanner."*

Orelia pressed her hands together to signal her acknowledgment, a gesture vaguely approximate to a Quatran one. "Stand over there," she said to Zafir, gesturing at a faint circle on the floor. "They need to scan us."

Zafir did as he was told, and a few seconds later, his eyes widened as lines of transparent moving symbols began to wrap around his body. "They're your vitals," Orelia explained quietly, self-conscious about speaking Quatran in front of the soldiers. "Your height, age, body mass, blood oxygen levels, antibodies, and a bunch of other stuff. It would also identify any concealed weapons, of course."

"Enough," a slightly older female soldier snapped in Sylvan. *"You've already handed over enough secrets to the enemy."*

Orelia fell silent, cold dread seeping down her spine. Criticizing a fellow soldier in this manner was taboo in the Sylvan military, yet none of the other four soldiers seemed put off by the woman's brazen breach of protocol and decorum.

"Follow us," the young male soldier said. *"General Greet is waiting."* They didn't restrain Orelia or Zafir, but the soldiers flanked them closely as they walked, prepared to spring to action at the first sign of trouble.

Her heart had begun beating so fast, she was sure the sound would rouse the guards' suspicions. Yet, to her surprise, Zafir seemed too fascinated by his surroundings to be afraid. "This is remarkable," he whispered, craning his head and swiveling it from side to side to take in everything they passed. His eyes widened as something whizzed above their heads in one of the magnetic chutes that ran through the ship. Sylvan design centered on efficiency, cutting down on expense and waste, whereas the Quatrans considered buggy robot servants to be the height of technological achievement, a testament to how much they fetishized human labor.

"Where are they taking us? Your general's office?" Zafir asked quietly.

Orelia glanced at the guards before she responded in case this also counted as sharing secrets with the enemy. "She doesn't have an office."

"Or wherever the officers have private conversations on this craft."

"The Sylvan conception of privacy is very different from yours. We don't have the same obsession with secrets."

He raised an eyebrow and smirked slightly. She knew what he was thinking. *Says the girl who created an entirely fake identity.*

The soldiers stopped abruptly in front of an open door. *"You can go in,"* one of them said.

"Thank you," Orelia answered in Sylvan before turning to Zafir. "Come with me." He nodded and followed her into the space that served as the ship's dining room, though she realized Zafir wouldn't necessarily recognize it as such. It seemed small and spare compared to the grandeur of the dining room on the Quatran battlecraft but in a way that was comfortingly familiar. There was no lavish furniture. No paintings of famous military victories. For the Sylvans,

war was something to avoid, not celebrate. They celebrated peace, not bloodshed.

General Greet was alone, which was unusual for her. She tended to include her advisors at important moments, and Orelia couldn't imagine anything more important than her first face-to-face encounter with a Quatran. Her light blond hair had more gray in it than Orelia remembered, though most of it was tucked under her cap. And there seemed to be a few more lines around her eyes. But otherwise she appeared unchanged, which Orelia found surprisingly comforting. After spending weeks being torn apart by uncertainty—uncertainty about her loyalty, about her future, about Zafir—it was reassuring to remember that some things would remain constant.

Orelia saluted, though it felt strange doing so in Quatran civilian clothes. Everything about facing General Greet felt strange. Although it'd been less than a year since Orelia left Sylvan, it felt like several lifetimes ago. It *was* several lifetimes ago. She'd been a Sylvan agent embedded behind enemy lines. She'd been a Quatra Fleet cadet, forming the first real friendships of her life. And now she was a traitor, mistrusted by both sides. After all that, she belonged nowhere.

"*Orelia*," General Greet said in a tone that might've sounded neutral were there not five soldiers standing outside the door, awaiting orders to arrest Orelia the moment their commanding officer gave the word. "*You're well?*"

"*Yes, General Greet*," Orelia replied in Sylvan.

General Greet turned to Zafir. "Thank you for joining us, Lieutenant." Orelia had never heard General Greet speak Quatran before and was momentarily surprised by her confidence and fluency.

Zafir looked similarly startled but regained his composure. "It's an honor, General." He inclined his head, just as a Sylvan would've done in this situation.

"Perhaps you can explain to me why the Quatrans are suddenly so interested in peace."

Zafir nodded. "I understand that this overture is unexpected, and I appreciate your willingness to hear us out." He spoke calmly and with such assurance that Orelia felt a surge of pride. He was shouldering the pressure and expectations of this historic event—the first diplomatic conversation between Quatran and Sylvan leadership—with courage and poise. "Most Quatrans, including myself and the majority of the Quatra Fleet, have always believed that the Sylvans struck first when they bombed Tri fifteen years ago. But a few days ago, Orelia explained that this was a misconception, and that we were being deluded by a handful of leaders at the very highest levels of our military and government. While we still don't have concrete proof that this is the case, we're obviously deeply troubled by the possibility that this costly war might be the result of deception. At the same time, this revelation made the idea of peace talks seem possible, something we never would've considered when we believed you to be the aggressor."

General Greet remained silent as she scrutinized Zafir. Unlike the Quatrans, the Sylvans didn't feel compelled to respond right away and saw nothing strange or awkward in allowing time to think before speaking. However, Zafir seemed unruffled by the long silence.

"We can discuss it over dinner," General Greet said finally. Orelia wasn't sure whether this was a good sign or a bad sign. Sylvans never discussed important business or political matters over dinner. They rarely spoke at all; meals were for sustenance, not socializing.

The three of them sat at the simple metal table, and the place mats at each setting began to glow. Orelia and General Greet pressed their hands on top. Zafir followed suit, then let out a muffled yelp and snatched his hand away. "It stung me," he whispered to Orelia.

"It's just performing a nutrition assessment," she explained. "Put your hand back."

A moment later, plates emerged from the opening at the center of the table. Orelia smiled as she watched Zafir do his best to contain his confusion as he looked from his plate to Orelia's. His was covered with salad greens, while hers contained a mixture of grains and vegetables.

"The scanner must've identified a vitamin deficiency," she said to explain the difference.

"Remarkable," Zafir said, gazing around the table.

"You'll understand, Lieutenant," General Greet began, "that my highest duty is protecting the people of Sylvan. For years, that meant staving off attacks on our planet and trying to neutralize the enemy that seemed set on annihilating us. However, there is no greater protection than peace, which is why I intend to take your proposal seriously. But it'd be reckless and irresponsible of me to take your claim at face value, given the behavior the Quatrans have exhibited over the years, behavior that points to a most callous disregard for the value of life."

Zafir's face remained polite and inscrutable while she spoke, betraying neither frustration nor concern. He looked so relaxed that, for a moment, Orelia forgot how truly extraordinary this was, to be in a room with both General Greet and Zafir as two seemingly incompatible parts of her life collided. "I understand. And that's why I'm not asking you to make any sort of commitment. All we want is for you to attend the peace summit, hear what we have to say, and then make your own decision about what's best for your people."

"And how do I know that I'm not leading them into a trap?"

"It's not, I promise," Orelia said, speaking for the first time since they'd sat down. "I was there when they decided to send the envoy to talk to you. They're as desperate to stop the war as we are."

Orelia had spent most of her life on a Sylvan military base, training under General Greet's watchful, exacting eye, and she'd grown attuned to the subtle ways her commanding officer conveyed approval, irritation, and disappointment. Yet as she met General Greet's eyes across the table, Orelia saw something even worse—suspicion. She'd grown too close to the Quatrans for the general's comfort, that much was clear.

The knots in Orelia's stomach began to tighten. Orelia would never forgive herself for her role in the deaths of those Sylvans, but at the same time, she *had* completed her mission. She'd traveled to another solar system, created a fake identity, and infiltrated one of the most secure bases in the Quatra Fleet. She'd done exactly what had been asked of her, against monumental odds. She'd never shied away from her duty.

Orelia had been up for twenty-six hours and had reached a state beyond exhaustion. She was leaving for the Quatra System in six days, and there seemed to be no end to the final round of preparations, tests, and briefings.

This time, however, they'd purposefully kept her up all night to see how she performed under stress, to ensure that she'd be able to maintain her cover no matter the conditions. Now, sitting in one of the small, dark windowless rooms in the center of the military base that had been her home for the past twelve years, she felt more delirious than tired, which she supposed was the point.

"Good afternoon, Orelia," Colonel Nion said as he entered the room and sat down in the chair across from her. "How are you feeling?"

"Fine," she said. Over the years, she'd learned that there was no point in attempting small talk or—gods forbid—trying to joke with the humorless Colonel Nion. He wasn't unkind, and he was arguably one of the most gifted intelligence officers on Sylvan, but he took his job very seriously. When she was younger, she'd found his demeanor rather wearing, but that was when her mission had felt abstract. Now that it was actually happening, Orelia understood Colonel Nion's seriousness. While she'd never say it herself, she knew it was true: The future of Sylvan was resting on her shoulders. Failure was not an option. She had to transmit the Academy coordinates back to General Greet. And in order to do that, she had to pose as a Quatra Fleet cadet without arousing suspicion.

"All right, then, let's begin," Colonel Nion said in a tone that made it clear he would've gone straight into the exercise no matter how Orelia had answered his perfunctory question. "What's your name?

"Orelia Kerr," she said, using her fake Quatran surname for the first time.

"Where are you from?"

"Loos."

"What part?"

"A small island called Ariad off the coast of Merilene."

Colonel Nion frowned. *"Merileen,"* he said, correcting her pronunciation. *"These details are important, Orelia."*

"I know. I'm sorry." She closed her eyes and took a deep breath. *"I'll get it right."*

"What part of Loos are you from?"

*"A small island called Ariad off the coast of Meril*ene," she said, forcing her mouth to produce the unfamiliar sound.

"Who did you live with?"

"My parents and my sister."

"What do your parents do?"

"My mother works as a receptionist at a beach resort." No. *The word rose up so quickly, it nearly escaped her lips.* My mother was a teacher. She loved to sing with the children. I could hear her in the classroom when Dad and I went to pick her up from work. We couldn't go for a walk without one of her former students coming up to her, wanting to share a memory of their time in her class.

"What about your father?"

"My father is a boat mechanic in the harbor." My father was a rescue worker. He saved people who were swept away by summer floods. Sometimes he'd be gone for weeks at a time, but I didn't mind because I knew he was a hero.

What would her parents think about her upcoming mission? It was a foolish question. If either of her parents had been alive, she wouldn't be going on this mission. She wouldn't have been raised on a military base along with the other war orphans, and she wouldn't have been identified as an "ideal candidate" for the top-secret operation the Sylvan leadership had been planning for years.

"How do your parents feel about you attending the Academy?"

"They're proud of me," she said. They're glad that I'll have the chance for revenge.

But was that true? For a while, Orelia had devoted her whole life to destroying the people who'd killed her parents; it was hard to imagine either of them holding on to so much hate in their hearts. But then again, Orelia had only a few years' worth of memories of her parents. She'd been only six when the Quatrans bombed her city, transforming the vibrant metropolis into a wasteland . . . and transforming her from a cherished child into an orphan.

"What track are you hoping for?"

"However I can best serve the Quatra Fleet."

"And what do you want to do after you leave the Academy?"

I want to watch it burn.

There was another long silence, but this time Orelia was the uneasy one. "We will attend the peace summit," General

Greet said finally, and for one brief moment the knots of dread in Orelia's stomach began to unfurl. "But if you betray our trust or take advantage of us in any way, we will reduce your entire solar system to cosmic dust." She turned to Orelia, eyes even colder than before. "And we'll make sure that you go with them."

CHAPTER 14

VESPER

"See?" Arran jabbed the screen, uncharacteristically agitated. "It doesn't make any sense."

"*Quiet*," Vesper whispered as she looked around the library. There didn't seem to be anyone else in there with them, but you never could tell who might be eavesdropping from behind one of the bookshelves.

"You're the one who wanted to meet here," Arran said, confused. "Should we just go back to one of our rooms?"

"No, that's even worse."

"Didn't you say that our rooms are soundproof?" he asked with a knowing smile. "I distinctly remember you making a big deal about how glad you were not to worry about disturbing your roommates when you—" The smile vanished from his face as he cut himself off. "When you had...visitors," he finished lamely.

"I'm not going to burst into tears at the sound of his name," she said, both touched by his concern and annoyed that anyone would see her as the type of girl who required careful handling after a breakup.

"Sorry," he said with a wistful smile. "I guess you're stronger than I am."

Her face fell. She'd been so focused on her breakup with Rex that she'd almost forgotten that Arran was also nursing a broken heart. "I'm sorry, Arran. That was stupid of me. Everyone has their own way of dealing with stuff like this. Speaking of which," she said, purposefully changing tack, "I heard an interesting rumor about you and that Loosian kid Rees."

He shrugged and looked away. "I doubt it's *that* interesting."

Vesper decided to let the subject drop for now, knowing that Arran tended to shut down when pushed too far about his personal life. She was delighted that Arran had found someone to distract him from Dash, but there was part of her that hoped the distraction was only temporary. They were so good for each other. Her shy, reserved squadron mate had come out of his shell around the gregarious Dash, and her childhood friend had become a calmer, steadier version of himself. "Okay, so what exactly about that doesn't make sense?" she asked, gesturing at the schematic.

He showed her a diagram of the supply chain responsible for the battlecraft. "There's no way the Specters could've infiltrated the process at any stage. Whoever planted the malware was a Quatran, I'm sure of it."

"But *who*?" Vesper asked, puzzled and frustrated. Nothing irritated her more than a problem she couldn't attack head-on. "The rebels on Chetire and Deva couldn't have accessed the supply chain either, could they?"

Arran shook his head wearily. "Probably not. But then that means it was someone..."

"In the fleet," Vesper finished for him.

They fell silent, the troubling words hanging in the air between them. "Don't you think it's strange that Stepney's so against peace talks?" Vesper said finally.

She waited for Arran to react with puzzlement, but instead he shook his head. "Honestly? No, I'm not surprised. Did you know that he's on the board of Orion, that fyron-mining company?"

Orion. She knew that word. But how? She was about to

ask Arran, when a memory came hurtling from the recesses of her brain, a memory that she hadn't thought about in a very long time.

Vesper tugged on the delicate strap of her evening dress, willing it to stay in place. She wished she were like her mother, who, unlike other career officers, never seemed uneasy in civilian clothes and wore her elegant black evening dress with the same confidence as she did her uniform. Even her father was in full-on networking mode, chatting up the vice-chancellor of the Quatra Federation on the other side of the room.

"Relax, Vee," Ward said, giving her outfit a cursory glance. "You look perfect." But before she could respond, he'd already turned his attention to the party they'd just entered, scanning the landscape with the same focus and strategic scrutiny he used in the simulcraft. Their classmate Marcel's parents had a fancy solstice celebration every year to which he was allowed to invite a few friends. It'd always been a coveted invitation. When they were younger, the appeal had stemmed from the well-stocked, poorly supervised bar. But as they'd gotten older and acceptance to the Academy began to feel more important than stolen shots of nitro spirit, the opportunity to mingle with high-ranking fleet officers became the real draw.

The party was always held at Marcel's family's apartment—an enormous penthouse on the top floor of one of the most exclusive buildings in Evoline. No matter how many times she visited, Vesper couldn't help but marvel at the panoramic window that curved around the dining room. The soaring towers of the Tridian cityscape glittered in the pink twilit sky, and both moons—one full, one crescent—glowed with warm yellow light. Every few moments, a zipcraft whizzed past, and in the distance, the four towers of the Armory soared up from the horizon.

"So, what's our plan of attack?" Ward asked as he took two glasses of sparkling pearlberry juice from a passing attendant. "Can you see Commander Stepney anywhere?"

"He's not involved with Academy admissions. If you want to find someone to suck up to, you'd be better off with Laia Trow. She's the head of the admissions committee."

Ward made a noise somewhere between a laugh and a snort. "She's a bureaucrat who reads thousands of applications a year. If you want to make sure yours gets to the top of the pile, you need to have someone influential advocating for you."

"Come on, Ward. You really think a few minutes of party chit-chat will be enough to make the commander of the Quatra Fleet want to help you?"

"Don't be naïve, Vee. That's how this stuff works. Now come on—we need to find him before dinner starts."

Vesper gamely followed Ward through the crowd, smiling and exchanging quick hellos with her classmates and her parents' friends and colleagues. She suspected that Ward's time was better spent studying than stalking high-ranking fleet officers, but she knew better than to start an argument. When Ward had his mind set on something, he could be pretty pigheaded. He wasn't so different from her, she supposed, except that her stubbornness rarely led to arguments with other people. The only person she refused to let get in her way was herself.

"That's him," Ward whispered. He gestured with his glass, causing a little liquid to spill over the sides. Vesper followed his gaze to see a tall, distinguished-looking man with grayish brown hair. There were bags under his eyes and lines around his mouth, but there was something youthful about his expression. He was listening intently while a slim, angular woman with sleek black hair spoke about something Vesper couldn't hear. "Come on," Ward said as he reached for her hand.

Vesper leaned back slightly to remain in place. "Now? It looks like he's busy. I don't want to interrupt."

"Well, then we should at least get closer," Ward said,

sounding slightly annoyed. "Otherwise someone else will swoop in before us."

With a sigh, Vesper followed Ward through the crowded room, coming to a stop a few feet from Commander Stepney and his companion. "Okay, just act natural," Ward said before letting out the most unnatural-sounding laugh Vesper had ever heard.

Vesper rolled her eyes and was about to say something calculated to embarrass him when something the black-haired woman said caught her ear. "I have sympathy for them, of course, but honestly, I can't see how this strike helps anyone. I'd happily pay them more for a job well done, but the way they take advantage is just appalling."

They're talking about the miners' strike on Chetire, Vesper realized. There hadn't been much in the news, but she'd heard her mother talking about it the day before.

"You're the one who wanted to buy a seventh mine, Amia," Stepney said with a smile. "No one said it'd be easy."

"It's not the number of mines," she said curtly. "It's the rabble-rousers who devote their lives to causing trouble. They act so noble, but they don't care about the miners any more than we— I mean, they only care about their own interests."

Commander Stepney sighed. "It does seem like order is breaking down across the solar system. It's a shame that local law enforcement is making such a mess of things."

Amia gave him a knowing look. "I don't suppose there's any way you could..."

"That's not the way these things work and you know it."

"This is boring," Ward whispered to Vesper. "Let's go find Marcel and come back later."

"Just a second," Vesper said softly, looking at Ward but still straining to hear the conversation next to them.

"Horace, come on," Amia pleaded, pouting slightly. "Surely you could send one teeny, tiny regiment to help keep the peace. It's all in the name of law and order."

"I can't send fleet forces until the Federation authorizes it. It's not a private army at my disposal."

"Well, that's a shame," she said, shaking her head. "Because if the strike doesn't end soon, stock prices are going to plummet, and you know how that's going to affect our investors. You're on the board, aren't you?"

Commander Stepney glanced from side to side and lowered his voice. "Perhaps we should talk about this privately," he said, gesturing toward an empty hallway up ahead. He held his arm out for Amia, who took it with a smile, whispering to him as they sauntered off.

"Did you hear that?" Vesper asked as she and Ward left to find Marcel.

"Hear what?"

"Never mind," Vesper said. She wasn't entirely sure what she'd just witnessed, so perhaps it was better to keep it to herself instead of causing trouble. "I think he's over there. Let's go."

"Actually, I think I did know he was on the board. I just never realized it mattered," she said slowly. "But you don't think he could..."

"Sabotage peace for financial gain?" Arran said quietly. "I'm not sure. Maybe."

"But peace wasn't even on the table when we went out on that patrol," Vesper said. "And everyone already supported the war with the Specters. Why frame them for that attack?"

"There's a difference between supporting the war to stop the Sylvans from attacking us, and supporting the war so we can colonize them. Maybe Stepney wanted to push everyone to an extreme where they will think taking the Sylvan planet, subjugating its people and using it as a fyron mine, is acceptable."

Vesper's blood ran cold. "Do you think he's capable of that?"

"I don't know," Arran said.

Vesper's wrist buzzed and she glanced down to see a message from her mother. She frowned at the cryptic words: *Come see me.* The only other time her mother had summoned her to her office on her own, it'd been to scold her for losing the captain assignment to Rex. "I need to go," Vesper said as she rose wearily to her feet. "Let me know if you hear anything else."

She'd just turned into the hall when someone called her name, and she turned to see Ward heading toward her in what amounted to his version of a hurry. He was the type of person who ambled more than he walked, perpetually confident that the world would be happy to wait for him. "Which way are you headed? I'll walk with you."

"I'm actually heading to my mother's office, so I should probably go on my own," she said.

Ward's face fell for just a fraction of a second before his jolly affability swept it aside. "Not a problem. What are you doing after dinner? Want to meet me in the screening room? I think they're showing that one you like, about the girl who falls into the wormhole and goes back in time."

"What are you talking about?" she asked, befuddled. "They stopped showing holopics weeks ago, after the attack." With all the additional patrol shifts and extra duties, hardly anyone had time to fritter away in the screening room.

"Yeah, no, you're right." An uncharacteristic blush spread faintly across his cheeks. "It's just that…" He trailed off as he gripped the back of his neck nervously.

"Just what?"

He smiled sheepishly. "I pulled some strings and got the pic delivered. I meant for it to be a surprise."

"Oh…thank you," she said as a strange combination of emotions crashed and swirled inside her. "But I'm not sure—"

"I thought it'd be nice to spend some time together," he cut in. "I know things have been weird with us. Totally my fault, of course," he said quickly. "But, I don't know, it's kinda made me wish I could go back in time and not be such a fuckup. Though then again, I think I needed this learning experience. I needed to know what it was like to lose the respect of the person I cared about most, to understand what really matters."

"I appreciate that. I really do. But I don't think it's a good idea to make things complicated when there's already so much going on."

"Complicated? Vee, what could be simpler than going back to the way things were? We were *great* together. We brought out the best in each other."

If I'd brought out the best in you, you wouldn't have written Go home Edgers *in the corridor*, Vesper thought as a flare of anger rose up in her chest. "I'm not sure about that."

He smiled and shook his head with an exaggerated sigh. "Still as stubborn as always. That's okay—you have so many other attractive qualities, it doesn't really matter."

Ward placed his hand on her arm, but Vesper shook it loose as she recalled what Rex had said to her the other day when the topic of her stubbornness had arisen.

That's one of the reasons I lo—He'd cut himself off, but the rest of the sentence had sprung from the tip of his tongue straight into her heart.

She didn't want grand gestures and someone who "pulled strings." She wanted to be with someone who made the dark parts of herself feel like an asset instead of a stain.

She wanted Rex.

"I have to go," she said. "My mother's waiting for me. I'll see you later."

She started to turn away, but Ward grabbed her again, clutching her wrist. "This is about him, isn't it? That piece of space trash?" His voice was cold, and all traces of affability had drained from his face.

"No, it isn't," she said as she wrenched her arm free. "It's about you. Yes, I want to be with someone who brings out the best in me, but not someone who tries to hide away the rest. We don't belong together, Ward. You'll understand that someday, I promise. I'll see you later." She flashed him a friendly smile that he returned quickly, but not quickly enough to mask the flash of anger in his eyes. There was nothing Ward hated more than not getting his way.

As Vesper approached Admiral Haze's office, her apprehension thickened into dread as she tried to guess what her mother wanted to talk to her about. Did someone alert her to Vesper and Arran's research? Was she going to be reprimanded for poking her nose where it didn't belong? Yet the moment the office door slid open, Vesper's anxiety gave way to bemusement. It was clear from her mother's glowing face and the rapidity with which she sprang from her chair that she hadn't summoned Vesper to deliver bad news.

"I'm glad you're here," she said with uncharacteristic warmth. "The news is going to break soon, so I figured there was no harm in telling you directly. Something remarkable has happened."

"What is it?" Vesper asked eagerly. She couldn't remember the last time her mother had seemed so obviously excited about something.

"The Specters have agreed to attend the peace talks."

Vesper stared at her, momentarily too stunned to speak. Although she'd known that this was the goal of Orelia and Zafir's mission, the odds had seemed dismally low. "That's incredible," she said finally. "Do you think we'll actually be able to settle on a treaty?"

"I do," Admiral Haze said firmly. "This war has gone on for far too long and cost far too many lives." She met Vesper's eye and her face softened. "I almost lost you...*twice*. In a matter of weeks. It's time to put a stop to the bloodshed."

"So there's going to be a peace summit?"

Her mother nodded. "Our two delegations are going to meet halfway between our respective solar systems in three days."

"Three days?" Vesper repeated incredulously. "Who's going?"

"That's why I wanted to be the one to tell you about the summit. A group of cadets will be going as support crew, and you've been selected as one of them. You won't attend the talks, of course, but you'll be on the site. You're going to be a part of history."

A tingle of excitement coursed through Vesper as she imagined standing on the deck of the battlecraft, saluting the delegates as they disembarked, then waiting with breathless anticipation for news. Being one of the first people in the entire solar system to learn that the war was over, and knowing that she'd played a very small part in the process. But her excitement faded slightly as she imagined standing next to Rex, unable to throw her arms around him in celebration.

"I just wish we could've arranged a cease-fire before the most recent attack," Admiral Haze said with a sigh. "Though, if everything goes according to plan, Sula will be the last casualty of the war."

Vesper hesitated, unsure how much to share with her mother about her and Arran's suspicions. On the one hand, she knew Admiral Haze would be far from pleased to learn that Vesper and Arran had taken something like this upon themselves. But on the other, it seemed important that the fleet leadership have the most accurate information at their disposal going into the peace talks. What if the Quatrans brought it up only to have the Specters deny it? It could derail the entire conversation. "I think there's something you need to know going into the peace talks," she said carefully. She took a deep breath and explained what Arran had discovered during his research. "There's just something… off about the whole thing. And I figured you'd want to know about it before heading out to the peace summit."

"That's a pretty serious accusation," Admiral Haze said, surveying Vesper carefully.

"I know. But right now, it's the only option that seems to make sense."

Admiral Haze pressed her lips together, her brow furrowing in thought. "I wonder if…"

"Wonder what?" Vesper asked carefully. It wasn't often that her mother confided in her.

"I'm not quite sure," she said, sounding uncharacteristically vague. "It just seems to fit with—"

She cut herself off as her door hissed open and Commander Stepney strode in. His face was so full of fury that Vesper barely recognized him—she'd never seen the calm, measured commander in such an agitated state. "What the hell is going on here?" he spat out, either unaware of Vesper's presence or too angry to worry about yelling at a subordinate in front of her daughter.

Without a word, Vesper rose from her seat and started to head for the door, cheeks burning with embarrassment and indignation. "Stay right there," Stepney barked. "The sooner you learn the truth about your mother, the better."

"What are you talking about?" Admiral Haze asked, seemingly unfazed by her boss's ire.

"You've sent a peace envoy? To the *Specters*? Are you out of your mind?! You don't get to make a unilateral decision like that. It's *mutiny*." Stepney began to pace around the office. "You know that the Specters aren't interested in peace. They're only interested in one thing—Quatran genocide. The only way we'll ever know peace is to kill every single one of those monsters."

"The situation has changed," Admiral Haze said calmly, as if she weren't the one essentially committing mutiny. "The Specter—I mean Sylvan—we had in custody has convinced her people to meet with us for a peace summit."

"She's a *spy*, Svetlara," Stepney cut in. His anger seemed to be fizzling out, leaving only exhaustion and frustration in its wake. "You can't trust her. You can't trust any of them! The naïveté you've displayed here is distressing, if I'm being frank."

"You don't know Orelia," Vesper said. The words flew

out before she'd had the chance to assess them. Before her brain had time to remind her mouth that contradicting the commander of the Quatra Fleet was a really, really bad idea. "She's the one who saved the Academy by telling us how to destroy the Specter ship. She understands what's at stake, and if she says she's going to help negotiate peace, then I believe her."

"It looks like insubordination and delusional tendencies are a family trait," Stepney said coldly. "You're dismissed, cadet."

Vesper saluted and hurried out of her mother's office, her cheeks still burning as she cursed herself for her foolish behavior. But under it all, she couldn't help but wonder at the strangeness of the situation. Yes, her mother had acted rashly—Stepney hadn't been overreacting when he'd used the word *mutiny*—but surely the prospect of peace mattered far more.

Unless Arran was right and Stepney had his own nefarious reasons for keeping the war alive.

CHAPTER 15

CORMAK

"This is *madness*," Frey said as he dropped onto the common room couch next to Cormak; a few of the first-year cadets had gathered to discuss the shocking revelation about the peace summit. "They've been launching vicious attacks on us for years with one aim: to wipe out every Quatran in the solar system and colonize our planets. So why the hell would they suddenly be interested in peace? It makes no sense whatsoever. It has to be some kind of trap."

It was strange to see the normally placid, ironic Frey so worked up. Cormak hadn't spent a great deal of time with him, but he couldn't recall ever hearing him speak so emphatically...about anything. "It's definitely unexpected," Cormak said, hoping that response would be enough to satisfy Frey. "Sorry, I have to run. I'll see you all later." He didn't have time to talk things through—not when he was preparing to attend the summit himself. Just thinking about it was enough to make him shiver. He'd been flabbergasted when Admiral Haze, never his biggest fan, had told him that he was one of the cadets chosen to attend as support staff.

"Okay." Frey let out a long sigh and then forced a cheery smile. "I'll see you at dinner…assuming the Academy isn't blown to smithereens before then."

"At least you'll die looking your best. No one rocks formal wear like you, Frey."

He nodded gravely. "You make an excellent point."

Cormak stepped into the corridor as a sea of cadets, guards, and Quatra Fleet staff dashed in all directions, making frantic preparations for the peace summit. He glanced down at his link. He had just enough time to swing by the canteen before he needed to report to the launchport to help load supplies. But just as he set off, a glint of shiny black hair in the crowd caught his eye. Even from a distance, Cormak could tell something was wrong with Vesper. Instead of striding along with her trademark assurance, she walked slowly down the bustling corridor, moving with the flow of traffic rather than darting impatiently through the crowd.

He'd been trying, somewhat unsuccessfully, to avoid her over the past few days. The only way to maintain his ridiculous "we're better off apart" stance was to keep as far away as possible, as one look at Vesper's face was enough to make him break.

Turn around, he told himself. *She hasn't spotted you yet.* But his stubborn feet remained firmly in place. It was physically impossible for him to run away from Vesper when she was clearly upset, Ward's threats be damned.

She spotted him and hesitated, causing the person behind her to bump into her. He could tell she was torn between seeking comfort from the person she'd once trusted most, and exposing herself to even more heartache. The look of indecision on her face sent a stab of pain through Cormak's chest. He hated himself for making her suffer like this.

But even if she'd wanted to escape, there was nowhere to go, and a few moments later, the surge of the crowd brought her alongside him. "What's wrong?" he asked, pulling her to the side of the crowded hall.

Vesper looked around warily. "I'm not sure I should talk about it here."

"Okay. Where do you want to go?" He winced inwardly as a trace of pain flashed on Vesper's face. Just a few days ago, it would've been the most natural thing in the world for them to sneak back to the residential wing and hole up in one of their rooms.

"Let's go to the library. No one's ever there this time of day."

"Sure," Cormak said lightly, although that was actually the second-worst place he could think of. He'd never admit it to anyone, but a few times when he'd been studying in the library, he'd amused himself by imagining it was a room in the house he'd share with Vesper someday. The fantasy had always felt a little foolish, even when they'd been together—it seemed audacious, or perhaps even delusional, for someone who'd snuck into the Academy by posing as his dead brother to have such outlandish hopes for the future. Cormak would be lucky if he graduated, forget about making enough money to have a room full of *books*. Yet he'd wasted an embarrassing number of hours imagining what it'd be like to build a life with Vesper, probably because he had no home to go back to himself. He didn't even know where he'd spend his leave. He didn't have the money to go back to Deva and would have no one to stay with when he got there.

The library was as empty as Vesper had predicted, and they settled into a pair of blue velvet chairs nestled against the wall. "So, what's going on?" Cormak asked as Vesper drummed her hands nervously on the arms of her chair.

She took a deep breath and then, in a shaky voice, told him about the confrontation between her mother and Commander Stepney.

"I'm sorry, Vee. That's a hell of a thing to witness. Are you okay?" He reached for her hand out of habit, then jerked his arm back when she flinched.

"Yeah, I guess so. I just wish I knew what was going to happen. What if Stepney forces her to call the whole thing off?"

"She'll figure something out. Your mother doesn't give up that easily. Maybe if she just apologizes?"

Vesper let out a short, brittle laugh. "I can't remember *ever* hearing her apologize. For anything. I guess she and I have that in common. We don't spend much time thinking about how other people feel."

"Are you serious?" Cormak said incredulously. "You were the glue that held our squadron together. You made sure everyone felt challenged *and* appreciated. You could always tell when someone was having a bad day and knew exactly what to say to make them feel better."

"That was because I wanted to *win*."

Cormak laughed. "Fine. So your motives weren't one hundred percent altruistic. But that doesn't matter. Kindness is kindness. People like being around you. You make them feel like the best versions of themselves."

"Not everyone, clearly," Vesper said softly, looking at Cormak with an expression he'd never seen before, full of sadness and regret.

"What are you talking about?"

"I obviously didn't make you feel like the best version of yourself."

Whatever had been holding the pieces of Cormak's fractured heart together finally snapped, flooding his chest with pain. "Oh, Vee." He reached for her hand and this time held it tightly even when she tried to pull away. "You have no idea how happy I was with you. The happiest I've ever felt, actually." He reached over to wipe the tears that had begun to slide down her cheek, and then, without thinking, tilted his head forward and kissed her.

For one brief, exquisite moment, everything in the world felt right again. Then she pulled away and looked at him with tears clinging to her long, dark lashes. "I don't understand. If you were so happy, why'd you break up with me?"

"It's... it's complicated."

"Why won't you tell me what's really going on?" she asked quietly. She was staring at him so intently, it felt like she was reading the secrets he'd taken such care to stow away, like she was looking directly into the deepest part of his mind. He wished that were possible. Then she'd understand why they couldn't be together, why Cormak had to take such extraordinary measures to protect himself... and her.

"I can't." There was no point in pretending that he wasn't hiding something. He didn't need to make her feel crazy on top of everything else he was putting her through. "I wish I could, but I can't."

"Then I'm going to go. Good luck with everything, Rex," Vesper said as she began to turn away.

"Vesper, wait." Cormak grabbed her hand and tried to

pull her toward him, but she shook herself free and hurried away.

Cormak headed to the canteen in a daze. He wasn't hungry, but it was better to grab something now so he could shut himself up in his room after his shift ended. The last thing in the world he felt like right now was facing the crowded dining hall.

But even the canteen was too bright and bustling for his current mood. Cormak was surprised to see the canteen's monitors, which were usually turned off, flickering with light and color as he walked in. It didn't take him more than a few seconds to recognize the soaring music coming from the speakers—it was the rendition of the Quatra System anthem that always played during fleet recruitment videos.

Cormak felt his brow furrow as he stared at the familiar images. He'd seen the ads so many times over the years, he could recite them from memory. *There are two types of people in the solar system: those who hide and those who fight. Which kind are you?* Then came the one that always made his brother laugh, the really old-fashioned one that showed a Settler soldier landing on his home planet launchport, where he was swarmed by beautiful women in skimpy out-fits. "Where the hell is that supposed to be?" Rex would ask. "They'd freeze to death on Chetire, be poisoned on Deva, and be eaten alive by fire gnats on Loos."

Next to Cormak, a second-year girl named Rielle was watching the videos with her arms crossed in front of her chest. "Why are they showing these?" he asked. "Everyone here has already joined up."

"To boost morale," she said with a withering look that he assumed was directed at the Academy, not him. "There've been rumors of defections."

"People are running away?" Cormak asked incredulously. A few weeks ago, when it'd looked like he wouldn't be able to replace his medical records in time, he'd been desperate enough to try stealing a ship. But, luckily, he'd realized the futility of his plan before anyone had gotten wind of it.

"Not yet, but it wouldn't be impossible. With so many active-duty troops and personnel coming and going at all hours, it'd be easy to blend in as a passenger on a transport ship."

"But *why*? Everyone here knew what they were getting into when they signed up."

Rielle shot him an even more withering look that, this

time, was clearly intended for him. "They signed up when they thought they were going to *kill* Specters, not negotiate with them."

When Rielle turned to resume glaring at the monitor, Cormak got in line and rose onto the balls of his feet to see which attendant was behind the counter. His favorite, the one programmed to make milkshakes, broke down a lot and was constantly being replaced by an older model with poor voice recognition who tended to hand you tea no matter what you ordered.

"I hope you enjoy whatever you're getting, because it's going to be your last meal as a free man," a now-familiar voice snarled behind him. With a grimace, Cormak turned to see Ward glaring at him with unabashed fury. Normally, the two-faced Tridian was all smiles in public, saving his vitriol for his private confrontations. But right now, he seemed to be almost shaking with anger. The only concession Ward made to the crowd was to lower his voice when he hissed, "What the hell were you just doing with Vesper? I thought we had a deal."

The bastard was spying *on us*, Cormak realized. But if that was the case, then he would've seen Cormak make his excuses and leave before anything happened.

By this point, at least half the cadets in the canteen were watching them. *Way to go, asshole*, Cormak thought. Ward probably thought he was threatening Cormak by mentioning their deal in public, but in doing so, he'd given up his power. The only leverage Ward had over him was the assurance that he'd keep Cormak's secret. Showing how little that mattered to him made Cormak a hell of a lot less likely to uphold his own end of the bargain. "Can we discuss this somewhere else?" he asked with what he was sure was infuriating composure.

"No. I'm done negotiating with you, Phobos," Ward said. He took a step forward until his face was mere inches from Cormak's. "I saw you two getting cozy in the library. Consider this your last warning. If I see you even *look* at her again, I'm going straight to Stepney. Do you understand?"

"Can you step back, please?" Cormak asked calmly.

"No, I fucking won't *step back*. Not until you tell me you understand."

"I'm not saying a damn thing until you get out of my face."

Ward's cheeks grew red and he clenched his teeth. "I don't take orders from Edgers," he spat out, shoving Cormak against the wall.

The impact shattered the shoddy barriers Cormak had built to keep his anger at bay, and it poured through his body like a surge of Loosian lava. He reached forward and shoved Ward's chest hard enough to make the taller boy stumble back a few steps. "If you touch me again, I swear to god I'll break your fucking arm," Cormak said, shoving Ward again for good measure while everyone in the canteen watched, dumbstruck. Fighting was strictly prohibited and severely punished at the Academy. But Cormak didn't care. He was sick of letting Tridians boss him around, and he sure as hell wasn't going to let the dumbest Tridian of all time control his life anymore. "And I'm done letting you tell me what to do. The last thing the fleet needs is one more imbecile giving orders."

"Then consider yourself a dead man walking, Phobos," Ward said with a sneer. "You know the punishment for treason."

Cormak did know, but he refused to give Ward the satisfaction of seeing the slightest hint of fear on his face. Without another word, he spun around and strode quickly but calmly out of the canteen, leaving furtive whispers and anxious stares in his wake.

He needed to get out of here, but stealing a ship was out

of the question. The last thing Cormak needed was to have *theft* added to the long list of potential charges. He'd have to find another way to thwart Ward. Maybe Cormak could reach Stepney first and convince the commander that an unhinged Ward had concocted an outlandish theory as a form of revenge. Perhaps, if he were lucky, Stepney would be far too busy with the peace summit to investigate the claims of a cadet who, only weeks ago, had vandalized the Academy with a hateful slur.

It's not the end of the road, Cormak thought as his fear and anger crystallized into resolve. He'd spent his life outwitting rich assholes who wanted to destroy him, and he wasn't going to give in now.

CHAPTER 16

ARRAN

"This is pretty wild," Rees said, sounding uncharacteristically awed as he surveyed the scene before them. The launchport was a sea of uniformed people: There were mechanics working on fightercraft, infantry troops loading and unloading gear, and officers performing inspections. The energy was unlike anything Arran had ever felt before, the air crackling with excitement and fear.

He felt the push and pull of those emotions as he checked his bag for the forty-third time since leaving his room. To his surprise and relief, the Sylvans had agreed to a peace summit. Admiral Haze, Commander Stepney, and a few top Federation diplomats would be leading the talks, but they weren't going alone. They'd be accompanied by nearly a quarter of the fleet's battlecraft, ready to provide backup should negotiations fail, and a handful of top cadets had been assigned to the crews, including Arran, Rex, Vesper, and Rees.

"That's definitely one word for it," Arran said as he watched a grave-looking Commander Stepney stride across the launchport, flanked by members of his staff.

"Did you hear about the big blowup?" Rees asked quietly. "Apparently, he accused Haze of staging a coup."

"How do you know about that?" Arran asked before realizing that it might've been better to play dumb. Although Vesper had told him what she'd seen in her mother's office, it seemed as if word hadn't spread beyond her inner circle and the fleet leadership.

"I told you," Rees said with a smile. "I pay attention to these things."

"I can't decide if your powers are impressive or terrifying. Maybe it depends on who you're paying attention to."

Rees raised one eyebrow and shot Arran a knowing smirk that made him blush. Ever since their kiss in the greenhouse, they'd spent most of their free time together. It'd been a very welcome distraction from all the chaos of the past few weeks, but while Arran could feel himself growing fonder of Rees—his intelligence, his sense of justice, his irreverent humor—he didn't really feel like they were growing *closer*. It still felt like there was some kind of wall between them, like Rees was keeping part of himself closed off in some way. But perhaps this mission would change all that. They were going to be a part of history together, forming a bond that would last the rest of their lives, regardless of what happened with their relationship.

"There's not a lot of officer gossip floating around the first-year common room," Arran said. "What's your source?"

Rees looked from side to side and lowered his voice. "The attendants record conversations. It's a backup mechanism so they don't forget orders before they carry them out. The files are supposed to be erased at the end of every day, but I wrote a code that captures the data."

"So you're eavesdropping on private conversations," Arran said, startled. "Isn't that a little…unethical?"

Rees's face hardened. "Don't you think we have a right to know why our commanders are risking our lives? Especially when Stepney has such close ties to the fyron companies."

"No, you're right," Arran said quickly, eager to change the subject. "But if Stepney was so opposed to the peace summit, why do you think he's going?"

"You think he'd let Admiral Haze change the course of Quatran history without him?" Rees scoffed. "If the peace talks end up working, he'll want to take credit for it, regardless of what he might've said in the past." Rees glanced down at his link and frowned. "It looks like I'm supposed to help load supplies on Dock B. See you later?"

"See you on board," Arran said. Their battlecraft was due to depart in less than three hours, and then the journey to the site chosen for the peace summit would take just two days, since both sides would be able to travel at light speed. In two days, the Quatrans would come face-to-face with the enemy they'd spent years merely imagining. In two days, he'd get to see Orelia again, a prospect that filled him with both excitement and apprehension. How were you supposed to greet someone who'd betrayed you? Who'd been one of your closest confidants while simultaneously putting your life in grave danger? At least now, after his research, he was positive that neither Orelia nor the Specters had been responsible for the explosion that killed Sula. He'd never be able to face her otherwise.

Arran had reported his findings to Captain Mott, but there was no sign that the information had been passed along to anyone else. A sharp twinge of anxiety momentarily overpowered the nerves that had already taken hold. Right now, the Quatra Fleet leadership was under the impression that the Specters had launched a deadly attack just days ago. If that wasn't true, then the misunderstanding could potentially have the power to derail the peace talks. With a glance over his shoulder, Arran began to compose a message to Orelia on his link. He doubted it'd reach her so far out of range, but it was worth a shot.

He sent the message and was just about to swing his pack over his shoulder and head up the gangplank when someone called his name. He turned to see Dash, breathing heavily, as if he'd run to catch up with Arran. "Can I talk to you for a second?"

"Now's not a good time, Dash." He gestured toward the massive battlecraft. "In case you haven't noticed, we're about to ship out for the most important operation in the history of the Quatra System."

Dash sighed. "I know my timing is awful...my timing's *always* been pretty awful. But none of us knows what's going to happen over the next few days, and I can't let you leave without telling you how I feel."

"I really don't have time for this right now," Arran said. Part of him was desperate to hear what Dash wanted to say, but it wasn't quite as big as the part that wanted to make Dash suffer as much as he had.

"Arran, please," Dash said, grabbing hold of Arran's arm. The feeling of his touch was enough to make Arran's chest swell with a painful mixture of nostalgia, longing, hurt, and anger. "I made a huge mistake. I'm sorry for being such a coward. Will you give me another chance?"

Arran stared at Dash, wondering if he were hallucinating. He'd imagined Dash saying those exact words countless times over the past few days, but the rational part of his brain wouldn't let his heart believe it. "I don't understand. What's changed? Your dad made it pretty clear what would happen if you insisted on dating a Settler."

"I told him I wouldn't let him threaten me like that. I explained that you were too important to me…I told him that I love you."

I love you. The words seemed to flow straight from Arran's ears into his heart, filling his chest with warmth. But even that sensation wasn't enough to dispel the hurt that'd calcified like scar tissue.

"I'm sorry, Dash," Arran said softly. "But it's too late. I'm with Rees now. I'm not going to shove him aside just because you say you've changed your mind. How do I know you're not going to do it again?"

Dash's face fell. "I won't. I promise. Oh, Antares... Arran." He reached out to squeeze Arran's hand. "What do I have to do to make you believe me?"

The pressure of Dash's hand sent another surge of warmth though him, but it wasn't enough to settle his spinning head. "I don't know," he said honestly. "You've said some awful things. You've *done* some awful things. You know how hard it was for me to trust you in the beginning; it was hard for me to believe that you liked me, that you weren't playing a cruel trick on me. And then it felt like all my worst fears came true."

"I know. I'm sorry..." Dash's voice trailed off and he shook his head, as if to dispel the painful thoughts gathering like storm clouds. He loosened his hold on Arran's hand, and for a moment Arran thought Dash was going to pull away. But Dash merely moved his hand to Arran's lower back. "I'm sorry," Dash said again, though this time it was a whisper against Arran's ear.

Arran shuddered at the sensation of Dash's breath on his skin but managed to take a step back. "No, I can't. I'm not trying to hurt you. I'm not doing this to make some kind of point. I just know that it's never going to work out between us. We're too different—you can't close that kind of gap."

"Is that why you want to be with Rees? Because he's a Settler?" Dash asked, his voice cracking.

"It's one of many reasons. I really like him, and I want to give him a fair shot."

Dash fell silent, looking at Arran with the expression of a small animal that'd just been kicked in the ribs by a beloved owner and then shoved out into the cold, snowy night. "Okay...if that's what you want, I'll leave you alone." His shoulders slumped, making him look smaller and more fragile than Arran had ever seen him. "Good luck, Arran. Take care of yourself."

"You too, Dash."

It took all of Arran's self-control to let him go, to not call after the first boy he'd ever kissed, the only boy he'd ever loved.

The journey to the peace summit location took two days, though between his various drills and duties, Arran barely slept more than a few hours in total. Not that he would've been able to sleep much, anyway. Between his unexpected conversation with Dash, his concerns about who'd caused the explosion, and his anxiety about seeing Orelia for the first time since her arrest, Arran spent those two days with his brain whirring like one of the badly wired, rusty old attendants back on Chetire that was always short-circuiting. The only silver lining was that, with so many things on his mind, it was impossible to fixate on one problem for long enough to truly agonize.

He and Vesper were just coming back from one of the daily mandatory sessions in the battlecraft's conditioning area when a trio of beeps rang through their monitors and the comm system—the signal that the ship was slowing from light speed to standard travel mode.

"We must be getting close," Vesper said, her measured voice belying the hint of fear in her eyes.

Before Arran could respond, his monitor blared a message in his ear. *"We are approaching the target. You have ten minutes to report to your battle stations."*

Arran and Vesper exchanged startled looks. "They probably should've updated the wording of that alert," Vesper said with a nervous laugh.

"Yeah, I'm not sure *battle stations* is quite the right term when it comes to attending a peace summit."

But underneath their forced playfulness, they both well knew why six battlecraft and nearly a hundred officers, cadets, and crew members had been sent to the summit.

As they hurried down the corridor, they saw dozens of people gathered near the large window on one of the observation decks. Sound carried in the cavernous battlecraft, and any populated space echoed with footsteps and chatter. But as Arran approached the window with Vesper, he couldn't hear anyone speak. He couldn't hear anyone *breathe*.

None of the assembled officers and cadets even looked at one another. Everyone seemed lost in their own world, absorbed by their own thoughts as they stared at the shapes in the distance.

The black outlines of a fleet of Specter battlecraft.

Despite his preparations, despite his yearning for peace, Arran couldn't keep the cold fear from seeping down in his spine. Like every kid in the entire solar system, Arran's childhood had been consumed by thoughts of the Specters— wondering what they looked like, what they wanted from the Quatrans, and most important of all, when they were going to strike again. When he was eight, he'd had a recurring nightmare about being the sole survivor of an attack on Chetire. Every night, he saw himself wandering through the smoking rubble until he stumbled across an enormous black fightercraft right in the middle of the ruined town square. And every night, the sight of the hatch slowly opening filled him with terror. The dream always ended just before Arran glimpsed the monster inside, when he'd wake up screaming.

And while the logical part of Arran's mind knew that they weren't monsters at all, that the Specters had far more right to look at the *Quatrans* as monsters, it was hard to undo so many years of instinct.

"It's going to be okay," Vesper whispered, more to herself than to Arran.

"Definitely," he said hoarsely. "Come on. Let's get ready."

CHAPTER 17

ORELIA

Orelia stood in front of the narrow mirror in the tiny cabin she'd been assigned on the Sylvan battlecraft. Or perhaps it only felt tiny compared to her room back at the Academy, the largest she'd ever had all to herself.

The ship was approaching the site that'd been chosen for the summit, but there wasn't much she needed to do to prepare. She wasn't one of the planned speakers, thankfully. Her role was mostly symbolic. Unfortunately, she didn't have any Sylvan clothes with her and knew it'd likely rub her people the wrong way to see her in Quatran wear. Though perhaps it'd make her an even more powerful symbol—the girl who, to everyone's surprise and confusion, seemed to belong to two worlds.

There was a knock at the door, which meant it could only be Zafir. Knocking was a distinctly Quatran custom. Privacy was a foreign concept on Sylvan, where few interior doors even closed. Doors were meant to keep out scorching heat, ice storms, and dangerous floodwaters—not other Sylvans.

General Greet had invited Zafir to travel to the peace summit on the Sylvan ship instead of rejoining Captain Avar and Colonel Beaune. She'd phrased it as an invitation, but it'd been clear to both him and Orelia that he wouldn't have a say in the matter. Until the summit began, he'd remain with the Sylvans, part guest, part hostage.

"Come in," Orelia called, wondering vaguely if this was the last time she'd ever use that phrase. Even if the peace summit was a success, she couldn't imagine a scenario in which she'd return to the Quatra System. She'd attended the Academy as a spy; she highly doubted anyone would suggest that she continue her fraudulent studies.

Except they hadn't been fraudulent. When she hadn't been worried about being captured and executed, she'd actually liked her classes, and had really enjoyed training and competing in the tournament with her squadron mates. And most of all, she'd loved spending time with the first real friends she'd ever had.

Zafir appeared in the doorway, already attired for the summit in his dress uniform. Her stomach fluttered when she took in the striking contrast between his white jacket and his warm, light brown skin. "The Quatran ships are about to dock. There's a pretty good view from the viewing deck," he said. "Would you like to come with me?"

She nodded and followed him down the narrow hall that opened into the deck. "It looks like everyone's right on time," Zafir said, staring out the window with an inscrutable expression on his face. Orelia peered out the window and shivered as her gaze fell on three Quatran fightercraft flanked by nearly a dozen Sylvan fightercraft. There was something unsettling about seeing so many Sylvan and Quatran ships so close together, like watching someone waving a lit match over a bundle of dynamite. One false move, one misstep, one misunderstanding, and they'd bear witness to the bloodiest conflict in the history of the war.

To her surprise, her wrist buzzed. Her link had originally been confiscated by the Sylvans, but they'd returned it to her yesterday. She didn't think it would work this far from the Academy, on a Sylvan ship. When she saw the name, her heart lurched, propelled against her rib cage by both joy and apprehension. She hadn't heard from any of her friends since she'd left the Academy and didn't know if they'd even still consider her a friend now that they knew the truth about her. She took a deep breath in an attempt to steady her racing pulse, then opened the message.

```
Orelia—


I'm not sure if you're going to get this,
but I think there's a chance now that
you're back in range of the Quatran Fleet.
I sent you a bunch of messages last week,
but your connection had been disabled. I was
so worried about you. At first, I assumed
there'd been some terrible misunderstanding.
I couldn't imagine that you'd ever pass
information to the Sylvans.
```

Orelia smiled to herself as she imagined Arran typing *Specters*, then deleting it and writing *Sylvans* instead. She kept reading.

```
It took some time for me to process everything.
I watched your video message close to twenty
```

times. And I want you to know that I'm not
angry. You were doing the job you were sent
to do, and I can only imagine how difficult
and scary it must've felt at times. We have a
lot to talk about, obviously, and I hope we
get the chance to do it soon. I'm part of the
envoy heading to the peace summit, so maybe
there's a way we can meet up before it's all
over. I guess that's assuming everything goes
well, but I'm hopeful that it will.

There's something I think you should know
first, though. Everyone thinks a Sylvan pulse
caused the explosion on a patrol ship last
week, but it's not true. I'm ninety-nine
percent sure it was a Quatran who planted the
malware on the ship—maybe someone in the fleet.
Check out the images below to see what I mean.

Good luck. I'm rooting for you. I'm rooting
for all of us.

—Arran

"Everything okay?" Zafir asked, looking at her with concern.

"Yes," she said distractedly, then paused for a moment, considering. "I'm actually not entirely sure." She showed Zafir Arran's message, and then they both examined the images he'd sent of the vents that were supposedly damaged by the electromagnetic pulse.

"What do you think?" Orelia asked.

Zafir didn't respond right away, his gaze fixed on the images, which Arran had annotated. When he finally spoke, his voice sounded tight. "I think we might have a problem."

Before Orelia could ask another question, General Greet appeared around the corner, flanked by four guards. "It's time, Lieutenant," she said. "Let's go meet your compatriots."

The summit was to be held on the Quatran battlecraft, since its larger cargo hold could accommodate more people. The Sylvan ship had docked alongside the Quatran ship close enough to form a bridge between their two airlocks. The Quatran delegation would enter the cargo hold from one entrance, and the Sylvans from the other, though Zafir would go ahead first to rejoin his own people.

He and Orelia stepped to the side of the airlock for some

semblance of privacy. "I guess I'll see you soon," he said in a cheerful voice at odds with the tension in his face.

"Definitely," she said, doing her best to match his tone.

A heavy silence fell between them, full of all the things they couldn't say in front of General Greet and the Sylvans, and all the things she couldn't quite say to herself, let alone to him.

He extended his hand toward her, ostensibly to touch her arm, but then he saw General Greet watching them and thought better of it. He flashed her a warm smile, but by the time he'd turned toward the airlock, his expression had become focused and grave. He nodded at General Greet and the other Sylvans, then disappeared into the tunnel.

A few minutes later, it was time. General Greet stepped through the airlock first, moving with calm, businesslike assurance, as if she were heading to a staff meeting rather than her first face-to-face encounter with the enemy who'd slaughtered millions of her people. She was followed by the magistrates of Sylvan's six largest provinces and the High Priestess of a self-governing theocratic island in the Southern Sea.

The air buzzed with tension as the two delegations filed in from separate ends of the storage facility. Orelia entered fourth, which gave her just enough time to witness the initial reactions from the Quatrans. Although by this point they knew that the Sylvans were far less alien than they'd imagined, they clearly still found it startling to look at faces so similar to their own.

Orelia did a double take after glimpsing a familiar face and found herself locking eyes with Vesper. Her heart lurched against her chest and, momentarily paralyzed by Vesper's cold expression, Orelia almost walked on without acknowledging her. But then Vesper nodded slightly, and Orelia nodded back.

For a moment, the only sounds echoing through the cavernous space came from the scrape of chairs as everyone took their seats around the long table, with the Quatrans on one side and the Sylvans on the other. General Greet and Commander Stepney faced each other from opposite ends. "Thank you all for joining us," Admiral Haze said, her voice strong and steady. "And special thanks to General Greet for helping to organize this historic event in such a short amount of time."

General Greet inclined her head, a decidedly un-Sylvan gesture she'd no doubt been advised to do.

"It is our feeling, and I believe it's yours as well," Admiral Haze continued, "that the fighting between our people has gone on for far too long."

"The fight you started," General Greet said. One of her advisors shot her a look of warning, but she continued unabashed. "I think it'd be helpful to understand why you attacked Sylvan in the first place. Otherwise, why should we believe that you won't do it again?"

The Quatrans exchanged uneasy looks. Orelia wondered if Admiral Haze had told anyone about their conversation. Either way, she doubted they'd been interested or able to accept such a disquieting revelation quite so quickly.

"We're not here to rehash the past," Admiral Haze said. "We're here to ensure a peaceful future, and while we'll never forget the lives that were lost, the families that were torn apart, and the years of fear and bloodshed, it's time to move on. We propose an immediate cease-fire and have prepared some terms that we think you'll find very reasonable."

"Peace is always our goal," General Greet said carefully, "but you'll understand our skepticism, given the history. We'll need proof of your good intentions before we'll be able to trust you."

"Trust *us*?" Commander Stepney said incredulously, speaking for the first time. "It seems rather suspect that you'd be willing to negotiate a cease-fire just *days* after attacking one of our patrol ships. A cadet was killed, and the rest of the crew nearly died."

Arran was right, Orelia thought anxiously as confused murmurs rippled along the Sylvans' side of the table. One of the magistrates leaned over to whisper something to General Greet, who nodded along with a frown.

"There was no attack," General Greet said. "We did send a ship a few weeks ago, but it was destroyed before reaching its target."

"Forgive me, *General*," Stepney said, injecting the word with a note of scorn. "But I'm not sure how we're meant to trust one another if you insist on lying to everyone here."

Orelia cringed, and gasps rippled along her table as Stepney's words were translated for those who didn't understand Quatran. To accuse someone of lying was the gravest possible insult on Sylvan, where honesty was prized above all else. Even the word *lie* was considered a form of profanity.

Admiral Haze spoke up quickly. "What Commander Stepney means is that we're still investigating the matter."

"We're not investigating anything, Admiral," Commander Stepney snapped. "They used an electromagnetic pulse to destroy the oxygen converter on our ship, resulting in a fatal explosion."

General Greet stood up, the sound of her chair scraping against the floor ringing through the cargo hold. "It seems as if this summit was premature," she said as her guards closed in around her.

No, Orelia thought desperately as the Quatran guards followed suit. They couldn't let everything fall apart like this. How many thousands more would perish just because of a Quatran intelligence failure? She glanced over at Vesper and saw Arran whispering something to her, his face white with panic.

Someone needs to say something. Someone had to explain what Arran had told her before they missed their one, fleeting opportunity for peace. But the thought of interrupting the proceedings sent a jolt of cold fear through her chest. The breach of protocol—a low-ranking agent interrupting the most crucial diplomatic event in history—would border on mutiny, to say nothing of how the Quatrans would feel about an enemy spy contradicting the commander of the fleet.

"Can everyone wait just one moment?" Every head turned to look at Zafir, who'd stood up to address the room. "I recently received intelligence that might help put this matter to rest. There's proof that the explosion was caused by malware planted inside the ship—not from a pulse. If someone would be kind enough to project the applicable images, I'll show you what I mean." He shot a quick, meaningful glance at Arran, who froze, his eyes wider than the larger of Sylvan's two moons, until Vesper nudged him in the ribs. Arran looked down at his link, and a moment later, the images of the undamaged hydrogen vents appeared in the air between the two long tables.

As Zafir pointed out details on the images, Orelia watched Commander Stepney's face grow slightly red as, next to him, Admiral Haze suppressed a smug smile.

"Just to make sure I understand you correctly, Lieutenant," General Greet said, "are you suggesting that this incident is an internal matter?"

"Yes," Admiral Haze said quickly, answering for him. "One that we'll be investigating seriously, but that should have no bearing on this summit. If you're happy to proceed, then so are we." She turned to Commander Stepney, who managed to nod despite the fury in his face.

A couple of hours later, the delegates decided to break for the day. Orelia rose from her seat in a daze and was about to follow General Greet and the other Sylvans back to their own ship when she felt a hand on her shoulder. She turned to see Vesper and Arran standing next to her. Vesper was beaming and Arran looked nearly as stunned as Orelia felt.

"That was incredible," Vesper said, her voice just as warm as it'd been back in the simulcraft after a hard-earned victory. "You were brilliant to show Arran's message to Zafir."

"It was all Arran. He saved the day." Orelia turned to him with a smile, but to her confusion, he merely stared at her. "Are you okay?" she asked, worried that perhaps seeing her in person made the sting of her betrayal even worse. "I'm so sorry for everything that happened. I...I never wanted to lie to you."

Arran flung his arms around her and hugged her tightly. "I'm just so glad you're okay," he said, his voice muffled. "I know you didn't have a choice. And I know how much you risked to protect us during the attack." He let her go and stepped back, his cheeks flushing at his uncharacteristically effusive display of emotion.

Orelia was blushing too, but more from pleasure than embarrassment. "Is Rex also here? Or is he back at the Academy?"

"He's here somewhere," Vesper said, glancing over her shoulder. "He's probably on duty in another part of the ship. We'll make sure he finds you before the peace talks continue tomorrow. I know he's dying to see you."

"Can I talk to you a moment?" a soft, deep voice said. Orelia turned to see Zafir standing next to her.

"Of course." She glanced at Vesper and Arran, who saluted and said hasty goodbyes, leaving Zafir and Orelia on their own.

"Do you think you have time for a quick walk before you return to your ship?"

Orelia looked over at General Greet, who was speaking to Admiral Haze, both of them looking relaxed and engaged. "I think so. If we're quick."

She followed Zafir out of the cargo hold and down a series of narrow corridors until he stopped suddenly and turned to face her.

"I owe you an enormous apology," Zafir said. "What

I said the other day, about not being able to trust you, it wasn't kind and it wasn't true. I was just…taken aback by the revelation. I was confused, embarrassed, and honestly… I was a little scared, which is why I lashed out. I'm sorry."

"What were you scared of?"

"You got past my defenses, literally and figuratively," he said, his voice a mixture of tenderness and bewilderment. "I had to face a number of unsettling facts: I didn't notice that a first-year cadet was an enemy spy, *and* I developed feelings for a student. It made me feel like a failure, like I was out of control."

"I understand that." Orelia had spent most of her life learning how to put herself in other people's heads, but she'd never stopped to imagine what Zafir must've been feeling over the past few weeks. He hadn't just been angry with her; he'd been furious with himself. "Though we're nearly the same age. I had to pretend to be younger than I was to pose as a cadet. I'm sorry about that."

"You're done apologizing." He took her hand and squeezed it. "Because of you and your friends, the war could be over soon."

"It's a little hard to wrap my head around," she admitted. "So what happens next?"

"I have no idea," Zafir said with a laugh. "I guess I'll have to redo the syllabus for my counterintelligence classes, to start."

Orelia smiled. "I wasn't going to be the one to say it, but your lecture on 'what we know about the Specters' could use some work."

"You're right. I'll need to add a whole section about how staggeringly intelligent they are, how brave...how beautiful."

She shivered at the word and felt bold enough to whisper, "I was scared that you were going to hate me forever."

He brought his face toward hers. "And I was afraid you'd only pretended to care about me."

"I'm not that good a liar," she said into his ear, then brought her lips to his mouth and kissed him lightly.

"I'm glad," he murmured as he placed his hand on her lower back and gently pulled her toward him.

A current of electricity shot through her, burning away every thought, every sensation except for the warmth of Zafir's touch. But then the sound of distant footsteps made her start.

"What's wrong?" Zafir whispered in her ear, his breath tickling her skin.

"I thought I heard someone."

But instead of glancing over his shoulder to investigate the source of the sound, he wrapped his arm around Orelia's waist and pulled her closer. "It doesn't matter. You're no longer my student. The war is almost over. There's nothing to hide anymore."

CHAPTER 18

CORMAK

The success of the first day of peace talks had left the attendees in an almost giddy mood, and a decidedly un-military, festive atmosphere had spread throughout the ship. Superior officers turned a blind eye as lower-ranking crew members abandoned their duties to discuss the day's events. A few of the cadets had clearly had too much to drink, and Ward was leading a particularly rowdy bunch in a series of increasingly loud toasts, his cheeks growing red as his eyes turned glassy.

Cormak found himself standing apart from the crowd, watching everything with a strange air of detachment. Intellectually, he knew he was witnessing history unfold around him, and that years from now he'd marvel at the fact that he'd been there. Yet it was nearly impossible to focus on anything except his mounting fear about whether Ward would follow through on his threat to turn Cormak in. *Relax*, he told himself. *You need to act natural.* There was no immediate cause for concern. He never would've gotten anywhere near the battlecraft, let alone been allowed to attend the peace summit, if anyone besides Ward knew that Cormak was an imposter. Either the big-talking Tridian had wimped out, or else he hadn't found anyone to take him seriously.

Cormak was just about to slip away when Ward's gaze fell on him. His eyes narrowed, and for a moment, the glassy look gave way to a cold shrewdness. "Whatcha doing, *Cormak*?" he called loudly.

Get out, Cormak thought. *Get out now and no one will notice.* They'll just assume Ward was being drunk and ridiculous as usual. But as Cormak turned around and began to walk casually away, Ward's voice grew louder and sharper. "I'd like to introduce all of you to *Cormak* Phobos. Turns out there was a little mix-up with his application, but good ole Cormak didn't let a little thing like *not getting into the Academy* stop him."

All around him, Cormak could hear confused murmurs

and felt the weight of curious, confused gazes. No one told Ward to shut up, and emboldened by the attention, he stood and staggered over toward Cormak. "Bet you thought I wouldn't do it, right? But I just had a nice little chat with Commander Stepney, and he seemed *very* interested in what I had to say. The game's over. You lost."

He's bluffing, Cormak thought, willing himself to stay calm. "What'd you do? Spray-paint it on his office? That's your preferred method of communication, isn't it?"

Ward smiled, a response Cormak found far more ominous than a scowl. "Stepney stormed out of the summit, furious about the fact that someone in the fleet planted the malware. I heard him shouting at his staff, so I decided to help out. I told him that you were here under false pretenses, which proved you were capable of shady shit. He thanked me and sent one of his underlings off to look into your records."

Get out. Get out. Get out, Cormak's heart thudded, like someone banging on the window of a room filling with smoke. Ward wasn't nearly smart or creative enough to come up with a lie like this just to mess with him. He didn't know what Stepney's aid would discover now that the medical records had been updated, but he wasn't going to stick around to find out.

He never should've gotten on the battlecraft bound for the peace summit. At least back at the Academy he would've had a chance, albeit a miniscule one, of stowing away on a shuttle or transport ship bound for Tri. He probably wouldn't have lasted long as a fugitive on an unfamiliar planet, but at least he would've had a shot. Whereas now he was trapped parsecs away from the Quatra System, surrounded by every top-ranking official in the fleet.

As he watched two officers behind Ward clink glasses of "borrowed" nitro spirit, he realized this was his one shot. If he was going to leave, it had to be now, while everyone was distracted by the successful first day of peace talks. Everyone's guard would be down, and there might even be less security on the top deck, where the fightercraft were docked. Without another word to Ward, Cormak spun around and hurried into the corridor. It took every ounce of self-control not to break into a sprint. Time was of the essence, but if anyone spotted him looking sweaty and frantic, it was all over. His life depended on looking like his life wasn't in danger at all.

The chance of gaining access to a fightercraft and then flying it off the ship was a thousand in one, but he had to try. He refused to spend what remained of his life in a Quatra Fleet prison, counting down the moments until his execution.

The top deck was normally a sea of activity with mechanics working on fightercraft, infantry troops loading and unloading gear, and officers performing inspections. But to his relief, there were only a handful of people, none of whom seemed particularly interested in the sudden appearance of a cadet.

"*You have entered a restricted area,*" his monitor announced. "*Access denied.*"

"Dismiss," Cormak said under his breath. The monitor was only supposed to be removed by a medic, but there was obviously no time for that. He brought his hand to his ear, clenched his teeth, and yanked, grimacing as he tore the small metal device from his skin.

He took a deep breath and began walking across the launchport with the calm, purposeful strides of someone following orders—not trying to make a desperate escape before he was arrested for treason.

He didn't know if he'd actually be able to fly a fightercraft on his own. He'd only flown simulators, and since he'd been their squadron's captain, not the pilot, it'd been a long time since he'd done that much. And even if he somehow managed to take off without being shot, fly it without crashing, *and* land without attracting the attention of the local police, Cormak had no idea where he was supposed to go. He didn't have any money, and there was no one in the solar system who cared about him enough to risk their life to hide him. He supposed there was a chance his old boss, Sol, the Devak arms dealer, would help him in exchange for ten or twenty years of indentured servitude, but that option seemed only marginally more attractive than moldering in an icy, subterranean prison.

The thought landed in his chest with a painful thud. The only people who cared about him were here, on this battle-craft, parsecs from civilization. And the only way to save his life was to leave them behind forever.

He imagined Vesper's look of hurt and confusion when she realized that he'd left without a word, and the image was almost enough to make him reconsider his plan. His chances of surviving his escape were so low, perhaps it was better to stay, to get to say a proper goodbye, to save her the pain of a second betrayal.

I need to send her a message, he thought, fumbling with his link. But what could he possibly say? He'd spent the past few months searching for the words to explain everything to her, and he'd always come up short.

Vesper, he began. *I don't think there's anything I can say that'll keep you from hating me, but I have to try. My real—*

The shrill blare of an alarm cut through the drone of fightercraft, and the lights began to flash. *"Intruder alert… intruder alert…Cease all operations immediately and secure the area…Intruder alert…"*

"No," Cormak whispered, cursing under his breath. He looked around wildly, unsure what to do. It'd be stupid to run and draw attention to himself if the alarm was just part of a drill. But then another sound filled the silence between the alarm beeps—the sound of stomping boots. With dread expanding in his stomach, Cormak turned to see about a half dozen guards coming his way, the looks on their faces a far cry from the easygoing expressions of the people celebrating downstairs. They were led by a grave Commander Stepney, who shouted, "That's him!"

Cormak didn't resist as the guard wrenched his arms behind his back and snapped restraints on his wrists.

"Cormak Phobos, you're under arrest for suspicion of a terrorist act resulting in loss of life," Commander Stepney said, a note of triumph in his voice.

Cormak had replayed this moment so many times in his head, there was something almost surreal about seeing it play out in reality. He felt strangely detached, as if watching it from a distance, the sounds muted and indistinct. He almost didn't notice Stepney's confusing choice of words.

"*Terrorism?*" Cormak repeated. "What are you talking about?"

Commander Stepney's face twisted into a mask of disgust. "There's no point in playing dumb, cadet. We know you're an imposter. It was you who installed the malware that caused that fatal explosion."

"What?" Cormak spat out as the accusation jolted him back to alertness. They thought *he* was responsible for the explosion that killed Sula? "Why the hell would I have done that? My friends were on that ship." *The girl I love was on that ship.*

"Because you're a Devak terrorist, that's why," Commander Stepney said. "And you're going to pay for what you've done."

Cormak didn't answer. He couldn't have spoken even if

he'd wanted to. It felt like every cell in his body was paralyzed by fear. He couldn't move. He couldn't breathe. The only muscle that hadn't turned to ice was his heart, which was beating so fast it nearly drowned out all other sounds.

He didn't resist as they began marching him across the launchport, a thousand curious eyes boring into him. *I'm sorry, Rex*, he thought. And for the first time since Rex's death, Cormak found himself wishing, praying, that his big brother wasn't watching over him.

CHAPTER 19

VESPER

Vesper jogged along the corridor. If she didn't hurry, she'd be late for her shift patrolling the weapons bay. It was unlike her to run behind schedule like this, but in all the excitement of the peace talks, she'd lost track of time.

"Vesper!" At the sound of her name, she turned to see Frey running toward her, looking uncharacteristically ruffled himself. "I've been looking for you everywhere," he said, breathing heavily.

"What's wrong?"

"Rex was just arrested. I was finishing up a maintenance shift, and I saw it happen. They've taken him to the brig." The words poured out of him at a speed at odds with his usual languid demeanor.

"What do you mean *arrested*?" Vesper asked, praying that she'd misheard.

"Commander Stepney had Rex arrested for planting malware on your patrol ship," he said, wringing his hands as he spoke.

"But that doesn't make any sense. Why would he even *want* to blow up the ship?"

"Stepney says he's a...terrorist," Frey said with a wince.

Vesper let out a high-pitched laugh of disbelief. "A terrorist," she repeated. "That's the most ridiculous thing I've ever heard. Anyone who's spoken to him for five seconds would know he's the last person who'd ever do something like that."

"I know, I know," Frey said, a bit too quickly. "But Stepney seems convinced..."

"This is all just a misunderstanding," Vesper said firmly. "I'm going to talk to Stepney. We'll sort this out." Her confident tone belied the panic bubbling in her chest. She knew it was no misunderstanding. Stepney was looking for someone to blame, and for whatever reason, he'd chosen Rex as his scapegoat.

Vesper expected Frey to protest against doing something so rash, in such obvious breach of protocol, but he merely nodded, which somehow made the situation feel even more terrifying. "You'd better hurry. I heard from one of the guards that they're planning to transport Rex back to Tri in a few hours."

A wave of panic-tinged nausea filled her stomach at the idea of Rex in shackles, being led onto a transport ship. She could see him with his head held high, doing his best to put on a brave face but unable to mask the panic in his eyes. She couldn't let that happen. She had to do something, even if it meant putting her career on the line. She'd rather be dishonorably discharged from the Quatra Fleet than let Rex go through that sort of ordeal.

She hastily thanked Frey for his help, then took off at a run, ignoring the looks of confusion and alarm on the people she passed. She sprinted to the officers' mess hall, and when she found it empty, she ran to the command deck but was stopped by a guard before she could reach the stairs. "I need to talk to Commander Stepney," she said breathlessly.

"You need to return to your post, cadet," he said with a frown. "The commander's busy."

"Please," she insisted. "It's urgent."

"And you urgently need to return to your post before I report you for insubordination."

"I have a message from my mother, Admiral Haze," she said desperately. She'd never used her mother's name like this before, but she couldn't imagine a better time to try it out.

"If it's that urgent, then she should contact the commander directly instead of sending her *daughter*," the guard said with a sneer.

"It's too sensitive for the network. That's why she sent me."

The guard sighed. "He's gone back to his quarters. But if you wait here for a few minutes, I might be able to..." He trailed off as Vesper spun around and, without another word, began sprinting down the corridor toward the officers' private quarters.

I won't just get dishonorably discharged for this, she thought as she ran. *I'm going to be arrested myself.* But it didn't matter. Nothing mattered except for saving Rex. For in that moment, she knew with absolute assurance that she loved him, would always love him, even if he didn't love her. And if she let something happen to him, she'd never forgive herself.

But by the time she reached Commander Stepney's door, her courage began to fail her. What was she going to say?

What evidence did she have that Rex was innocent except for a feeling in her gut, an unshakable belief in his honor, bravery, and innate goodness?

The sound of her heart slamming against her rib cage was louder than the pounding of her fist against the door. She waited for a moment, but there was no answer. She knocked again and felt somehow both disappointed and relieved when there was still no response.

Vesper jumped back in surprise as the door swung open. "Are you in there, Commander?" she asked tentatively, then cringed. That was how you called for your roommate, not the head of the Quatra Fleet. There was no response, of course. The commander wasn't in his quarters.

If she hadn't known she was on a battlecraft, Vesper would've believed herself to be in an elegant estate outside of Evoline, where many of her Tridian friends, like Frey, had country homes. The sitting room wasn't huge, but it was sumptuously decorated with a leather couch, a set of green velvet chairs, and a number of oil paintings in gilded frames. The most striking item was a large, ornate wooden desk with various sea creatures carved into the legs, an antique from the days when the fleet patrolled the seas instead of the skies. It had been updated, of course, the top replaced with a link monitor.

Vesper took a few steps toward it for a closer look. Perhaps Commander Stepney's schedule would be open and she'd be able to track him down. She'd just take a very quick look and then hurry away as fast as possible. There didn't seem to be anyone around, and while she was risking severe punishment by trespassing in the commander's quarters, she had to do whatever necessary to help Rex before it was too late.

She held her breath and inched toward the desk, as if afraid that her mere presence would trigger an alarm. The commander's schedule wasn't pulled up, but his messages were.

Stop it. Turn around right now, Vesper ordered herself. If she was caught reading Commander Stepney's correspondence, she'd be put into the cell next to Rex. Yet some kind of invisible force seemed to be pulling her closer to the desk. Nothing about the events of the past few days made sense— Arran's discovery about the explosion, Stepney's strange behavior during today's conference with the Sylvans, Rex's arrest. She needed answers, and this seemed like the best possible place to start.

The first few messages would've been interesting if she'd been driven by pure nosiness, but they didn't contain any information pertinent to her mission. She kept scrolling, and her dismay grew. What the hell was she doing? She wasn't going to help Rex by reading about salary budgets and new guidelines for safety inspections. She was just about to give it up as a lost cause when a word caught her eye. *Malware.*

Heart pounding, she began to read from the beginning. It was a message assuring Commander Stepney that chips had been installed, and that the malware could be activated remotely to destroy an oxygen converter and close the hydrogen vents. "Arran was right about everything," Vesper whispered, dumbstruck. The explosion had been caused by someone in the fleet—Commander Stepney. She read one of the lines again, her shock freezing into horror. The *chips* had been installed. Did that mean he was planning to do it again?

"What the hell are you doing?"

It wasn't easy to overwhelm Vesper Haze. She was known for keeping a cool head in every situation, whether in the simulcraft, where she could land on an asteroid without breaking a sweat; in the classroom, where she answered trick questions with confidence and poise; or in the dining hall, where she responded to taunts from her rivals with charm and wit. But as Vesper spun around, she felt her heart scramble into her throat for safety.

"I was sent to leave you…this," she said, fumbling for a file on the side of his desk. "I was just looking for a safe spot, since it's confidential."

"You don't have the security clearance to handle those types of documents," Stepney said coolly. "And if you did, you would know that delivering them to my room would be an absurd breach of protocol."

Even if Vesper had been able to think of a response, there was no way she'd be able to form the words. Her heart was beating so quickly she thought she might actually pass out.

"Do you want to tell me what you're actually doing here? Did your charming mother send you?"

"No." Vesper managed to force the word out, desperate to make it clear that this had been her decision, her mistake. Not her mother's.

"I'm not sure whether that makes it better or worse," Stepney said, shaking his head. His disappointment looked so genuine that, for a moment, Vesper felt a flash of shame. She'd spent so much of her life trying to impress high-ranking members of the Quatra Fleet that it was a hard habit to break.

But not him, Vesper reminded herself. Stepney might wear a fleet uniform decorated with medals for bravery and valor, but underneath, he wore the skin of a traitor. It didn't matter what he thought about her, save for the fact that he had the power to punish her for gross insubordination. Or, worse, treason. But looking into his strangely cold eyes, she realized it was over; there was nothing she could do to protect herself now. The realization felt like being submerged in icy water—painful and shocking, but clarifying at the same time. With nothing to lose, there was no reason not to indulge her curiosity. "Why'd you do it?" she asked.

With a sigh, he pressed a button on his link. "There's been a security breach. Please send backup," he said wearily, before looking up at Vesper. "Do what?"

"Cause that explosion on the patrol ship and let everyone believe it was a Specter attack."

Commander Stepney forced a laugh. "You're out of your mind."

"No, I'm not," Vesper said, no longer afraid of insubordination. She was already in such profoundly deep trouble, one more charge hardly seemed to matter. "They're giving you orders, aren't they? The fyron corporations. They want access to Sylvan's supply and you're making it possible."

"The world is a far more complicated place than you seem capable of understanding, young lady," Stepney said icily. "I'd worry about your naïveté, but that hardly matters now that you're going to spend the rest of your life in prison."

"You're going to do it again, aren't you?" Vesper said, nearly shouting. The bubbling anger in her chest had subsumed her fear. "You're going to cause another explosion and blame it on the Sylvans. The peace talks are going to fall apart, the war will continue, and millions of people are going to die."

The door hissed open and Vesper spun around to see that the room had suddenly filled with helmeted guards pointing their guns at her. She lifted her arms over her head in a gesture of surrender, but none of them lowered their weapons. "I'm afraid this cadet is in league with the Devak terrorist," Stepney said, arranging his features into an expression of pity. "We'll need to keep her locked up until we determine what sort of danger she poses."

Vesper felt her arms being jerked behind her, her wrists bound together by restraints. It was painful but she didn't cry out, nor did she resist as they dragged her out. She kept her eyes locked on Stepney the entire time. If she was indeed executed for treason, this could be the last time

Stepney ever laid eyes on her, and although her heart was beating so frantically she thought it might crack through her chest, she wouldn't let her fear show. His final image of her would be one of defiance. But what would that matter once he sabotaged the fragile peace treaty, ripping it out of the ground before it had time to take root? She needed to tell someone—anyone—about Stepney's plan before it was too late.

CHAPTER 20

ARRAN

"Arran? Are you listening?"

Arran glanced at Rees, slightly startled. His mind had been a jumble of thoughts since the first session of the peace summit earlier that day, and he hadn't realized he'd zoned out while Rees was speaking. He still couldn't believe Orelia had pulled it off, that she'd gotten Zafir to do what he'd been too afraid to do. Because of their joint efforts, the summit would continue. Peace was on the horizon.

He'd tried to send her a message, but she was once again out of range. After the session, both the Quatran and Sylvan ships had dispersed and docked in undisclosed locations. They'd meet back up for the next day's talks, but until the peace treaty was actually signed, it was too risky for their battlecraft to remain in such close proximity.

"Sorry," Arran said, shaking his head with a smile. "What were you saying?"

They were having dinner in the battlecraft's spare, utilitarian mess hall, which Arran found to be a refreshing change. While eating flavorless food at a slightly dented metal table wasn't as elegant as dining with antique silverware under a chandelier, it was nice to escape the slightly oppressive sense of history in the Academy's dining hall—a history that'd excluded people like him.

Rees glanced at the cadets at the other end of their long table and lowered his voice. "I was asking if anyone's figured out it was you who told Orelia about the malware."

Arran shook his head. "No. But I'm sure it's just a matter of time. Do you think it counts as passing secrets to the enemy?"

"If the peace talks are successful, then she won't be the enemy."

"I'm not quite sure it works that way," Arran said, forcing a smile to hide his growing nerves. Eager to change the subject, he asked, "It's going to be strange going back to the

Academy, won't it? I mean, for decades it's been synonymous with the war against the Specters."

"Oh, don't worry," Rees said grimly. "They'll keep us plenty busy quashing rebellions on Deva and shooting at striking miners on Chetire."

"You think so? We haven't seen that type of violence in a while."

"Don't be naïve. Without the threat of the Specters, the Federation is going to have to find something for the Tridians to worry about. That's how the government and the fleet maintain their power—they create an enemy and then convince people that they're the only ones who can protect them."

As Arran struggled to process this unsettling thought, a commotion rose up from the other end of the table. A young Tridian officer had run over and was saying something to a group of startled-looking cadets. One of them nudged Fabien, a friend of Dash's, and they both turned to stare at Arran.

"Why are they looking at you like that?" Rees asked, narrowing his eyes.

"I don't know. Maybe I should go see," Arran said.

But before he could rise from his seat, Fabien jumped from his chair and hurried over. "Something's happened," he said, looking uncomfortable. "Rex was arrested. They think he has ties to the rebels on Devak and that he was the one who caused the explosion."

"What?" Arran said, rising quickly from his own seat. "That doesn't—"

Fabien cut him off. "That's not all. They're saying Vesper helped him. She's been arrested too."

"That's ridiculous. And who the hell is *they*?"

"The fleet, I guess. Commander Stepney was there when they took Rex. Frey saw it happen."

Of course, Arran thought, as his heart began to race with fear and fury. "Everyone knows that's a lie. There can't be any evidence. I have to go talk to someone."

Fabien took a step back, as if he were afraid Arran would ask for his help. "I just thought you'd want to know. So, yeah..." He trailed off awkwardly.

"You were right. Thank you."

Fabien shuffled back to his seat, leaving Arran standing. He knew he had to do something, but he had no idea what that was.

Rees stood up and came around the table. "You okay?" he asked, rubbing Arran's arm.

"No, not really," Arran said, shaking his head. "I can't believe they've blamed the explosion on *Rex*. It's absolutely insane. Even if he'd had access to the tools *and* to the battlecraft—which he didn't—there's no way in hell he would've put me and Vesper in danger like that."

"Unless he did it before he knew that you and Vesper would be assigned to that crew," Rees said, a strange light in his eyes.

"What? No. He wouldn't have done it regardless."

"I'm just saying that maybe it's not as awful as it sounds. If he didn't know that you and Vesper would be on the ship, then you can't really blame him for what he did."

"He didn't *do* anything," Arran snapped. "It's all a lie. But it seems like you want to believe it."

Rees raised his chin. "And what's wrong with that?"

"For the love of Antares, Sula *died* in that explosion."

"Sometimes it's about the greater good."

Arran stared at Rees with growing horror. "I can't talk about this right now," he said.

As he hurried out of the mess hall, Arran's confusion and

disgust over Rees's comments faded. Every buzzing thought in his previously frenzied mind was pushed aside by one overwhelming question: How the hell was he going to rescue his friends? He began to tap on his link, searching for the message Rees had sent him with the master lock code. If ever there was a time to follow Rees to the "dark side," this was it.

CHAPTER 21

VESPER

The door shut with a heavy thud, leaving Vesper alone in the tiny cell. If she sat on the edge of the metal bench and stretched out her arms, her fingers would brush against the opposite wall. It was even smaller than a simulcraft, smaller than the tiniest closet in her parents' house. *I'm never going home again,* she realized. What would she have done differently if she'd known she was leaving forever when she'd departed for the Academy? Would she have gone around the house touching the surfaces to commit them to memory? Would she have gotten up early to watch the sunrise in the panoramic living room windows, marveling at the spectacular view she'd taken for granted for too long? How would she have said goodbye to Baz, their faithful attendant who sometimes seemed to care about Vesper more than her parents did?

"Vesper, are you in there?" The voice was so heartbreakingly familiar that she wondered if her exhausted, terrified brain had imagined it. Perhaps that's what happened when you knew you were going to die—you heard the voices of the people you loved. Even if you never had the chance to tell them that you loved them.

Even if you weren't sure whether they loved you back.

"Rex?"

"What are *you* doing here?" he asked, his tone going from confusion to panic. "I heard your voice when they were bringing you down the hall. What happened? Are you okay?"

She told him about getting caught breaking into Stepney's quarters, and what she'd discovered before he'd arrived. "He's going to sabotage the peace summit," she said, her voice trembling with frustration. "We have to do something once we get out of here."

Rex cursed under his breath, then she heard a thud that sounded like him banging his fist against the wall. After a long pause, he said, "I think...I think this might be it for me."

"What are you talking about?" Vesper asked. The despair in his voice kicked her into a new gear, rendering her determined to find a sliver of hope for them to cling to. "As soon as my mom finds out what happened, she'll force them to release us." She wasn't sure if she believed it herself, but she had to convince Rex of the possibility.

"There are things I haven't told you...things I couldn't tell you." He paused and she heard him take a deep breath, as if summoning the strength to extract words buried deep inside his chest. "My name's not Rex, it's Cormak. Rex is... *was* my older brother. He was the one admitted to the Academy, not me. But he..." He trailed off as his voice cracked. "He died before he ever got to go. He knew there was a chance that would happen, so he left me a note telling me to take his place. That way at least one of us would make it off Deva."

For the umpteenth time that day, Vesper's brain felt on the verge of short-circuiting. "I don't understand," she said, picturing the face of the boy who'd dominated her thoughts since she'd arrived at the Academy. "You've been lying to everyone the entire time?"

"I didn't have a choice. I felt like I owed it to Rex. He died trying to earn enough money for me to go off planet, so he wouldn't have to leave me behind when he went to the Academy. If I hadn't tried to take his place, it all would've been in vain, and I...I couldn't let that happen." She could hear the pain in his voice and could imagine it written on his face. Before she realized what she was doing, Vesper raised her arm and pressed her hand against the wall separating their two cells. "I couldn't let my brother die for nothing."

The words *I understand* flew to Vesper's lips, but she didn't release them. Because the truth was that she didn't understand, couldn't understand. She couldn't imagine the grief of losing a sibling. "Tell me about him," she said softly.

"Tell you about Rex?" She could almost hear the smile in his voice. "He was goofy, scarily smart, immensely kind, and the best person I ever knew. Because of him, it really seemed like I was going to have a future...even if it's one I didn't actually deserve."

"What do you mean?"

"I didn't pass the entrance exam. I don't really belong here."

"That's bullshit," Vesper said with so much conviction that, for a moment, it pushed aside her fear. "You got the highest score on the aptitude test, made captain, *and* led your squadron to victory in the tournament. No one belongs here more than you do."

To her surprise, he laughed. "You don't really do things by half measures, do you? When you're angry, it's like facing the fury of a thousand suns, but I have to say, you being supportive is almost as scary."

"So what happened?"

"For a little while, it looked like I was in the clear. That's what I needed the money for—I paid someone on Deva to hack into the Academy's medical database and swap out Rex's files for my own. And it worked. But your charming ex-boyfriend grew suspicious and ended up talking to my contact. Ward doesn't know everything, but he knew enough to blackmail me. He told me that if I didn't break up with you and keep my distance, he'd report me as an imposter. And then he did it anyway."

"Are you *kidding* me?" Vesper leapt to her feet, buoyed by a surge of fury. "I'm going to kill him. I don't care what I have to do, but I'm going to kill him."

"Forget about him," Rex—no, *Cormak*—said. "Ward doesn't matter anymore. All that matters is figuring out how to get you out of here."

"How to get us *both* out of here," Vesper corrected.

Although, deep down, she knew there'd be no escape, it was comforting to think that Cormak hadn't given up hope.

"No matter what happens, I'm glad I got the chance to tell you the truth. It's been killing me, keeping this from you. Letting you think that I didn't want to be with you. You're the best thing that's ever happened to me."

Vesper felt a surge of tenderness for the boy who'd been through hell but hadn't let it break him. She pressed her fingers against the wall even harder, wishing she could reach through it and take his hand. "We'll figure it out, I promise."

Cormak laughed again, but this time, it was tinged with a sadness that made her chest ache. "I know you're the most stubborn girl in the solar system, but there are some things beyond even your control."

A violent jerk shook Vesper from the bench, sending her tumbling onto the floor. "What the hell?" she muttered. In the next cell, she heard Cormak making similar noises. "Are you okay?" she shouted.

The walls began to vibrate and a loud rumble drowned out Cormak's response. The lights began to flicker as the ceiling shook, sending bits of debris drifting toward the floor. Vesper covered her head with her hands and half crawled, half wriggled under the bench, drawing her knees up to her chest. "Take cover!" she shouted as loud as possible, to be heard over the din. In the distance, she heard the piercing wail of an alarm and beyond that, faint shouts.

He did it, Vesper realized, fighting back tears of anger. *Stepney activated another corrupted chip and he's going to blame it on the Sylvans. The war's never going to end.*

And then a more urgent, chilling thought took hold.

We're going to die in here. Her heart seemed to realize it before she did—it'd already lurched into a frantic sprint as if urging her to run for her life. But there was nowhere to go. From the sounds outside her cell, it was clear the guards had abandoned their prisoners, leaving them to their fate. The ceiling shook again, more violently this time. Vesper rolled onto her side and pressed her back against the wall. She closed her eyes and tried to imagine Cormak doing the same thing. If she focused hard enough, she could almost feel the warmth of his skin against hers. Could almost hear his heartbeat.

"Vesper! Come on!" She opened her eyes to see Arran, sweaty and panting, standing in the now-open doorway. Vesper rolled out from under the bench, scrambled to her feet, and ran unsteadily into the corridor just as Cormak slipped through the gap in his own cell door. "Follow me,"

Arran said, then spun around and broke into a run. Cormak grabbed Vesper's hand and they took off after him. The main deck had erupted into chaos as cadets, staff, officers, and fleet personnel darted in all directions—some heading to help the injured, the rest running to their battle stations.

"Those slimy fucking Specter bastards," Vesper heard a woman in a pilot's uniform say as she helped a limping officer down the hall. "We never should've trusted them for a second."

"Stepney's given the order to blow them all up," the injured man said through gritted teeth. "They'll get what they deserve."

It wasn't them, Vesper wanted to scream. But now wasn't the time. They had to find a way to get a message to the Sylvans, to warn them about the attack so they had time to put up their shields before it was too late.

Vesper's and Cormak's links had been confiscated, so they used Arran's to send a message to Admiral Haze, who told them to meet her in her quarters. They found her standing in the doorway, and she ushered them inside. She pulled Vesper into a hug, then stepped back to survey her worriedly. "I was on my way to find you when I got your message. What the hell's going on? Stepney had you *arrested*?"

Vesper told her mother what had happened, with Cormak and Arran filling in their parts, then explained her plan. "Stepney triggered another explosion to make it look like the Sylvans violated the cease-fire. He wants to have a reason to destroy them all and colonize the planet for its fyron. We have to warn them."

Arran was fiddling furiously with his link. "I keep trying to contract Orelia, but the message won't go through now that the Sylvan ships have returned to their location. She's out of range." He glanced up at them, looking grave. "We have to get closer and tell the Sylvans to put up their shields. And convince them *not* to retaliate or run. The Sylvans can't give the fighters any reason to think they started this battle."

Vesper waited for her mother to dismiss the idea as too complicated or too dangerous, but Admiral Haze closed her eyes, let out a long breath, and nodded. "Yes, I think that's our best option. We'll find you a ship and get you in range."

"Okay," Arran nodded. "But...who's going to fly it?"

To Vesper's astonishment, her mother turned to her and smiled. "Think you're up to the task, pilot?"

CHAPTER 22

CORMAK

Cormak felt nearly giddy with relief as he stepped onto the fightercraft. He didn't know what would happen in the next five minutes, let alone the next five years. Whether he'd be pardoned for his crimes or spend the rest of his life as a fugitive. But none of that seemed to matter right now. After months of deception—dealing with the guilt and loneliness of keeping such an enormous secret—he'd finally told Vesper the truth and, miraculously, it hadn't driven her away.

"Go on," Admiral Haze urged, motioning for them to hurry. "If you leave now, you should be able to send the message before Stepney has time to attack. The fightercraft are faster than the battlecraft transporting the weapons." On their way up to the top deck, she and the other top-ranking officers had received their orders from Commander Stepney. He was indeed planning a retaliatory attack and had ordered the mobilization of the entire fleet. When the Quatrans attacked the Sylvans, it would be with the full force of their military might.

Stepney wasn't aiming to reignite hostilities—he'd created an excuse to wipe out the entire population. There was just the faintest hint of a silver lining: Since Stepney had to wait for the rest of the fleet to arrive, the cadets would have a head start. If they got within range of the Sylvan ships before they realized the Quatrans were planning an attack, they could possibly avert the bloodiest battle of the entire war. Admiral Haze would stay behind to contact the Quatra Federation and explain Stepney's treachery.

Admiral Haze stepped into the fightercraft to say goodbye. She gave Vesper a quick hug, and gave Arran and Cormak each an affectionate if slightly awkward pat on the shoulder. "Good luck, all of you. I'll see you soon." And then she was gone, leaving the three of them on their own.

Vesper hurried over to the pilot's seat while Arran settled himself into the chair next to the tech bay, where he'd be able to monitor fuel, engine function, and all other mechanical issues. But Cormak remained standing until Vesper spun around and asked, "Everything okay?"

"Yes, fine. I just didn't want to…I mean, I didn't think it was right to assume…" Cormak stammered, feeling slightly sheepish.

"Assume what?"

"I didn't want to just assume that I'd continue as captain. The tournament is over—we can take whatever positions feel right to us. It feels like something we should at least discuss."

Arran eyed the pilot's seat warily. "The trip is going to require some intense flying—way beyond my capabilities. I'd rather stay here, if that's okay with everyone."

Cormak turned to Vesper. "I could probably handle flying, if you feel like you should captain this mission. The tournament aside, you have a ton more experience than I do."

"I think we all know who belongs in that seat…Captain Phobos." Vesper gave a playful salute and smiled, sending a surge of warmth through Cormak's chest. It didn't matter that his name was Cormak, not Rex. Or that he'd secured a spot at the Academy through subterfuge. She still cared for him.

Admiral Haze had the power to authorize their departure, but the sight of a fightercraft leaving suddenly, on its own, was going to raise some red flags. They needed to leave as quickly and unobtrusively as possible—no small feat considering it was only their second time flying an actual ship. For Arran and Cormak, it'd be easy to pretend they were back in the simulator, but it was an entirely different situation for Vesper, who'd have to take off from the crowded top deck of the battlecraft.

With anyone else, the stress would be evident. But as she prepared for liftoff, Vesper looked confident and focused. Cormak felt a surge of admiration as he watched her perform her usual ritual, tilting her head from side to side to stretch her neck and rolling her shoulders a few times before her fingers began to move deftly over the controls, as she retracted the docking mechanism and fired up the engine.

A moment later, they were airborne.

As they pulled away from the battlecraft, Cormak found that he felt more excited than nervous. This was where he belonged—in this fightercraft and, more important, with this team. The last time he, Vesper, and Arran flew together, they'd managed to destroy an enemy ship and save the Academy. They might be first-year cadets, but they were all gifted in their own way, and together, they were unstoppable.

"Arran, how long until we're in range of the Sylvan ships?" Vesper asked as she deftly steered around an enormous chunk of metal that must've broken off from the Quatran battlecraft during the explosion.

"Not long," Arran said as his fingers flew over the controls of the radar panel. "If we go at max speed, maybe forty minutes?"

The communications panel lit up and Admiral Haze's voice poured out of the speakers. "Stepney decided not to wait for the rest of the fleet to launch his attack. The first wave of ships is taking off now. You have to hurry." Cormak had never heard her sound so distraught.

"We'll be fine," Vesper said calmly. "We have a head start. We'll make it to the Sylvans in time to send the message."

"That's not the only problem. Stepney knows I authorized you to take the fightercraft, and he's figured out the plan. He's…" She took a deep breath. "He's going to try to stop you from reaching the Sylvans."

"So what do we do?" Arran asked, looking from Cormak to Vesper anxiously. "What if he orders us to turn around?"

"You keep going," Admiral Haze said resolutely. "Even if he tries to use force."

"Force?" Vesper repeated. "You think Stepney will *fire* on us?"

"As far as he's concerned, you've taken the ship illegally and you're harboring a fugitive."

Cormak's heart sank as silence filled the fightercraft. Vesper and Arran had risked their careers to rescue him— and now it looked like they'd risked their lives too. He clenched his teeth as a wave of nausea crashed over him. This is exactly what had happened with Rex. Anyone who cared about Cormak ended up paying for it.

Arran must've seen the dismay on his face, because he sat up straighter and said, "Then we'll show him what happens to people who try to go up against Squadron 20."

"Hell yeah!" Vesper called from the pilot's seat.

Their enthusiasm wasn't enough to sweep away the guilt and anxiety bubbling up in Cormak's stomach, but he tried to remain focused. After everything Arran and Vesper had done for him, Cormak owed them his best effort. As they flew on, he began to relax into the comforting rhythms of flying with his friends, using the shorthand they'd developed during their countless hours practicing in the simulator and competing in the tournament. It felt so familiar that he was surprised to glance over and see the intelligence officer's seat empty; there was part of him that'd almost expected to see Orelia sitting there.

"How much farther?" he asked Arran.

"It's impossible to know for sure, but I estimate that we'll be in range in about ten minutes. I'll try sending the message now, just in case." Keeping an eye on the control panel, Arran began to tap on his link. "Still too far."

The light on the comm system began to flash again. Cormak assumed it'd be Admiral Haze with another update, but this time an unfamiliar male voice filled the cabin. "This ship was not authorized for departure. You have ten seconds to turn around. After that, your ship will be considered an enemy craft and treated accordingly."

This is it, Cormak thought. *This is the moment I get my friends killed.* "We should do what they say," he said. "There's no reason for you two to get hurt."

"No way," Vesper said in a fierce voice that made Cormak's heart swell. "We have a mission to carry out."

"Arran, what do you think? You're not a wanted felon."

"I'm pretty sure I am now." He sounded strangely calm, almost amused by the absurdity of the situation. "And I say we keep going."

"Incoming missile detected...Prepare for impact," the warning sounded.

Cormak gripped the sides of his chair. "Vesper, get us out—"

"Already on it," she called as she turned the craft into a sharp, inverted dive.

"Impact avoided."

"Yeah, we know..." Cormak said as he let out a ragged breath. "Great job, Vee."

Cormak took a few deep breaths to quell his nausea. Arran did the same, though Vesper appeared unruffled. "How far away are we from the Sylvan battlecraft?" Cormak asked.

"Just three parsecs," Arran said. "We'll be in range in five minutes if..."

"If that ship doesn't blow us up first," Vesper finished for him. "And we're not going to let that happen."

Like hell we're not, Cormak thought, his fear hardening into resolve.

"So what am I supposed to say to her, exactly?" Arran asked.

"You have to explain that Stepney went rogue," Cormak said, still breathing heavily. "And then *she* needs to convince her commanding officer to put up the ships' shields but hold off on returning fire."

"Great. No big deal, then," Arran said with a short laugh.

"You can do this," Cormak called from the captain's chair. "If anyone can avert a violent showdown, it's you. Besides, you're just talking to your friend. Our friend. She'll be willing to listen to us."

Arran took a few deep breaths. "Okay..." He sat up straighter, rotated his shoulders a few times, and pressed his link again and frowned. "We're still not in range. I'm not sure what's going on..."

"I think that's our problem." Vesper lifted one hand from the controls to point out the window. "It looks like there's an asteroid belt between us and the Sylvans. The signal's probably getting scrambled. Arran, how big is it? Should I go around?"

Arran leaned in to look at the radar screen. "I'm not sure there's time. If we don't send that message soon, the Sylvans will notice Stepney's forces on the move and prepare their own counterattack. Do you think you can make it through?"

"We're about to find out."

"*Incoming missile detected... Prepare for impact,*" the warning sounded again. But this time, Vesper didn't seem to be adjusting their course.

"Prepare for impact in ten...nine...eight..."

"Vesper!" Cormak shouted. "You have to—"

"I've got this. Trust me."

"Seven...six...five..."

The craggy outline of an asteroid filled the window, and Cormak's breath caught in his chest. If they weren't blown up by the missile, they'd crash and cause an explosion themselves.

"Four...three...two..."

Just as Cormak closed his eyes, he felt the ship dip slightly. He opened them and saw that Vesper had taken them under the asteroid—the fightercraft cabin turned dark as jagged shadows filled the windows.

A moment later, the ship began to rumble. Cormak turned around and peered out the back window just in time to see a flash of orange flames. "What was that?"

"The missile hit the asteroid instead of us," Vesper said calmly. "And if I'm correct, the ship Stepney sent after us was just pummeled with about a thousand pieces of debris."

"I think you're right," Arran said, sounding slightly awed

as he examined the radar screen. "The ship's not following us anymore."

"I told you to trust me."

Cormak couldn't see Vesper's face, but he could hear the smile in her voice.

"Okay, try messaging Orelia now," Cormak said as they emerged from the asteroid belt a few minutes later. "Arran, are we in range?"

"Yes…I think so. Hold on." Arran cleared his throat. "Orelia? Are you there?"

CHAPTER 23

ORELIA

Orelia hadn't realized such a thing was possible, but for the first time in her life, she felt too happy to sleep. Every time she closed her eyes, she saw Zafir's face, his expression a combination of tenderness and intensity that made her shiver despite the fact that her small sleeping chamber automatically adjusted to her body temperature. The situation was fixable, of course; years of training had taught her how to clear her mind. But tonight, Orelia had no interest in quieting her thoughts and allowed herself the rare luxury of lying awake, replaying her kiss with Zafir over and over again.

Although the first session of peace talks had ended on a promising note, General Greet still "invited" Zafir to return

to the Sylvan ship at the end of the day. Despite the defer-
ence and politeness he was shown, it was clear he was more
hostage than guest and would remain in that position until
a treaty was signed.

He'd been assigned a sleeping chamber a few doors down
from Orelia, and the thought of him in bed so nearby made
her feel tingly and restless. She wished she could send him
a message to see if he was awake, but his link had been confiscated for "safekeeping" while he was aboard the Sylvan
ship. Would he find it nice or strange if she snuck into his
chamber to say good night?

Orelia rose from her cot and hesitated, wondering
whether or not to change out of her loose Sylvan sleep
clothes into something more flattering. But surely it'd look
even stranger for her to appear in his room late at night
fully dressed? She forced herself to stop overthinking and
padded quietly from her chamber down the empty hall
toward Zafir's room.

Sylvan doors didn't lock, so she simply opened it and
slipped inside the chamber, prepared to retreat immediately
if Zafir turned out to be asleep. Yet as her eyes fell on his
curled form, she felt a surge of affection that kept her gaze
locked on him. He hadn't brought his shaving kit with him,

and four days' worth of dark stubble shadowed his sharp jaw. Instead of the Sylvan sleep clothes he'd been given, he wore only his underwear—dark blue shorts that covered little of his muscular legs, one of which ended at the knee. It was easy to forget that Zafir had been seriously injured in a Sylvan attack a few years ago; with his prosthetic, he moved with more agile grace than most people Orelia knew.

She was just about to turn around when he murmured something she couldn't quite hear and his eyes fluttered open. "Orelia?" he asked, his voice thick and scratchy with sleep.

"Did I wake you up? I'm sorry, go back to sleep. I was just..." She realized she didn't have an excuse other than wanting to see him.

"It's okay. I was dreaming about you," he said with a smile. "But this is much better." He glanced down at his chest, then up at her sheepishly. "Sorry, I'd normally pull the blankets up to preserve my modesty, but you Sylvans don't seem particularly keen on bedding."

"That's what the sleep clothes are for. The fibers expand and constrict according to your body temperature. Are you cold?"

"Maybe a little." He moved over to make room for her in the narrow cot. "Want to help me warm up?"

"Is that the line you always use in situations like this?" Orelia asked, doing her best to keep her voice light despite her growing nerves. Growing up on a military base had given her a ton of experience in some areas, like code cracking and hand-to-hand combat, but it hadn't provided many opportunities for romance. Until she'd met Zafir, Orelia had never even thought of herself as someone who *could* be loved. She'd spent most of her life training for the mission to the Quatra System, which had left her convinced that she was more valuable as a weapon than as a person.

"I can't say I've been in a situation quite like this," said Zafir.

"You've never had a girl sneak into your room in the middle of the night? I find that hard to believe."

He grinned. "I'm not sure what I've done to give you the impression that this is a regular occurrence for me, but I think I'm just going to roll with it."

His warm smile melted her nerves away, so she walked toward him and was about to lower herself onto the cot when her wrist buzzed, startling her. Her link hadn't been confiscated, since the Sylvans were less concerned about Orelia receiving messages from the Quatrans than they were about Zafir sending them. But this wasn't just a message—it was an incoming call from Arran. "I'll be back in a minute," Orelia said to Zafir before slipping into the hallway and hurrying toward her own sleeping chamber.

She pressed accept and a moment later, Arran's face appeared on the screen. "Hi," she said, unable to mask the concern in her voice. "Is everything okay?" She leaned in and squinted. "Are you in a *fightercraft*?"

"Thank Antares," Arran said with a heavy sigh, then glanced over his shoulder as if looking at someone just out of sight. When he turned back to her, his face was pale and haggard. "We need your help."

What am I doing? Orelia thought as she sprinted up the stairs toward the command deck, a hastily dressed Zafir right behind her. General Greet was already suspicious about Orelia's loyalties, and now she was going to try to interfere with high-level military and diplomatic strategy? But if it meant saving countless Sylvan lives and avoiding the deadliest battle of the entire war, then it was worth a try, regardless of the consequences.

"*Where's General Greet?*" Orelia gasped as she stumbled onto the command deck, which was empty save for the pilot and a weary-looking navigator.

"*Sleeping,*" the navigator said, eyeing Zafir warily. "*Why?*"

"*I need to talk to her. Immediately.*"

"*You can talk to her tomorrow.*"

"*Call her. Now,*" Orelia said, marching over to the communications panel.

"We don't have any time to waste," Zafir said as he peered over the navigator's shoulder at the radar screen. "They'll be here any minute."

The navigator scowled and was apparently about to refuse when something on the screen caught his eye and he blanched. He slammed his hand down on a button and spoke into the panel. "*I'm sorry to wake you, General, but you're needed immediately.*"

A few minutes later, General Greet arrived looking alert and composed, bearing no sign of being roused from sleep. "What's going on?" she asked in Quatran as she strode across the deck toward them.

"I just talked to Arran. He says that Stepney was the one who planted the malware and that he staged another explosion to make it look like we'd broken the cease-fire." The words were tumbling out of her mouth so quickly, Orelia could barely catch her breath, but there was no time to lose. "Stepney's being paid off by a fyron mining company. That's why he doesn't want peace—he wants an excuse to colonize Sylvan."

General Greet remained so still and silent that for a moment Orelia thought she'd spoken too quickly to be intelligible. "Then we'll destroy them all," she said, her voice so low and cold that Orelia shivered. "I'd already dispatched a stealth craft to the outskirts of the Quatra System in case they could not be trusted. It's carrying a bomb capable of reducing a planet to dust."

"You can't target civilians." The words tumbled out of Orelia's mouth before she had time to stop herself. "It's not the Quatrans who've violated the terms of the cease-fire. Commander Stepney's gone rogue. If we just hold off for a little bit, you'll see that—"

"They're greedy, bloodthirsty *liars*," General Greet snapped, cutting Orelia off. "And if you'd like to return to your treacherous friends, Orelia, that can be arranged."

"Please, General," Zafir said. "Admiral Haze is contacting the Quatra Federation as we speak. As soon as they learn what Commander Stepney's done, they'll order him to call off the attack. Forgive my impertinence, but we think the best thing you can do is put up your shields and wait."

"And *wait*?" General Greet spat out as she pressed a

button on the command console, triggering an alarm. Almost immediately, Orelia began to hear distant shouts and the thud of echoing footsteps. "Raising the shields requires so much power that we'll have to shut down all other operations. We won't be able to communicate with the rest of the fleet, let alone fire our own weapons. We'll be helpless. But I'm sure you know that already, don't you, Lieutenant?" Her eyes were so full of fury, Orelia felt she might order the guards to kill Zafir on the spot. "This was part of your plan all along."

"No, General," Zafir said, shaking his head. "I know none of this looks good, but you have to believe us."

"Please," Orelia said. "Don't you see this is exactly what the Quatrans want? We can't give them any reason to believe we actually started this attack or want this war. A diplomatic approach is the best way—"

"*Enough.* I don't want to hear another word." General Greet turned to Orelia. "I'm not sure if you're a traitor who betrayed her people or a fool who was too stupid and weak to be trusted. Either way, any Sylvan blood that's spilled tonight will be on your hands."

CHAPTER 24

VESPER

The three of them sat in anxious silence while Orelia went to relay the message to General Greet. "Do you think it's going to work?" Vesper asked, no longer able to keep her thoughts to herself.

"It has to," Cormak said in a flat voice she'd never heard him use before.

They fell quiet again for a moment until Arran jumped from his chair, startled by his buzzing link. "Orelia? What's going on? What'd General Greet say?"

Vesper and Cormak hurried over to stand behind him, peering over Arran's shoulder so they could see Orelia on the screen. Vesper's stomach plummeted when she saw the frustration and fear in her friend's face.

"I'm sorry," Orelia said, breathing heavily. "She won't order the ships to put up their shields, and she's preparing to attack." She glanced over her shoulder and lowered her voice, leaning in closer to the link. "Apparently, she had a backup plan all along in case something like this happened. There are ships in position near the Quatra System. She... she said they're carrying bombs powerful enough to..."

"To do what?" Vesper asked as the anxiety in her stomach turned to dread.

"To reduce every planet in the solar system to dust."

There was a pause as the cadets' brains raced to process the horror of Orelia's words. Arran was the first to speak. "You have to stop her. You just have to stall for a little bit, until the Quatra Federation orders Stepney to call off the attack."

"Zafir and I both tried, but without proof, there's no way to make her believe us."

"Maybe she was bluffing," Cormak said. "The fleet would've noticed Sylvan battlecraft on the edge of the solar system, right?"

"Sylvans don't bluff," Orelia said.

"Then try *again*," Arran snapped. "Disable her if you have

to. You can't let millions of people die just because your commanding officer doesn't trust you."

Cormak put his hand on Arran's shoulder to steady him and looked to Vesper for help, but she barely noticed as she turned her attention to something Orelia had said. General Greet didn't believe that Stepney had gone rogue because there was no proof that he was acting on his own against the wishes of the Quatra Federation. Except that Vesper had *seen* proof when she'd snuck into Stepney's room and read the message about the malware.

"We have to get into his messages," Vesper said, thinking aloud.

"Whose messages?" Cormak asked.

"Stepney's. If we can find a way to show General Greet the note about the malware, then she'll believe us when we explain that Stepney's not carrying out the fleet's orders, and that there's no reason to launch such a devastating counterattack."

"You're right," Cormak said, nodding as he began to pace around the fightercraft cabin. "But how the hell do we do that in the next hour?"

"The next ten minutes," Arran said hoarsely. He was

staring at the radar panel with a look of stunned terror. "General Greet wasn't bluffing. There's a Sylvan destroyer headed toward Tri."

"We have to warn them!" Vesper said, dashing back toward the comm system. "They have to evacuate whatever planet it heads toward."

"You can't evacuate an entire planet," Arran said, suddenly sounding very tired.

"Then they can try to disable the weapon before it detonates. Or maybe knock it off course," Cormak said desperately. "Vesper, you have to tell your mother."

Vesper adjusted the frequency on the control panel and pressed the button. "Mom? Are you there? Can you hear me?" She paused to listen, but there was only static. "Shit." She slammed her hand against the control panel and tried again. "Is anyone there? Can anyone hear me? Hello?"

"There's no time," Cormak said, rubbing his temples as he paced. "Arran, is there any conceivable way of hacking into Stepney's account and stealing that message?"

"Anything's conceivable. That doesn't mean it's possible. But I can try." He frowned and pressed something on his link, then looked up at one of the monitors on the control panel. "I'm going to run a rainbow table of passwords against Stepney's account. It contains about a million combinations, but I doubt the commander of the Quatra Fleet's account would be so vulnerable." The icons on Arran's screen disappeared and were replaced by lines of rapidly flashing numbers. Vesper held her breath, then cursed when the words ACCESS DENIED appeared.

"Keep trying," Orelia urged. "I'm going to talk to General Greet again. I'll let you know if anything changes."

Arran's fingers flew across the controls, then he slammed his hand against the console when the same error message flashed on the screen. "I don't know what I could possibly do. The local encryption is too sophisticated. The only thing we can do now is wait…and hope."

"For the love of Antares," Cormak whispered as his head fell into his hands. Then he stood and walked over to squeeze Vesper's shoulder. "It's going to be okay. There's still time."

The three of them fell silent again, subsumed by their own terrifying thoughts. Vesper began to tremble as she imagined all her family and friends back on Tri, going about their day, completely unaware that, in a few hours, the sky would darken as the Sylvan bomb passed between Tri and the sun. Would they have time to grab the people they loved for a desperate, hasty goodbye before the world exploded around them? Would their final sensations be one of terror or pain? *No,* Vesper thought as she closed her eyes. *Please, please don't let that happen.*

"They'll take out the Academy too," Arran said hoarsely. "Dash is going to die thinking that I hate him."

"Don't talk like that," Cormak said. "There's still time. We can't give up. There has to be a way." He took a deep breath and began to pace again. "You said the local encryption's too sophisticated, but Stepney's files can't be stored locally. It's too dangerous. There has to be a backup somewhere, right?"

"Sure, I suppose. But there's no way to…wait, hold on." Arran rubbed his eyes and leaned toward the screen. "The radar scanner keeps picking up a small but consistent burst of signal from the Academy. It happens every fifteen minutes like clockwork. That might be the regularly scheduled backup."

"Can you track it?" Vesper asked, hurrying over to stand next to Arran.

"Maybe…yes, I think so…hold on. There!" A prompt for credentials appeared on the screen. "I'll try the rainbow table again."

Out of the corner of her eye, Vesper saw Cormak frown. "But why would it work this time?" he asked.

"There's a chance the backup server has a generic system administrator password. It wouldn't necessarily have the same safeguards." The same lines of flashing numbers appeared and Vesper had to resist the urge to look away, lest she see the devastating error message appear again. *Please, let it work*, she prayed. *For the love of Antares, please let it work.*

She heard Arran's cheer before her brain had time to make sense of the images on the screen. It was Commander Stepney's in-box. "We're in!" Arran shouted. "Vesper, show me where you saw the message about the malware."

"Just do a keyword search," Vesper said as she drummed her fingers along the control panel. "It should be the most recent result—there!" She skimmed the message to confirm it was the same one she'd read earlier, then clapped her hand on Arran's shoulder. "Can you send that to Orelia to show General Greet?"

"Already done," Arran said. "And I can do one better— I've forwarded it to the entire Quatra Fleet listserv." He glanced down at his link, then closed his eyes for a moment and took a deep breath. "Orelia says she's going to show it to General Greet now. It's out of our hands."

"How will we know if it worked?" Cormak asked. His voice was steady, but there was a hint of fear in his eyes that made Vesper take his hand and squeeze it. After everything he'd been through, after all the trauma and pain he'd endured just to survive, was he going to have to watch everything he'd fought for slip away?

Arran pointed to the radar screen, which he'd configured to show the Quatra System on one side and the Sylvan battlecraft on the other. "We'll either see the Sylvan ships go dark, which means Orelia convinced General Greet to raise the shields instead of attack..."

Vesper took a deep breath and finished the sentence for him. "Or we watch the Sylvans decimate their first Quatran target."

An eternity passed before anyone spoke. Before anyone even *breathed*. Vesper, Arran, and Cormak watched in tense silence as the fightercraft peeled off and then began to retreat. Finally, Arran extended a trembling arm toward the monitor. "The Sylvan ships seem to have shut down power—they're not emitting any signals. It worked...Orelia convinced them to stop."

Cormak let out a sound that was somewhere between a laugh and a sob. "Using information that *you* sent"—he clapped one hand on Arran's shoulder and grabbed Vesper's hand with the other—"and *you* found. Seems like another pretty big win for Squadron 20."

"So what do we do now?" Vesper asked, looking from Arran to Cormak. She felt like she was still in a daze.

A moment later, the static coming through the speakers faded, and a voice emerged. It was Admiral Haze. "Well done, you three," she said, sounding slightly dazed herself. "The Federation has authorized Stepney's arrest and military police are on their way. It looks like his ship was disabled trying to cross the asteroid belt. It's functioning just enough for him to try to make an escape. Think you can keep him from getting too far? I just need you to hold him off long enough for the military police transport ship to arrive."

Before Vesper could respond, Cormak leaned past her to talk into the speaker. "We're on it, Admiral Haze," he said with a smile. "I can't think of anything we'd like to do more."

CHAPTER 25

ORELIA

"Do you have any more surprises in store for me?" General Greet asked wryly as they stepped out of their ship onto the Quatran battlecraft. It'd been two days since the thwarted attack, and peace talks were about to resume. This time, the Sylvan delegates had arrived on a fleet of fightercraft instead of docking their own large ship to the airlock.

"Not that I'm aware of. But there's no knowing what might happen," Orelia said blithely. She'd never really bantered with General Greet like this, but the giddy relief she'd felt since the thwarted attack hadn't quite dissipated, and she was feeling strangely buoyant.

She wasn't the only one who seemed to feel this way. There was a very different energy on the Quatran ship than there'd been the last time they'd arrived. Instead of the tension and hostility Orelia had expected, both the Quatrans and Sylvans seemed almost relaxed as they greeted each other on the top deck of the battlecraft and prepared to make their way down to the cargo hold for the summit. Orelia supposed there was nothing like narrowly averting genocide to put people in a good mood.

Arran, Rex, and Vesper were waiting for her at the top of the stairs. Orelia glanced at General Greet and thought that perhaps she'd be expected to stick with the Sylvans until the summit began, but to her surprise, Greet nodded at Orelia's friends. "Go on," she said with a small smile. "They risked their lives yesterday to get that message to you. They've proved their trustworthiness."

Orelia felt slightly self-conscious as she approached her former squadron mates. Although their previous encounter had lifted an enormous weight off her chest, she was still hyperaware of her outsider status. Yet there was hardly any time to feel awkward, for as soon as she was within arm's reach, Vesper pulled her into a hug. "Thank you for

everything," she said. "I don't know what would've happened without you."

"I do. We'd all be dead," Rex said cheerfully before hugging her himself.

"Out of my way, Captain Positivity," Arran said as he
playfully jostled Rex aside in order to give Orelia a record-
breaking third hug. It was more physical affection than
she'd experienced during a lifetime on Sylvan.

"Thank you," Arran whispered in her ear. "You were
amazing yesterday."

As he pulled away, Orelia blushed and shifted her weight
from side to side, unsure how to respond to her friends'
un-Sylvan behavior. But luckily, she was granted a short
reprieve by a commotion on the other side of the deck. They
all turned to see a group of guards escorting a haggard-
looking man toward one of the Quatran transport ships.
Orelia stared for a moment, taking in the man's disheveled
hair, rumpled, dirty uniform, and bound wrists before she
realized who it was.

Commander Stepney.

"Good riddance," Vesper said as she watched the guards
load him into the ship.

"It looks like *he's* the one who's going to spend the next few years getting familiar with the inside of a Chetrian prison," Rex said, his voice full of disdain.

Orelia looked from Rex to Stepney, then back to Rex. "I think I might've missed something," she said. "Who else would've spent time in a Chetrian prison?"

Rex, Vesper, and Arran exchanged a look Orelia couldn't quite read. "Don't worry," Arran said to Orelia with a smile. "We'll fill you in on everything after the summit."

"You'll only be able to do that if it goes well," Orelia said. "Otherwise, I doubt we'll be hanging around long enough to chat." The thought gave her a pang. There was no reason for Orelia to go back to the Academy; she was no longer a spy, and she was no longer a cadet. The only logical option was for her to go home with the returning Sylvan fleet, except that she wasn't sure Sylvan would feel much like home anymore either. She'd spent the majority of her life on a military base preparing for this mission, a mission no one ever expected her to survive. There was no plan in place for her return. Where would she live? What would she *do*? And most important, how would she manage to see Zafir again?

"I'm feeling cautiously optimistic," Vesper said with a smile as she nodded at something behind Orelia. She turned around to see Admiral Haze speaking animatedly to General Greet and then shaking her hand warmly. "I think everyone wants this to work."

Vesper was right. Without Commander Stepney present, the talks were productive and diplomatic, and less than three hours after they'd sat down at their respective tables, General Greet and Admiral Haze rose to shake hands again—and sign the treaty that'd been drafted during the conference.

The cheers that'd echoed through the cavernous cargo hold was one of the loveliest sounds Orelia had ever heard in her life.

"We did it," Zafir said as he walked Orelia back up to the top deck, where the Sylvan crafts had docked. He smiled and shook his head, as if he needed the incredible truth to settle into his mind before he could fully process it. "The war's over."

"Are you worried that you'll be out of a job?" Orelia teased, trying to push aside the knot of dread that'd taken root in her stomach. As the initial wave of elation receded, it became impossible to ignore the heart-wrenching downside of peace—that she'd be returning home, possibly forever.

"I doubt it. I just imagine my job will be slightly less stressful for a bit."

"What are you going to do with all that free time?"

"Who knows?" He gave her a significant look. "Maybe I'll do some traveling."

A surge of warmth spread through her, partially dissolving the prickly knot of anxiety. "How far do you think you'll go?"

"As far as it takes," he said quietly, reaching out to brush her cheek with his thumb. "I'd cross the galaxy for you, Orelia."

"You don't have to cross the *whole* galaxy," she said as her heart began to race. "Sylvan's only a few light years away."

Orelia and General Greet were alone on the command deck. Greet had dismissed all nonessential personnel to give the crew a chance to rest before they began their journey back to Sylvan. "I owe you another thank-you," Greet said.

"I didn't do much this time. I was just delivering a message."

"A message from people who trusted you, despite knowing you were a spy. That's a remarkable achievement, Orelia. You were sent to infiltrate an enemy base and you came back with allies. You should be very proud of yourself...I know I am."

It was the moment Orelia had spent years dreaming about, finally earning General Greet's respect and approval. Yet the thrill of pride wasn't enough to temper the guilt churning in her stomach as she thought about the crew of the ship she'd helped to destroy. "There's something I have to tell you," Orelia said, taking a deep breath.

General Greet stared at her inquisitively, probably more perturbed by Orelia's use of the Quatran phrase than by anything else. Sylvans didn't announce that they *had something to say*. They simply said it. "I know I let you down when I wasn't able to stop the Quatran fightercraft from..." She paused, suddenly unable to give shape to the words that had been echoing through her head for weeks.

A Quatran would've completed the sentence for her or simply nodded to make it clear that she knew what Orelia was trying to say. But that wasn't the Sylvan way either. They didn't risk confusion or misunderstandings by making inferences. They asked direct questions and expected direct answers. *Just say it, you coward,* Orelia thought. The fear pulsing through her veins couldn't possibly compare to the terror the Sylvan crew must've felt in their last moments, as the flames engulfed their ship. "I told my squadron mates about our spread spectrum. That's how they were able to fry the battlecraft's shield."

At first, she wasn't sure whether General Greet had heard her. Her commanding officer didn't respond and her expression didn't change. Finally, after the longest moment of Orelia's life, she closed her eyes and said, "That must've been a very difficult decision."

"It was," Orelia said carefully, unsure what Greet was implying. "And it's haunted me ever since. Some days, it's all I can think about."

"I'm not sure what I would've done in that situation."

Orelia stared at Greet, startled. "You would've done everything in your power to protect your people. I'd already completed my mission by then; I'd sent you the coordinates. At that point, the only reason I needed to stay undercover was to protect myself."

"That's a strong motivator."

"But it was selfish. The lives on that ship should've mattered more," Orelia said, no longer able to keep the pain out of her voice. If General Greet wasn't going to chastise her, then she'd do it herself. "Dozens of people died because I was too scared to sacrifice myself."

"Was it all selfishness?" Greet asked, sounding surprised. "I would've thought you were also protecting your friends. Your squadron mates, as you call them."

"I was," Orelia said quietly as she allowed the terrible memories to crawl out from the darkest part of her brain. She recalled her anguish as she looked around the cabin and realized that her friends' lives were in her hands. If she hadn't told them about the spread spectrum, they would've died. Kind, generous Arran, who'd insisted on being Orelia's friend long before she was able to give him anything in return. Loyal, brave Rex—no, *Cormak*—whose cocky swagger was always overshadowed by the sympathy in his eyes. And Vesper, a fiery ball of ambition who wasn't afraid to incinerate any obstacle in her way...or any person who dared to hurt the people she cared about. "But they're Quatrans. I wasn't supposed to worry about them."

General Greet smiled sadly. "Orelia, do you really think we'll punish you for protecting your friends? Your loyalty to them led to the cease-fire. You saved many more lives than you lost."

"I didn't want to lose any," Orelia said, no longer trying to hold back her tears. "I didn't want anyone to die because of me."

"No one ever does. But that's what happens during a war. And that's why we're all immensely grateful for everything you've done in the name of peace." She placed her hand on Orelia's shoulder. "It's time to forgive yourself and move forward. Are you ready to go home?"

"I don't even know what I'm supposed to do now," Orelia said as she wiped her eyes with the back of her hand. "I'm not sure I'd do a very good job as a spy."

"I'm not worried about you," General Greet said with a small smile. "I have a feeling you'll figure something out."

CHAPTER 26

ARRAN

Arran could barely hear the cheers as he, Vesper, and Cormak staggered down the steps onto the Academy's launchport. He was so tired, his ears couldn't muster the energy to send sound waves up to his brain. He'd never been this exhausted in his life—not after the all-nighters he pulled cramming for the Academy entrance exam, not even after their near-death encounter with the Sylvan ship a few weeks ago. It felt like someone had cranked up the gravity on the track *and* changed the setting to viscous mud.

The delegates from the peace summit had just returned to the Academy, and despite the cheerful chaos, nearly everyone on the launchport stopped what they were doing to applaud Arran, Cormak, and Vesper as the three squadron mates exchanged bewildered looks. Arran heard a squeal and a second later saw Cormak being embraced by Orelia's old roommate, a Loosian girl named Zuzu. "We heard what you did," she said after hugging a dazed Arran and a slightly affronted Vesper, who'd never particularly warmed to Zuzu. Probably, though Vesper would never admit it, because of her undisguised crush on Cormak. "You saved the negotiations with the Specters!"

"The Sylvans," Vesper corrected.

"Well, whatever. You guys are heroes... again."

Arran shrugged and looked around the launchport uneasily, searching the crowd for Dash and feeling simultaneously relieved and disappointed when he didn't find him. Arran would have to break things off with Rees immediately, that much was clear.

For the few, terrible minutes when it'd looked like the Sylvans were going to attack the Quatra System, Arran had been consumed by thoughts of Dash. In that moment, he'd realized that Dash was the only boy he'd ever loved, could ever imagine loving, and that he'd been a fool to brush off his apologies. He'd let his hurt pride stand in the way of true happiness, and now it was probably too late. How could Dash ever forgive him for all the terrible things Arran had said to him?

As Zuzu wandered off, Cormak looked around the launchport uneasily. "I'm not actually sure whether or not I'm allowed to be here." Arran understood his concern. Cormak had left the Academy as an escaped felon, and unlike Vesper, his crimes had nothing to do with Stepney's corruption. He was still a trespassing imposter, no matter what acts of bravery he'd performed.

Vesper took Cormak's hand. "It's going to be okay," she said quietly. "We're going to figure this out."

"Right now, it appears," Cormak said as he caught sight of Admiral Haze striding toward them.

"You three have certainly become accustomed to making an entrance." She pressed her lips together in an unsuccessful attempt to contain the smile spreading across her face. "I hope you won't find it anticlimactic when you arrive next term on the shuttle, like the other cadets."

Cormak stared at her for a moment. "Hold on. Does that mean that I…"

Admiral Haze nodded. "Yes, I've requested an official pardon." Vesper let out a decidedly un-Vesper-like squeal. "But I'd keep a low profile for a while, until the paperwork's completed."

"Yes, ma'am," Cormak said.

She shot him an irritated look. "And don't do anything to make me regret it." Then her face softened. "The Quatra Fleet is lucky to have you, cadet. We're lucky to have all of you."

As Admiral Haze walked away, Cormak looked from Vesper to Arran in stunned amazement. "So I guess that means I get to stay?"

Vesper reached out for Cormak's hand and interlaced her fingers with his. "I'm not letting you go anywhere, Cormak Phobos." He grinned, and then there on the launchport, in front of everyone, he kissed her.

Arran took a few steps back to give his friends their space, feeling a strange mixture of pleasure and pain at the sight of their happiness. Their love for each other had been tested by the most extreme challenges—life-threatening secrets, blackmail, and war—and they'd come out stronger for it. Yet Arran and Dash hadn't been able to survive the pressure of coming from two different planets.

Arran turned and began to wander across the launch-port, unsure of his destination. What was he supposed to do now? Go back to his room and stare at the wall until it was time for dinner? What was he going to do tomorrow and the day after that? The war was over and a new future was beginning, but Arran had driven away the only person he wanted to spend it with.

The corridor was deserted as Arran made his way back to the residential wing, eager for a shower and maybe a long nap. Yet to his surprise, someone seemed to be standing outside his door. Arran felt a flash of annoyance—all he wanted right now was to be left alone—until he realized who the person was.

It was Dash.

"Hey," he said with a smile as Arran approached. "I was looking for you. I hope you don't mind." He shifted his weight from side to side, looking uncharacteristically nervous, as if unsure how Arran would respond.

"Mind?" Arran repeated, then let out a long sigh. "Dash, you have no idea…" He shook his head and started over. "The thing is, I realized…" He smiled, embarrassed. "This isn't really going the way I thought it would. Or, at least, the way I'd hoped it would."

Dash nodded seriously. "Okay, let's start over and you can show me how you wanted it to go." He turned to face the wall, then spun around again. "Hey, I was looking for you. I hope you don't mind."

"Seriously?" Arran asked with a smile.

"Yes, come on. How often do people get a second chance like this?" Dash paused as a look of pain flashed across his face. "Though I suppose not everyone deserves one."

"Dash, no. I'm the one asking for a second chance. I'm so sorry for what I said. I guess I just needed time to figure everything out."

"I'll give you all the time you need. I just want to make sure you know that I'm sorry for being an idiot." Dash shook his head. "When I'd heard about the explosion during the peace summit, I thought I'd lost you. It was the worst moment of my life. And I knew that if you made it back, I was going to devote the rest of my life to making things right."

Arran was vaguely aware of people approaching from the other end of the hall, but he couldn't tear his eyes from Dash. He wanted to drink him in and make up for every agonizing moment they'd spent apart. He leaned in and brought his lips to Dash's ear. "I love you," he whispered, then kissed him.

Dash wrapped his arms around Arran and pulled him closer until Arran wasn't sure where his body stopped and Dash's began. Just the way it was supposed to be. The way it would stay forever.

CHAPTER 27

CORMAK

A few months later

As he walked out of the Quatra Fleet registrar's office, Cormak regretted telling Vesper not to wait for him. The streets of Evoline were like something out of a fever dream—slender, soaring towers stretched into the sky, a moving sea of zipcrafts buzzed in all directions. But as much as he wanted to stare at the startling scene overhead, he couldn't look up for too long lest he knock into one of the countless people rushing along the street. He'd just accidentally bumped into an elegantly dressed older lady who'd released a stream of curses that would've turned heads in the seediest Deva bar.

He'd never seen so many people in one place before: people hurrying to work, hurrying home, or hurrying to one of the hundreds of restaurants lining the pristine streets. There were bistros with piles of tantalizing Loosian shell-fish in the windows—Cormak didn't even want to think about how much it cost to import fresh seafood from off planet—pastel-colored cafés full of pastries as ornate as jewelry, and restaurants serving smoked meat from animals Cormak had thought were extinct. He couldn't imagine what it was like to *choose* what you wanted for dinner.

Cormak glanced down at his link. It was a twenty-minute walk from the registrar's office to Vesper's family's apartment, which meant he had some time to explore before it was time to pack and catch the shuttle back to the Academy. He glanced down at the new badge on his uniform, *Cadet Cormak Phobos*, and felt a mixture of pride and sadness. For while it was an enormous relief to have this burden lifted, part of him missed wearing Rex's name on his chest. Yet he knew that, wherever his brother was right now, he was proud.

He definitely didn't feel equipped to tackle ordering in a restaurant, but he figured he should be able to hold his own in a bar. He wound his way down a series of side streets until he found an establishment that looked a tad shabbier than the ones on the main street. Cormak walked in and, for a brief moment, was relieved to see the seats filled with the Settlers who performed most of the service jobs on Tri— cooking, cleaning, and executing tasks that were better carried out by people with opposable thumbs than attendants. But then he noticed that everyone was staring at him, at his uniform in particular. *Of course*, he realized. This was the first year Settlers had been admitted to the Academy, which meant that he must look like a Tridian. A Tridian with the gall to strut into a working person's bar in Evoline. "Ah, must've taken a wrong turn," he said awkwardly before turning around and hurrying out.

He spent the rest of his walk in a strange mood. On the one hand, he was thrilled that he was going to stay in the Quatra Fleet. But on the other, it was a little frightening to enter such uncharted territory. Would people at home be proud of him? Or would they now count him as one of the enemy? He didn't even know when he'd get to return to Deva. He'd stopped paying his rent when he left for the Academy, which meant that he'd surely been evicted from his apartment. And with his father and Rex gone, there was no one he was particularly desperate to see.

As he turned onto Vesper's street, his thoughts were

pushed aside by the overwhelming scent of flowering trees. Cormak closed his eyes and inhaled, marveling at the way the fragrance washed over him. Until he'd landed on Tri a few days ago, he'd literally never taken a breath of fresh air. He'd never been outside without a gas mask. He was looking forward to returning to the Academy, the only place where he'd ever felt like he truly belonged, but part of him wished he could spend a bit more time on a planet where the atmosphere actually sustained life.

Although he'd been staying with Vesper and her parents for a week, he still felt uneasy coming and going as he pleased. Whenever he'd make deliveries back on Deva, the wealthy tower residents had made him feel like a trespasser. But today, in his uniform, Cormak felt like he could enter any building with his head held high; no one would dare question what a Quatra Fleet cadet was doing in one of the most exclusive residences on Tri.

He strolled through the large lobby, admiring the black-and-white tiled floors and the enormous palm trees in the center atrium. He stopped and pressed his hand against the glass, and a moment later a large red-and-purple bird flapped over, tapping its curved orange beak against the enclosure. "Hello, Ralphie," Cormak said. *You like that creature more than you like me,* Vesper had said affectionately when Cormak started making daily visits to the bird. He was partly driven by curiosity—he hadn't seen a real animal since his visit to the zoo all those years ago—and partly by a strange feeling of kinship with the exotic, captive bird put on display for the residents' amusement. For while Cormak knew he deserved to be a part of the Academy and was proud of his accomplishments, some people were already treating him like an oddity, as if a Devak in a fleet uniform were no different than a rare animal in captivity.

He stepped into the elevator and took a few deep breaths to keep his nausea at bay as he zoomed skyward. Perhaps this was what had given Vesper her edge as a pilot—she'd been training in stomach-churning high velocity her whole life.

Although Vesper had added Cormak's fingerprints to the security system, he still felt more comfortable ringing the bell than scanning in. He buzzed, and a moment later the door slid open revealing Baz, the Hazes' longstanding attendant. "Hi, Baz, it's me…Cormak. I'm back," he said awkwardly, remembering Vesper's warning. *Don't take it personally if he pretends not to remember you. He acts buggy around new people,*

*especially boys. Ward came over three or four times a week for two
years, and Baz never acknowledged him.*

Yet, to Cormak's surprise, the attendant glided to the
side in a gesture of welcome. "Of course. Please come in.
Would you like a refreshment?" The compartment in Baz's
chest slid open to reveal a glass of the fresh spineberry juice
Cormak had marveled over at breakfast a few days ago.

"Um, sure, thank you." Cormak carefully removed the
glass and took a sip. "This is delicious." He wondered if
Vesper had somehow programmed the famously prickly
attendant to be extra solicitous to him. According to Dash,
Baz had once thrown away a pair of shoes he'd left by the
door.

"Ms. Haze will be home shortly. She suggests that you
change into your evening attire now, as there won't be time
once you arrive at the Academy. May I show you to your
room?"

"It's the same one I've been staying in all week, isn't it?"
Cormak asked.

"This way, sir."

Slightly confused, Cormak followed Baz through the
immaculate apartment into a hallway he hadn't seen yet. At
the end, Baz glided to the side so that Cormak could step

into the room. It was twice the size of the guest bedroom he'd been staying in, with a stunning view of the Evoline botanical gardens. Cormak reached over to touch the cloud-like white comforter on the bed, just like the one that had caught his eye the other day when he'd been out with Vesper. *I'm going to get one of those someday,* he'd said.

In a daze, he made his way to the closet, where a variety of civilian clothes hung—all new, and all in his size. "What is all this?" he asked Baz.

"Ms. Haze thought you might like a room of your own on Tri, for holidays."

"Just when you can't make it all the way to Deva," another voice clarified. Cormak turned to see Vesper in the door, grinning at him.

"You did this?" Cormak asked, staring at her with wonder and disbelief. It'd been a long time since anyone had taken care of him. After Rex died, he'd been completely on his own. There wasn't a soul in the solar system who'd cared if he had enough to eat, if he had somewhere to sleep. He'd managed. He'd survived. But the thought of Vesper going to all this trouble and expense for him made something in his chest crack open.

"Oh, Antares…I didn't mean to upset you," Vesper said, rushing over to squeeze his hand.

"I'm not upset." He wiped his eyes quickly. "I'm just...I don't know what to say."

"You don't have to say anything. I only wanted you to know that you have a home here if you ever need it."

"Thank you." He tilted his head to kiss her forehead. "Though home is anywhere you are, Vee."

CHAPTER 28

ARRAN

"Cadet Korbet, please report to the launchport. Based on your current location, your estimated travel time is . . . twelve seconds."

"Right," Arran grumbled to himself. "Because I'm *on* the launchport."

"Depart immediately. If you require directions, say—"

"Dismiss!" Arran ordered loudly enough that a few members of the construction crew turned to stare. As the engineer overseeing the reconstruction of the Academy's launchport, Arran had to exude competence and expertise. Arguing with his monitor in public was not the way to inspire confidence.

"Korbet!" a booming voice called. Arran turned to see Sergeant Pond waving him over. Arran tugged on the hem of his jacket, trying to straighten everything into place. He wished he'd anticipated one of Pond's "casual" inspections today so he could've prepared a bit. His team had made tremendous progress since Pond's last visit, but it wasn't immediately apparent, and he doubted he could convince Pond to put on a space suit to examine the supports they'd just finished installing underneath the launchport.

When he reached Pond, Arran saluted, then stood at attention. Pond fixed him with a critical stare. "Why are you standing like that, Korbet?"

"It's the proper way to greet an officer of the Quatra Fleet, sir."

"There's no time for any of that nonsense. You have a launchport to build, cadet! Are you still on schedule?"

Arran nodded. He'd been charged with adapting the launchport to accommodate the Sylvan ships that would soon be traveling to the Academy with considerable frequency.

"And did Admiral Prateek send along his requirements for the new simulcrafts?"

"He did. They're a bit more complex than we anticipated, but we'll get it done." After Admiral Haze had succeeded Stepney as commander of the Quatra Fleet, Zafir had been promoted and named the new superintendent of the Quatra Fleet Academy. He'd wasted no time redesigning the school's curriculum, and to support the new focus on cross-cultural studies, he'd requested that the simulcrafts have a "diplomacy mode" to allow cadets to practice problem-solving.

"Good. I'll leave you to it. So I'll see you at the dinner for the new ambassador?"

"Certainly, sir."

"See you tonight then, Korbet. It should be quite the evening."

Arran was still attending classes on top of all his new responsibilities, something he certainly didn't resent, for as Admiral Prateek had rightly explained, "Just because you're already one of the most accomplished engineers in the

Quatra Fleet doesn't mean we can let you graduate without knowing who settled Loos." Arran did, in fact, know who'd settled Loos—he'd received the highest history marks on the Chetrian exams last year—but he agreed with Zafir's general sentiment.

He was ten minutes late to Advanced Theoretical Cosmophysics and tried to sneak in without drawing attention, but the moment he slid into his seat in the back row, Brill's head whipped around. "You missed the quiz," she whispered. "Though I suppose it doesn't matter now that the Edger-lovers are in charge."

"Cut it out, Brill," Frey snapped. "You're making yourself look ridiculous."

As they spilled out of the classroom at the end of the period, Frey sped up to walk alongside Arran. "I'm sorry about Brill," he said, his voice equal parts exasperation and embarrassment. "She's not going to last long here if she keeps talking like that, but I'm sure that's not much comfort to you."

"I appreciate that, but I have more important things on my mind at the moment," Arran said.

"I'm sure," Frey said with a knowing smile. "So I guess things are going well with you and Dash."

Arran felt heat rise to his cheeks. "That's not what I was talking about."

"I'm just teasing you," Frey said with a laugh as he slapped Arran on the arm. "Tonight's the fancy dinner, right?" he asked as they turned into the residential wing. "You'd better get ready."

"I don't think my beauty regimen is quite as...involved as yours," Arran teased.

"If I had skin like yours, I wouldn't bother either," he said, pinching Arran's cheek playfully. "Dash is a lucky man. Have fun tonight."

"Formal attire is required this evening," the attendant said as Arran approached the entrance to the dining room.

"This *is* formal attire." Arran gestured at his dress uniform. "Pretty much as formal as it gets."

"I apologize for the inconvenience, but all guests at tonight's event are required to wear formal attire." The attendant's voice took on a slightly superior tone, which was particularly infuriating given the fact that Arran had specifically told the engineers to remove that setting from the new models. The Academy was about to welcome a whole new group of Settler cadets, and Arran wasn't going to let any of them be bullied by a robot.

When Arran didn't move, the attendant continued, "If you do not have formal attire, you may attend in the nude. That is also acceptable."

"*What?*" Arran sputtered, blushing as he stared at the attendant in horror. "What the hell—"

"That would be my preference," a deep, playful voice called. Arran turned to see Dash striding down the hall in a slim black suit, a slightly upgraded version of the one that had made Arran's heart flutter at their first Academy formal.

Arran tried to fix Dash with a disapproving scowl, but it was impossible to suppress the smile tugging at his lips. "You did this, didn't you?"

"Did what?" Dash asked, eyes widening. "You can't *possibly* be suggesting that I bribed one of your engineers to write a special program for this one attendant, could you? Because, frankly, I'm insulted that you think I have that much free time."

"It was a pretty risky prank. What if I'd decided that it

was better to strip and go in naked than miss the dinner altogether?"

Dash grinned and ran his hand down the front of Arran's jacket. "Then the ambassador and her guests would've received the greatest treat of their lives."

CHAPTER 29

VESPER

The shuttle docked at the nearly finished launchport. One of the walls was still unsealed, so the passengers had to exit through a temporary tunnel that had been erected in lieu of a real airlock. A few of their fellow passengers looked a bit wary as they walked through the tunnel, which appeared to be made of fabric. One tear and they'd all asphyxiate within seconds. But Vesper felt completely relaxed as she took Cormak's arm. She knew that Arran had built this structure, which meant that it was perfectly safe.

"It must feel a little different this time," Vesper whispered with a smile as they followed the well-dressed crowd through the construction site into the Academy proper.

"You mean because I'm not trespassing and committing identity fraud?" He smiled. "Yes, it's a nice change."

She and Cormak had only been away from the Academy for a week while he sorted out his paperwork, but when they reached the dining room, Vesper did a double take. The lighting was exactly the same, a soft glow that combined with the starlight to make the room feel both welcoming and elegant. The large, round tables scattered throughout also looked relatively unchanged. At first, it looked like all the regular portraits were in place, but as Vesper moved toward the wall for a closer look, her breath caught in her chest. Next to her, Cormak murmured something she couldn't make out. She reached over and squeezed his hand without tearing her eyes from the wall. The portraits of the famous Quatra Fleet leaders had been interspersed with portraits of some of the countless civilians who'd been killed in the senseless war against the Sylvans. She felt a twinge of pain in her heart as she gazed at the faces of those who'd paid the ultimate price for a few people's greed.

"Pretty amazing, isn't it?" Zafir had appeared next to them, looking particularly impressive in his new uniform.

"Admiral," Cormak said respectfully as he and Vesper saluted.

"I'm glad you two made it back in time. Everything in order, cadet?"

Cormak nodded. "Yes, sir."

"Excellent. I have to say, I'm glad I was named superintendent of the Academy before anyone asked how the head counterintelligence instructor failed to notice that one of his students had fake papers and another was an enemy spy." His mouth twisted into a shape that was half smile, half grimace. "I'd better keep circulating. Enjoy yourselves tonight."

"We will," Vesper said, looking around the dining hall packed with politicians and fleet officers in their finery. Across the room she spotted her mother, wearing her new commander's uniform, talking to someone whose face was partially blocked by the crowd.

"I think she wants us to come over," Cormak said. Sure enough, Commander Haze was gesturing for Vesper and Cormak to join her. "Who's she talking to?"

"I'm not sure," Vesper said as they wove through the crowd. "Where are we going?" she whispered as she followed Cormak on a circuitous route around a woman in dress whites.

"I didn't want to spill this on her." He held up his

precariously full cup of deep red sparkling pearlberry juice, and Vesper smiled, feeling a surge of affection for the boy whose secret sweetness couldn't be fully masked by his distinguished uniform. "Oh, Antares," Cormak said under his breath as they approached. "Is that—?"

"Yes," Vesper said as a current of nervous excitement shot through her. "That's President Hobart."

"I need to put this drink down," Cormak said, looking frantically from side to side.

"You'll be fine. Come on, they're waiting for us."

As they approached, Commander Haze stepped to the side to make room. "Madame President, may I present my daughter, Vesper Haze, and Cormak Phobos."

President Hobart was much shorter in real life than Vesper had expected, but that didn't make her any less formidable. Her white hair was pulled back from her face in a smooth bun, and she wore a dark blue tunic affixed with a gold Quatra Federation pin. "A pleasure to meet you both. The Federation is grateful for everything you've done."

"They have very promising careers ahead of them," Commander Haze said, giving Vesper a smile that sent heat rising to her cheeks. "I couldn't be prouder."

One of President Hobart's aides came over with another

guest for her to meet, and Vesper and Cormak excused themselves.

"So that happened," Cormak said. He sounded slightly dazed.

"Get used to it, Phobos. You're a big shot now."

An attendant glided up to them. "Please take your seats. The ambassador will be arriving shortly."

Cormak grinned. "Though not as much of a big shot as some people." He took Vesper's arm in his as they searched the names on the table settings until they found their spots.

"Thank Antares you're here," Dash said as he slid into his assigned seat next to Vesper. "If I have to make small talk with one more seventy-five-year-old colonel, I'm going to throw myself out of the airlock."

"Just wait until after they serve the appetizers," Vesper said, patting his arm. "If you delay dinner, I'll kill you myself."

A few older guests they didn't know—high-ranking Federation officials and fleet officers—sat down at their table, giving Cormak, Vesper, and Dash cursory nods before continuing their conversation.

Finally, Arran rushed over and took his seat. "Sorry," he said, slightly breathless. "I got tied up. Did I miss anything?"

But before any of them could respond, Zafir stood up, and the din of chatter died away. "Welcome, everyone. As you all know, we're here to honor a very special guest. The last time most of you were here, this school was the heart of our battle against the Sylvans. This was where we debated new tactics, developed new technologies, and trained the next generation of warriors. And the new Academy will continue to be the backbone of the Quatra Fleet. We'll be the guardians of our legacy—the good and the bad—and we'll use these hard-earned lessons to prepare our future leaders for a new world. A peaceful world. For we are no longer at war with the Sylvans. Nor are we at war against our own people." Zafir paused as a few people shifted uncomfortably in their chairs or exchanged knowing looks. "We claimed that we were training cadets to fight the Sylvans, yet the truth is that only a fraction of the Quatra Fleet ever engaged in direct battle. The majority were eventually sent to Chetire, Deva, and Loos, where their primary responsibility was to intimidate Settlers, enforce cruel laws, and suppress rebellion." Zafir's face hardened, and his voice grew slightly louder. "No more. That era is behind us, and while we won't erase it or hide it, lest we repeat the mistakes of the past, we're going to make good on the empty promises we've been making for generations. The Quatra Fleet Academy, and the fleet itself, will be devoted to protecting and uplifting every person in the solar system. We've been given an extraordinary gift in the chance to start over, to do better, and it begins now." He took a breath and smiled. "And with that, it's my privilege to introduce our honored guest this evening, a person who embodies this new era of cooperation and understanding. May I present the Sylvan ambassador to the Quatra Federation...Orelia Kerr."

The room broke into applause, and as Orelia made her entrance, looking dignified and splendid in her Sylvan robes, no one clapped harder than Vesper, Arran, and Cormak. Vesper put her hand in Cormak's and he squeezed it, wordlessly conveying everything they were both thinking. She would be excited to face any future with Cormak by her side.

CHAPTER 30

ORELIA

It was only the third party Orelia had been to in her entire life, and this time she wouldn't be able to skulk in the corner, observing from the safety of the shadows. She was the guest of honor and would have to spend the event making small talk with the dizzying array of important Quatrans who kept appearing at her side.

The dinner had been manageable, as there'd only been eight people at her table, but the post-dinner reception was beginning to feel overwhelming. A trio of musicians had been given special security clearance for the evening—the first time in Academy history—and the center of the room was a blur of swirling skirts and gleaming brass buttons as the guests danced beneath the star-filled windows. But Orelia barely had time to glance their way. Every few minutes, the vice president of the Quatra Federation would guide Orelia to a different cluster of people waiting to bombard her with questions about Sylvan.

"Don't worry," Arran had joked earlier that night. "No matter what you do, you'll still be the best Sylvan ambassador in history."

"But if I'm terrible, I might be the first and *last* Sylvan ambassador to the Quatra System," she'd responded.

She scanned the crowded room for Arran, but he was nowhere in sight. Vesper, Cormak, and Dash had also disappeared in the crowd. Orelia forced a smile and turned back to the Tridian commerce minister, who was talking about an elaborate trade deal he was hoping to propose to the Sylvans. *Trade deal, perfect*, Orelia thought grimly as her heart began to race. She'd grown up on a military base, where she'd never had any need to handle money, let alone think about trade deals. *Just smile and nod*, she told herself. It wasn't her job to discuss the minutiae of policy; she was here to foster "understanding and goodwill," which had sounded easy enough. Though now, looking at all the people eager to talk to her, she wasn't so sure.

"Sorry, coming through. Urgent diplomatic business." Orelia turned to see Vesper elbowing her way through the crowd while Arran and Cormak trailed after her, looking slightly embarrassed and amused, respectively. "We need to speak to the ambassador immediately." A few people looked askance as Vesper grabbed Orelia's hand and began to pull her away, but of course no one objected.

"Vesper thought you looked like you needed rescuing," Cormak explained as Vesper led them to the far side of the hall.

"Was it that obvious?" Orelia asked.

"Not at all," Arran said, shooting Cormak a look. "You're doing great. We just figured you needed a break."

They sat at one of the empty tables, and Vesper produced a flask of nitro spirit from her pocket. "What are you doing?" Cormak asked, glancing over his shoulder.

"Oh, relax. No one's looking over here. Besides, Orelia has diplomatic immunity."

Cormak rolled his eyes. "I meant, why would you smuggle in disgusting, cheap nitro spirit when we're at an official fleet reception with a full bar? We can just go up and order drinks."

"Oh, right." For a moment, Vesper looked uncharacteristically abashed, but then she grinned and shrugged. "Well, this will save us a trip to the bar."

"For the most ambitious girl in the solar system, you can be ridiculously lazy," Cormak said with an indulgent smile.

Orelia felt a flood of warmth as she looked around the table. The past few weeks had been so chaotic, she hadn't had time to think about how much she'd missed her squadron mates.

Vesper took a sip, then passed the flask to Orelia.

"Careful," Arran said, raising his eyebrows. "We don't want a repeat of last time."

"What happened last time?" Cormak asked, looking from Arran to Orelia.

"Nothing!" Orelia said quickly while Arran laughed. "Okay, *fine*. I had a little too much to drink and Arran had to help me back to my room."

"Really?" Cormak said incredulously. "How did I miss that?"

"Flirting with Vesper used to take up a *lot* of your time and energy," Arran said.

They all laughed, prompting a few curious stares from the dance floor, but Orelia didn't care. Her life no longer depended on keeping a low profile; she had nothing to hide anymore. She wasn't training fourteen hours a day for a top-secret mission that could determine the future of her people. She wasn't using a fake accent and a fake identity while embedded behind enemy lines. She sighed happily, releasing the tension that she'd been carrying for so long she'd forgotten what it was like to live without it.

But there was something else—it wasn't just the lack of tension that made everything feel different. Looking around the table, she felt a surge of affection for her squadron mates: people she cared about and who, for one reason or another, seemed to care about her. For the first time in her life, she had real friends.

"So what happens now?" Cormak asked her. "Are you going to be based on Tri? Or are you going to travel around?"

"I'm not actually sure," she said. "I think we're still figuring that out."

"Maybe you'll get to stay at the Academy," Arran said hopefully. "You can be the ambassador in residence."

"I think Tri is the likeliest option," Vesper said. "You can stay at my place if you want!"

"How many rooms do you have?" Cormak asked, shaking his head.

"I have a sneaking suspicion that the Federation will provide housing for Orelia. She's an *ambassador*," Arran said proudly. "Though maybe you can come back here to give lectures or something."

Vesper nodded. "That's an excellent idea. I'm going to mention it to Zafir."

"Mention it to whom?" a voice said. Orelia turned to see Zafir standing next to her, looking around the table with an amused expression.

"To Admiral Prateek," Vesper said, blushing slightly.

"Zafir is fine," he said. "I was just teasing you."

"Yeah, the thing is, it can be *really* hard to tell with you sometimes," Cormak said.

Zafir raised an eyebrow. "I'll take that under consideration."

"See! That's what I'm talking about!" Cormak looked to the others for backup, but they just smiled politely.

"If you'll excuse us, I need to borrow Orelia for some…"
He pressed his lips together. *"Urgent diplomatic business."*

"Was I gone for too long?" Orelia asked anxiously as Zafir led her toward the middle of the dance floor. "Who do I need to talk to now?"

Zafir took her hand and wrapped his other arm around her waist. "No one," he whispered into her ear. "I just wanted you to myself for a moment."

Orelia shivered as the tickle of his breath on her skin cleared her brain of every thought, including how terrified she was of dancing. Zafir began to sway from side to side, placing just enough pressure on her that she had no choice but to move in sync. For the first few moments, she felt stiff and awkward—and convinced that everyone was staring at her—but then the warmth of Zafir's hands seemed to spread through her body, making everything feel loose and limber.

Feeling confident enough to stop staring at her feet, she looked up and met Zafir's eyes. He was staring at her with a look she couldn't quite identify, but that made her shudder nonetheless. "Are you okay?" he whispered.

"More than okay."

He reached out to tuck a stray lock of hair behind her ear,

letting his fingers linger on her cheek. "Have I told you how beautiful you look tonight?"

"How am I supposed to remember?" she asked with a smile. "I've spoken to so many people tonight, it's impossible to keep all the conversations straight."

"Fair enough. I'll just have to keep telling you." He drew her closer to him until she was pressed against his chest. "You look beautiful."

Orelia was vaguely aware of music soaring around them, but it was drowned out by the thud of Zafir's heart beating in time with her own. At that moment, it seemed impossible that she'd ever put a foot out of place dancing with him. She'd never known that two bodies could move in sync like this.

"You have no idea how badly I want to kiss you right now," he murmured.

"What's stopping you?"

"It doesn't seem quite fitting for the superintendent of the Quatra Fleet Academy to make out with the new Sylvan ambassador during her very first reception."

Orelia sighed dramatically. "First you couldn't kiss me because I was your student. And now you're saying you can't kiss me because I'm an ambassador? What's with all the excuses?" She cocked her head to the side. "Though, if I remember correctly, I didn't take no for an answer that first time."

"No, you certainly didn't."

"And I don't see any reason why I should do so now." She raised her chin and let her lips brush lightly against his while her hand pressed against his lower back. Then she pulled back and surveyed him with a smile. "So, Admiral. Where exactly do diplomats sleep when they've been invited to late-night receptions at the Quatra Fleet Academy?"

"The VIP guest suite has been prepared for you. We had to downgrade President Hobart, but she was a good sport about it."

"And how far is that from the faculty quarters?"

"Very far." His fingers pressed harder against her waist. "But the superintendent's quarters aren't in the faculty wing."

"No? So where are they?"

"Quite close to the guest rooms, actually."

"And now that I'm not a cadet, I suppose I don't have to worry about curfew, do I?"

"Definitely not." He shook his head. "In fact, I think that, as ambassador, you have every right to arrange a conference with the superintendent at any hour."

"Does that count as *urgent diplomatic business*?" Orelia asked, rising onto her toes to whisper into Zafir's ear.

"Absolutely. In fact, I can't think of anything more urgent," he said with a grin that left Orelia suddenly short of breath. "Now come on. Let's get you back out there to wrap up your rounds. I'm not sure how much longer I can wait for our…policy discussion."

Zafir kept his arm around her waist as he guided her off the dance floor and steered her toward the Quatran vice president, who was scanning the room, clearly searching for Orelia. "You've got this," Zafir whispered. "You've been brilliant all night. You've been brilliant since the moment I met you." He slowed down and turned to look at her. "Is it strange for me to say that I'm proud of you?"

"Why would that be strange?" she asked, doing her best to keep her face from erupting into a decidedly unprofessional grin.

"I don't know. What right does an admiral have to be *proud* of an ambassador? It doesn't seem like quite the right word."

"It's all that I want," Orelia said quietly, realizing that she meant it. She'd been pleased to make General Greet proud, of course, but she'd done so by fulfilling Greet's vision for a secret agent, whereas Zafir was proud of her for being herself. Somewhere behind her, she heard Cormak's distinctive laugh and felt a wave of contentment wash over her. She might've discovered it in the unlikeliest of places, but she'd finally found the home she'd been looking for.

ACKNOWLEDGMENTS

None of my books would exist without the creativity and dedication of the team at Alloy. Thank you for believing in me and for giving me the opportunities of a lifetime. Special thanks to my fiercely intelligent, patient, unflappable editor, Viana Siniscalchi, whose storytelling prowess and clear-eyed vision informed every aspect of this book. Were it not for your encouragement and wisdom, I'd still be stuck on chapter three.

Huge thanks to everyone at LBYR and Hachette UK, especially my editor, Pam Gruber. Working with you has made me a stronger writer, a deeper thinker, and a better editor myself. Thanks to you (and Viana) for pushing me to grow and to elevate this story beyond anything I could've imagined. I'm also incredibly lucky to have Siena Koncsol, publicist extraordinaire, in my corner. Your energy, humor, kindness, and publishing savvy have made this adventure even more fun and rewarding. Many thanks to keen-eyed assistant editor Hannah Milton and copy chief Jen Graham for their excellent catches and suggestions.

I'm very grateful to the team at Rights People for giving me the opportunity to share my stories with readers around the world. Thanks to all the talented publishers, editors, translators, and designers responsible for the gorgeous foreign editions of my books. Seeing them is truly a dream come true. And thank you to the publishers who gave me the extraordinary opportunity to meet my international readers: Myrthe Spiteri and Lotte Dijkstra at Blossom Books, and Glenn Tavennec and Fabien LeRoy at Éditions Robert Laffont.

I'm privileged to have wonderful friends and family whose support never wavers, even when deadline stress makes me slightly unpleasant to be around. Thank you for all your encouragement, and for not minding when I disappear for long stretches of time. Extra thanks to my writing group: Laura Bisberg, Michael Bisberg, Laura Jean Ridge, Grace Kendall, Gavin Brown, Nick Eliopulos, and Matt

Gline. Your storytelling skills and fire-building talents are wondrous to behold.

Finally, heartfelt thanks to all the readers I've met at festivals and online. Your kindness and enthusiasm have been the most rewarding part of this journey.